The Wolf's Consort

Max Ellendale
with J.L. James

This is a work of fiction. Names, characters, places, and incidents are products of the author's imagination or are used fictitiously and are not to be construed as real. Any resemblance to actual events, locales, organizations, or persons, living or dead, is entirely coincidental.

Contributor: J.L. James
Cover Artist: Victoria Miller
Editor: Deadra Krieger

All rights reserved. No part of this book may be used or reproduced electronically or in print without written permission, except in the case of brief quotations embodied in reviews.

Max Ellendale
www.maxellendale.com

Copyright © 2019 Max Ellendale

All rights reserved.

ISBN-13: 9781797508016

CHAPTER ONE

"I got the story," I called out. "I'm on it."

"Fine. Parker, you get the hospital terrorist attack. That's what we're calling it, yeah?" The Editor-in-Chief pointed at me while tilting his head. I smirked at the shiny spot on his bald head where the fluorescents reflected.

"Right-o. Rebrand unknown explosive device to terrorist attack. On it." I saluted him.

"Watch it, Parker, or you're back on book reviews."

"Sir, she *likes* book reviews, sir." Heather, goddamn Heather, and her fucked up half-smile.

"Yeah well, then food reviews," he retorted, waving me off again. "All of you get gone."

"Aye Aye, Chief," Heather said, glancing at me before the small crew exited the even smaller newsroom. Considering only four of us made up the staff of the Fourth Corner Review, working out of a one-room storefront wasn't the worst thing in the world.

My boots hit the sandy street, and I clutched my padfolio closer to my chest. In early October, snow hadn't hit this area of Northern Utah just yet. Eventually, it would blanket the lower part of the Rockies. Moving here to the quaint town with single-story buildings all within walking distance, from Salt Lake City probably wasn't the best decisions I'd ever made, but I needed to get away from what I left behind. Here, no one knew me save for my name on a byline.

News crews pooled behind the police line around the local hospital. Unlike the rest of the town, the multi-storey tower loomed over us, almost ominous in the way it blocked out the autumn sun. Without a hitch, I ducked under the police tape and approached the big burly police officer from whom I made a habit of siphoning information.

"Steve-o, what've we got here?" I called out.

He turned to me, his copper cheeks lifting his sunglasses slightly when he tried not to smile. "Parker, do I need to place you under arrest for crossing a police line? Don't make me. I've done it before," he warned, playfully at best.

"You just get your jollies off slapping cuffs on my dainty wrists." I held my hands out to him, cocked my head to the side, and smiled.

He chuckled, deep and gutturally. "Don't even try to play."

"Why play when I've already won?" My smile melted to a grin and he glanced around, nodding for me to follow him. He led me away from the news crews, one of the reporters glaring in my direction, and around the corner of the building where two other officers stood with their backs to us while they sifted through a pile of rubble.

"Weston," he called out. The female officer turned to face us. "This is Miss Parker. She's a reporter at the FC Review. Give her an exclusive."

"Me?" Her voice deepened with the question. The moment her eyes fell on me, so green they nearly mirrored the sharpest corner of an emerald, I felt my face heat up as if the sun wrestled its way out from behind the building. A smattering of freckles across the bridge of her nose didn't do anything to soothe my intimidation. Cops weren't supposed to look like her. Flawless, bronze, and lithe. They were supposed to be short, stocky, and average.

"Yeah, you. If anyone's getting an exclusive on this, it's our own paper," Steve said, nodding to her. "Got a problem with that?"

"She's nosey." Weston gestured at me, a scowl marring her pretty face. "And the last time I saw her, I arrested her for trespassing at a crime scene."

"You did *not*," I fought back, crossing my arms over my chest. "I've never met you before."

"It was dark out, Parker. Don't get smart." Weston folded her arms in the same fashion, her eyebrow lifting in challenge.

"Trust me. I would've remembered *that* face," I said, stepping into the dispute.

"Ohhh," the male cop beside her called out, chuckling. "This is getting good, boss."

Weston elbowed him. "Shut up, Lightfoot."

"Enough already. Weston, take Miss Parker on the exclusive. Lightfoot, go help control the press out front." Steve pointed back toward the front of the hospital; a gesture that parted the group, and left me standing alone with the grumpy cop.

With one last glance at each other, she turned and led me toward the side entrance. Once inside, the heels of my worn-in Frye boots thudded heavily beside Weston's nearly silent steps. I waited a minute or so before continuing our argument.

"You did not arrest me," I said.

"Doesn't mean I wasn't right about you being nosey," she replied, grumpily.

"How'd you even know that I was picked up for that?" I glanced at her, though she kept her gaze ahead. "Are you stalking me?"

"No. It's a small town." She paused, lifting another line of police tape for me to step under.

I ducked, brushing my skirt down over my thighs on

the way. The hallway ahead of us appeared almost dismantled. Equipment littered the floor, and crime scene investigators gathered evidence while on their hands and knees.

"What happened here?" I asked, lifting my camera from my purse to snap a few shots.

"Some sort of explosive device."

"Was anyone hurt?"

"Not by the explosion." She grabbed my elbow, urging me away from the wall before a small piece crumbled. Her grip, firm and hot to the touch, startled me. "Stay in the middle of the hall."

"Ouch, Wonder Woman." I wriggled my arm and she let go. "Jeez."

"S-sorry," she said, glancing at me. "Just be careful."

"What did you mean 'not by the explosion'?" I pressed, side-stepping some debris.

"One was taken, but she's since been recovered." Weston stopped beside the stairwell.

"I don't understand. An explosion in a hospital without anyone getting hurt? And taken as in kidnapped?"

"Yes." She sighed, glancing over her shoulder then back to me. "Someone pulled the fire alarm and the hospital was evacuated before the explosion. I don't understand why I have to tell you any of this."

"Because someone targeted this hospital for a particular reason. Who was kidnapped?"

"A local doctor, but she's been recovered and she's fine."

"Who took her?"

"We don't know."

"What was the motive?"

"Don't know that either."

"Officer Weston, you're not very helpful." I frowned, turning away from her and heading off down the hall. "I'll find my own exclusive."

"It's why we call it an investigation, Parker!" she called

after me, but I rolled my eyes and carried on without her.

An hour or so later, I returned to the office, with not much more to go on than when I went in, save for a few tidbits of information.

"How'd you fair?" Ian asked as we sat down to lunch at our desks. Heather and the boss weren't in at the moment, so it gave us ample opportunity to catch up.

"Not very well. I did learn that a staff doctor was kidnapped briefly and that no one else was injured. The hospital was evacuated before the explosion after someone pulled the fire alarm. So...now I need to find out the name of the doctor."

"No one's scooped you yet?"

"Not funny, Ian." I crumbled up the wrapper of my sandwich. "You know I want this story."

"I know, Mack. Calm down."

"I'm going home to work on this. Tell the Chief for me." I swiped my laptop from my desk, and grabbed my bag, leaving with a chip on my shoulder.

Sometimes I wished I lived further away so that I could storm off for a lot longer. My loft, settled happily above the shop owned by a nice lady named Imogene, smelled of freshly burned sage. Over the years, the smell became a comfort. Of course, I never burned it myself. The incense from the shop below often permeated the floorboards. I pulled open the curtains that overlooked the main street and gazed down over the passing traffic and pedestrians. It was nothing like Salt Lake City, and for that I was eternally grateful.

The mid-afternoon sun cast beams across the patchwork quilt on my bed, and I watched as flecks of dust floated in the rays. In my quiet space, my thoughts settled and my aggravation over not having enough to write an exclusive story calmed. I set my computer down on the L-shaped desk, beside my second laptop and other equipment. With one last breath, and a glance over my shoulder, I sat down and decided, against my better judgment, to call upon the skills of my former life.

I pulled up the website for Stormhill Hospital, and began my attempts at gaining entry into their servers. At the very least, a staff database filled with schedules and names could be enough. Narrow it down to that night, and I had my interview pool. A few lines of code, a quick program to do the work for me, and all I had to do was sit around and wait.

≈

"You asked for me?" queried a bubbly voice.

"Are you Beth?" I turned to face the woman clad in a pair of pink scrubs.

"I am." Her brow furrowed. "Do I know you?"

"No. I'm Mack Parker, Fourth Corner Review." I extended my hand and she shook it like a floppy fish, her mouth hanging open a bit. "It's come to my attention that you were on duty the night of the explosion here."

"Um...yeah. Why?"

"Are you aware that a doctor was injured during the incident?"

"Yes...Why?"

"By any chance, do you know who that is?"

"Yeah. *Why?*" She folded her arms over her chest, frowning at me. "You're really a nosey little thing, ain'tcha?"

"I'm a reporter. It's my job to be nosey." I tapped my pencil against the notebook. "What happened to the doctor?"

"She...got knocked out while helping a patient during the commotion." Her answer, coupled with her shifting gaze told me that wasn't the whole truth. My mind spiraled through the list of doctors on the roster that I stole from my recent bout of law breaking.

"So *she* got knocked out. Is that right?" I pretended to scribble something on that pad. "And she was working with you here in the emergency room?"

"How'd you even find me, Miss—what's your name?"

"Parker. You were on staff that night. Small hospital. You're my fourth interview. No one else seemed to know anything about the doctor. But you do."

"I think you need to leave, Miss Parker. I'm not talking to you anymore." Beth moved away from me and back behind the reception desk of the emergency room. "Or I'll call security."

"Fine." I smirked, snapping my notebook shut. "But you gave me everything I needed."

"I gave you nothing. Go away."

With a smile plastered across my face, I nearly skipped out of the hospital. My hack turned up the entire employee roster of Stormhill Hospital, of which, had only three female doctors listed. Working that night, only one female doctor entered my search.

Shawnee Twofeathers, MD.

CHAPTER TWO

No phone. No email address. No property listing. On paper, Doctor Twofeathers presented as a formidable ghost. The only thing that kept her on the grid was her medical license, particularly the one she filed in Utah with a Utah address. And the tax I.D. number she used for her private practice. *Doctor Twofeathers, you're not as elusive as you think.*

Except for the fact that she lived in the most remote area of the county and I didn't own a car. No bus lines drove that far out. Uber didn't exist here, so the cab ride cost me more than a full day's pay even though it wouldn't take me further than the trailhead.

"Thanks," I said as I slid from the vehicle.

"You sure about this, lady? That trail is expert and leads into the national forest."

"I'm good, thank you."

"You got enough water in that pack?"

I chuckled. "I'll be fine. If I go missing, you can be the first to file the report."

"I got your name on this credit card receipt just in case. You got your weapon?"

"What weapon?"

"A gun, miss. You can't just go on out there unarmed." His sweaty face lifted with his concerned brow. "You'll be asking for it in these parts."

"Thank you for your concern, but I'm fine." I closed the car door, tossed on my pack, and embarked for the trail way.

As expected, about a mile in, the woods thickened and the afternoon light dimmed, giving the illusion of sunset. No signs of human life existed by the time I hit mile two. Did everyone around here live this far in the woods?

Eventually, the trail split in two. One direction pointed toward the continuing trail, the other toward nothingness. I examined the map I'd pre-programmed into my phone, and knew right away that into the *nothing* I must go. With a quick shifting of the weight of my pack, I headed toward no woman's land.

My feet tangled in fallen leaves, crunching louder than I expected. The ruckus I made echoed in the tranquil woods, announcing my presence to any predator within earshot. Despite the obvious nerves that accompanied this, enjoyment flooded me while I took in the dense nature. Sun shimmered in the treetops, birds chirped, and a cool breeze soothed me. Just being out here slowed me down from my usual rush. Part of being a reporter, the part that I found myself addicted to, was the constant rush. Chasing a story, following a lead, uncovering truths, shifted my focus away from my singular existence in the world. It brought me solace in the resolution, and in the exposé that followed. There wasn't a story that I ever left unfinished. I wasn't about to let this one go either.

It took me awhile, as I wandered further into the unknown territory, to realize how deeply I fell into my thoughts. The un-trail no longer ascended and instead, a sandier soil crunched beneath my feet. In the distance, the trickle of a stream echoed in the trees. I glanced down to my phone, the map still clear, and pondered my next move.

Rustling kicked up somewhere around me, drawing my attention away from the device. Before I had a chance to process the direction of the sound, a silhouette of something lurking by the base of a nearby tree shuffled. I froze, staring at it in hopes that its emergence would bring nothing more than a rabbit. A deep rumbling rose from the shadows, and the shimmering reflection of light in animal eyes blinked in my direction. The rumble turned into a growl, and my breath caught in my throat.

At first, I took a step back, and the thing lowered itself closer to the ground. A beam of sunlight clipped its shoulder, illuminating gray and brown fur. My body never moved so fast in its life when I twisted myself around and bolted out of there. I had no idea which direction I ran, but I tore off, hard and fast. My breath left me in heated exhalations, until I glanced over my shoulder when I heard the snapping of a tree branch. I never expected to see a *wolf*, a full-blown wolf, chasing me down.

A strangled scream left my throat and I burst out of the thicket of trees, into a clearing. Ahead of me, the vast expanse of a lake had me skidding to a halt. I swung around in time to see the wolf make a bounding leap at me, tackling me backward into a pile of loose earth. Rocks tumbled around me, and the weight of the wolf on my lower half forced a scream from me. I shoved at it, my hands pressing into its thick mane while it snarled and snapped at me. When it leaned back, teeth bared, I covered my face with my arm, bracing for impact.

Nothing.

An unexpected stillness fell around me, but the weight of the wolf hadn't disappeared. I peeked up, only to find the deep yellow eyes of the wolf only a few inches from mine. Breath left me in heaving gasps, but the wolf seemed to sniff my arm. Both of us locked in a stalemate.

"Hey!" someone shouted and the wolf looked up. "*Away.*" The wolf growled, backing off me. "*Away.*" Silhouetted in the sun, the looming form of a woman approached. "Bad," she said, waving her hand at the wolf. He snapped at her, glanced at me, and bolted back into the woods as if he understood what she said.

Relief flooded me, and I collapsed in a heap, gasping for breath. "Oh my God."

"What do you think you're doing out here, Parker?" the voice became suddenly familiar and I sat up. The woman crouched beside me, clad in nothing more than a brown leather halter top and matching shorts. Her tawny hair hung to her waist, natural in its beach-wave, cradling her face like she'd just fallen out of the Jurassic Period. I stumbled over my words, looking her up and down once before meeting her gaze. Her agile, well-muscled frame towered over me. Only when I noticed her sharp green eyes and smattering of freckles did I recognize her.

"Officer Weston?"

"Yeah. What are you doing out here trespassing on private property?" She knelt down beside me, her bare knees against the rocks didn't seem to faze her.

"I...um...a wolf. It chased me—"

"It nearly ate your face off." Her gaze flickered over me. "Are you hurt?"

"N-no. Why do you look like that?" I shrugged off my pack, taking a few deep breaths as my head spun from the adrenaline rush.

"Like what?" She gripped my elbow when I tipped sideways. "Easy."

"Like...a sexy cave woman or something," I blurted out.

"I don't. You're delirious. Let's get you up." She wrapped her arm around my middle, before rolling to her bare feet. "Can you stand?"

"Yeah. I'm just a little stunned." With her help, I rose to my feet and brushed off my jeans. "Thanks."

"Come on," she said, grabbing my pack effortlessly and leading me away from the lake toward the woods again. I dug my heels in when we drew closer.

"What if it's still there?" I gripped my chest, glancing

around us as my heart pounded.

"She's gone. Come." She urged me forward until we entered the cover of the tree line. After a few paces, my footing found me again. "You're lucky she was just a cub."

"A what?"

"A cub. Young wolf."

"Young? It looked fucking enormous to me." I sighed, reaching up and fixing my ponytail. "Where are we going?"

"My cabin isn't far," she said, gesturing ahead of us. "About a mile."

"A mile? How'd you know I was about to get my face eaten off from a mile away?" I asked, glancing to her with a knitted brow. She didn't answer me at first. Instead, she shifted my pack and met my gaze. "What?"

"I was fishing and heard you scream."

"Fishing? With what? A homemade carved spear while dressed in your leather-clad Blue Lagoon getup?" I waved at her outfit. "Which, by the way, I don't dislike by any means. I'm just saying—"

"What are you saying, exactly, Parker?"

I stammered and felt the heat rush my face. "You don't look like a cop, and that I'm not buying the fishing story."

"Well, that settles that then." She quieted after and we walked side-by-side for awhile longer. I watched her feet as they fell in step with mine. My boots crunched leaves and twigs, but she seemed unbothered by the debris on her bare soles.

"Do you always walk barefoot out here?"

"You ask a lot of questions."

"I'm a reporter."

"I'm not your story," she said, then her hush returned.

This Officer Weston wasn't like the broody one I knew from the streets. There wasn't anything hard about her. In fact, everything she did appeared nimble, deliberate, and gentle. And beautiful. How could I describe her as anything save for beautiful?

As we approached her cabin, I stumbled over the rough

terrain coupled with the emerging nighttime. The darkness didn't seem to bother her either. She waved toward the stairs and I preceded her. I couldn't make out what it looked like, but the faint scent of lavender made it to my nose. She opened the door, without a key, and ushered me inside.

"Did you drive up here?" she asked.

"I walked from the trailhead."

"Well, there's no going back to town until morning then. It'll be pitch black before you make it back."

"Why not? I can't just *stay* here."

"You can. I don't have a car and I'm not hiking with you back to town nearly ten miles in the dark when it's not safe," she said, setting my pack down on the floor. I stood by the door until she flicked on the lights.

I expected a cabin, but I didn't expect something as incredible as this. The single floor log cabin held all the modern conveniences one would expect from a home. The difference belonged to the decoration. Rustic furniture, cozy woven blankets, and hanging plants made up the main parts of the sitting room. A big stone fireplace, however, stole away the attention. To my left, the door to the bedroom hung open and I could see the made up bed from my position by the front door.

"How do you get to work without a car then every day?" I asked, looking back to her.

"Sometimes I walk. Sometimes Steve takes me in. He lives on the other side of the lake a few miles out," she answered, then nodded toward the hallway. "The bathroom's down there. Are you hungry?"

"Thanks. I'm okay." I folded my arms over my middle when a shiver struck my shoulders.

"You're cold. Come sit. I'll light a fire."

"Not going to argue that." I followed her into the living room and took up a perch on the sofa. "You know, I don't know your name."

"Officer Weston is fine," she said, smirking while she

crouched beside the fireplace.

I laughed at her. "When you're dressed like Wilma Flintstone, calling you Officer anything isn't the easiest."

"I might take offense to your jabs at my outfit if you keep it up."

"Are you Native?"

"No. Well, I don't know. But not to my knowledge."

"Were you role-playing or something?"

The flames whooshed in the hearth and I flinched from the heat that followed. "Give it a break, Parker."

"Mack."

"What?"

"My name's Mack."

"Mack?" She stood now, turning to face me. The glow from the fire beside her made her appear golden in the light. "What's your real name?"

"That *is* my real name."

"No it's not. What's it short for?"

"Makayla, if you have to be so nosey about it." I huffed, which only made her chuckle.

"Now you know how it feels," she said, joining me on the sofa. She reached down and pulled a fluffy blanket out from the basket beside it. "Here."

"Thanks."

"Welcome." She paused for a moment, staring off into the growing flames. "My name's Zara."

"Pretty name."

"I've always liked it," she said, pulling her legs up to sit cross-legged.

"You live here all alone?"

"I do."

"It's so secluded."

"I know."

"Why?"

"It suits me better. Someone like me does best away from others," she said, leaning her elbow on the back of the sofa.

"What's that supposed to mean?"

She shrugged. "Let's get back to you. What the hell are you doing wandering around up here? Someone could've shot you on sight. This isn't the friendliest of areas."

"I was following a lead on the hospital explosion," I confessed while pulling the blanket around my shoulders.

"What lead?"

"Why should I tell you?" I squinted and sent a scowl in her direction.

"Because I'm a cop and I said so."

"That's a lame ass reason."

She laughed and ran her fingers through her hair. Again, I found myself admiring her. I had to admit, I might've been a stickler for a woman in uniform, but tonight, I might just be a stickler for a woman in a loincloth. "Come on. I won't spoil your lead."

"No, but if you tell other news outlets, they'll scoop me."

"Honestly, no one else cares at this point. It's old news."

"Not to me."

"Then tell me."

I let out a sigh, watching her with heavy speculation. For an instant, when she glanced to the window, I could've sworn a green glow reflected in her eyes the same way it had with the wolf in the woods. A shiver raced up my spine and I pulled the blanket tighter around me. "I found out who the doctor was that got kidnapped."

"And how did you do that?" she asked, though her formerly relaxed posture tightened some.

"Revealing my methods would only get me in trouble, Officer Weston."

"Pretend I'm not a cop for a minute," she implored.

"Kinda hard."

"Is it?" She gestured down her body and it made me gulp.

"Not really…"

"How'd you find out?"

"Hacked the hospital database to find the work schedules. You said 'she' when you mentioned the doctor in question. There are only three female physicians at Stormhill. And only one of them on shift that night. So, Doctor Twofeathers it is. I was coming up here to try and get an interview with her."

"Fat chance. You're lucky you never made it to her house."

"Why?"

"More than one young wolf would've taken you out," she warned, rather flatly.

"And how come you know so much about wolves, *Zara*?" I frowned at her and the odd warnings she kept tossing out.

"I've lived here awhile. But listen to me, for real. This isn't something you need to be poking your nose in. The people behind this attack are dangerous and the last thing we need is for them to catch you butting in. Just...drop it, okay?"

"I can't do that. The people around here expect the truth. My boss plans to rebrand this as a terrorist attack, and unless I find some real answers, that's what's going to happen."

"If it'll keep you and other people away from it, then fine." Zara dropped her shoulders in a heavy shrug.

"Why do you even care what happens to me?" I asked, letting my hands flop in my lap.

"Because I do. Because I'm a cop and I'm here to protect citizens. Okay? And you don't deserve to get hurt by stumbling into someone else's battle. So please, just drop it. Make it go away somehow, Parker. But don't keep on this." This time, her warning held a heavier theme to it, and a dire tone.

"Then find me another story, *coppa*." I thumbed my finger against my nose and snorted.

"In this sleepy little town?" She scoffed. "Nothing ever

happens here."

"Something tells me you're lying."

"What exactly tells you that?"

"The words coming out of your mouth." I waved my hands in front of her face and she laughed.

"You're a horrible reporter." She pushed my hands away, though the slow drag of her fingers against my wrist sent a tickle up my arm.

"And you're a horrible cop."

"We fit well then." She glanced to the kitchen. "Want some hot cocoa?"

"Sure. Unless you plan to poison me."

"If it'll get you to stop asking so many questions, I'll consider it."

CHAPTER THREE

The sound of crazy birds woke me up the next morning. I found myself curled up on Zara's sofa, covered in three blankets, and sans shoes. She wasn't anywhere in sight, so I assumed she was still sleeping. I turned on to my back, looking out the window toward the early morning sunlight. It must've been about six o'clock, maybe a little earlier.

I took a deep breath, and thought about what Zara said last night about dropping the story. What was she hiding? What was *everyone* hiding? I looked down at the fuzzy socks still covering my feet, then stole the opportunity to examine the cabin further. On the mantle, small carved wood figurines lined the edge intermingled between candles that had the unevenness of a handmade product. There wasn't anything rough about the trinkets, the same way there wasn't anything rugged about Zara in this environment. With my mind scattered all over the place, I considered my predicament.

It'd been years since I'd slept over at another woman's home. Half a decade even. It wasn't a secret that I didn't have a line of friends gathered behind me or a bunch of happy family members celebrating my existence. I walked away from them the same way they walked away from me when they chose their beliefs over me.

I couldn't waste my time looking back anymore, but looking forward wasn't something I was good at either.

"You okay?" Zara's soft voice broke my reverie. "You look upset."

"I'm okay," I said, sitting up when she entered the room. Unlike last night, this morning she wore a pair of loose-fitting sweatpants, and a tank top. My eyes wandered over her to meet her gaze. She cocked a brow at me, her hands on her hips. "What?"

"What was that look for?"

"What look?"

"Like you've never seen anything like me before?"

"I haven't," I said, pushing myself up to stand. The minute I did so, I yelped when a sharp pain struck my elbow. I grabbed it instinctively and dropped back down on the sofa. Zara shot forward, dropping beside me.

"What's wrong?"

"My arm hurts." I gasped at the sudden pain. She jerked up the sleeve of my sweater and, like some sort of unusual force of nature, a purple bruise appeared over my arm. "Ouch."

"You must've hit it when you fell."

"I didn't feel it yesterday."

"Let me get you some ice." She hopped up and hurried off to the kitchen. When she returned a moment later, she had a dish towel, an ice pack, the first aid kit, and a bandage. "Let me?" she asked.

"Yeah." I pulled my sweater off, leaving me in a T-shirt. Zara wrapped the ice pack in the towel, pressed it against my elbow, then wrapped it in the bandage. She grabbed a few pillows to prop my arm and I leaned back with a sigh. "Thanks. Every part of me feels achy now."

"You were in a little bit of shock, I imagine." She shifted through the first aid kit until she found a bottle of ibuprofen. "How many do humans take?"

"As opposed to...amphibians?" I gawked at the odd question.

Zara's face reddened straightaway. "I was kidding. I take like four so I meant *normal* humans."

"Two, I guess," I said, laughing some as she handed them to me. I downed them without water and let my head drop back on the pillows. "Thanks."

"Welcome. Steve's going to drive us back to town in a little while. You sure you're okay? We can get that arm checked out."

"It's just bruised, I think. And I'm a little sore."

"Well, a hundred-something-pound wolf did tackle you to the ground, after all. It might've weighed as much as you do," she said, her eyes flickering over me in a clinical sweep. "And you slept on a sofa."

"It was pretty cozy by far. My loft isn't as nice as this."

"Where do you live?"

"You know that little Southwestern shop in town?" I asked, shifting my weight to test out the pain in my arm.

"Yeah. I shop there sometimes." She nodded, pulling her knee up to her chest.

"I live right above it. The shop owner is really nice. Her name is Imogene," I told her.

"She's Steve's sister-in-law. Did you know?"

My brows lifted with the surprise of her reveal. "I didn't. This town is *small*."

"You have no idea." She smirked, glancing to the door then back to me. "Are you hungry?"

"A little."

"I can fix us something. Eggs and toast perhaps?" Her delicate question, coupled with her quiet demeanor, reflected nothing of the woman-in-blue who normally grumped at me when I butted my nose into police business.

"Um...yeah, sure. That sounds nice. Can I help?"

"Not with that arm." She nodded toward it. "It'll take ten minutes. Coffee okay, too?"

"Coffee is always okay."

Together, we made our way into the kitchen, and I watched as she moved through the quaint space with practiced grace. She pulled two dishes down from the cupboard, along with two mugs. The way she juggled them had me ogling with awe. She chuckled when she set them down on the table.

"What?"

"You're gracefulness is pretty impressive. I would've dropped at least one thing. Are you sure I can't help?"

"I'm sure. Rest your arm up on the table," she urged, and I obeyed. "So, sunny side up or over easy?"

"I'm an over easy kind of gal," I said, smiling while I considered her caretaking.

"Me too."

Silence hung between us while she bustled about. Coffee brewed, bread toasted, and eggs fried all at the same time. Less than ten minutes later, we sat down together to share breakfast. The perfectly cooked eggs melted in my mouth and I nearly died from the deliciousness.

"This is yummy."

She chuckled, tucking a strand of hair behind her ear while she started on her third egg. "It's just eggs. Nothing fancy."

"Yeah, but I almost never have breakfast, let alone a home-cooked one. It's a nice change. Thank you." I sipped my coffee, holding the mug close to my chest. The soothing warmth of it, plus the heat that rose from the mouth of the cup, brought a sense of calmness over me like a gentle hug. "Not just for breakfast, but for saving my life. And letting me stay here."

"Something tells me it won't be the last time I save your life. *Nosey.*" She smirked around her bite of toast.

"And she's back." I laughed, shaking my head when she smiled at me. Her eyes twinkled with playfulness, and it warmed me almost as much as the coffee.

Sometime later, the front door open and Steve, in his work uniform, stepped inside like he owned the place. Zara acted as if she expected him to enter well-before his boots hit the floor. So much so, that she stood up beside the table almost at the same time.

"I heard you captured a wayward reporter in the woods out here, Weston. Charged her with trespass, have you?" he announced, his voice booming. In all the time that I'd known him, he'd always been *Steve* to me. I never even knew his last name.

"Cuffed and booked, sir." Zara smirked, gesturing to me. "There's your prisoner."

"Parker, what have you gotten yourself into this time?" he asked, chuckling. "Ready to roll?"

"Same ol'." I laughed and turned to Zara. "Not coming?"

"I'm off today," she said.

"Oh. Okay." I stood, patting my wrapped arm as I rose. "Thanks again."

"Of course. Get that checked out if it doesn't calm down in a few days," she said, walking with us to the door.

I grabbed my pack, and turned to her after tossing it over my good shoulder. "It was good getting to know you," I confessed, though I could feel the flush rising in my cheeks so I swung around quickly. "Take care."

"You, too." Zara's voice softened when she said it and bid us goodbye.

On the car ride back to town, Steve forced me to sit in the back of the patrol car so that he could laugh at me in the rearview.

"Not funny at all." Though I laughed, too. "How come the dog gets to ride up front?"

"He's well-behaved." He reached over and stroked the head of the regal German Shepherd. "Unlike yourself."

"Arrest me already then." I huffed, but he just laughed.

"My buddy Caden, his wife's name is Xany. You remind me of her sometimes."

"Zainy? What kind of name is *that*?"

"A damn suiting one if you ask me."

"Are you calling me crazy?" I kicked the back of his seat and he cracked up, jerking the steering wheel while he did so.

"I am, Parker, I am."

"You can call me Mack, you know."

"Nah. Parker is easier. So looks like you and Weston hit it off pretty well. At least she wasn't complaining about you this time."

"She's much less grumpy when she's not a cop."

"Aren't we all. I'm surprised she took you in," he said, turning off the dirt road after a good twenty minute ride through the woods. The tires no longer crunched and the drive became much smoother.

"What do you mean?"

"Weston's a loner. Doesn't take well to people in her space."

"Why do you say that? She seemed more than hospitable." My brow furrowed, and I leaned forward with my good elbow on the small window that sat open between the two seats. The dog turned and licked my cheek, chuffing at me afterward. I reached through and pet him gently while Steve and I spoke.

"Over the years, she's come across some unkind people. Hard to explain really, you'll have to ask her," he said, glancing at me in the mirror again. "So, what exactly were you doing in those woods?"

"What did Zara tell you?"

"That you got lost on your hike and she came across you getting mauled by a wolf. But something tells me there's more to the story."

"There always is with me." I offered him my cheekiest grin. "You'll have to buy a copy of The Review to read about it."

"Don't make me kill you, because I will."

"C'mon." I laughed hard. "Don't threaten me, *po-po*."

"Dear sweet Gaia. Save my soul from this one."

"*Gaia*? Is that how you avoid saying something more alarmingly offensive like 'Dear sweet baby Jesus' around these *conservative* parts?" I scoffed, which only made him chuckle again.

"Something like that. Where am I dropping you?"

"Home, please."

"You still above Imogene's shop?" he asked.

"Um… yeah. Are you stalking me?"

He sighed dramatically. "You know only about three-thousand people live in this town, right? And you know that I'm the only Police Chief? Which means I know everyone? And where they live?"

"Blah, blah, I'm the Chief and I'm special." I waved him off and he just shook his head at me. "At least your dog likes me."

"Better be careful. He's part wolf."

"Just what I need."

The rest of the ride continued with our ridiculous banter, and him trying to extract information about the story from me. I might've told Zara more than I should, but I wasn't about to divulge my law-breaking habits to the Chief of Police. Not only did he watch me like a hawk, but he was my main source of exclusive information.

Steve dropped me off at home, and I unwrapped my elbow first thing. The bruise appeared wider now, spreading up my arm and down toward my forearm in both directions. Even after a shower and a warm soak, the swelling didn't improve much. I settled on another ice pack, more ibuprofen, and propping it on my desk while I got back to work on the story.

The database hack, while useful for finding out the schedules of staffers, didn't give me active information about Stormhill Hospital. There had to be another way to find out what happened. It didn't take a genius to recognize that people around me kept secrets, especially the cops. I might have to get radical with my attempts at information…

I look down at my throbbing arm.

Like an impromptu visit to the emergency room.

∽∽∽

"The doctor will be in shortly to talk to you about your x-rays," one of the male nurses said, the next day after I'd embarked on my latest excursion into prying.

"Thanks." While I waited, I took the opportunity to scan the E.R. for the camera placement. On each floor, from the radiology department, back down to the E.R., I made quick notes about the cameras. And in one case, snapped a photo of the type of equipment. None of it appeared particularly high-tech, which would be of great benefit to me in the long run. The explosion took place in one of the halls leading away from the emergency room where Doctor Twofeathers worked. All I needed was access to the footage.

"Okay, Miss Parker. How are you feeling?" The doctor entered, his chipper smile, superficial at best, trained on his face while he pinned my x-rays up to the light box.

"Still some pain."

"The good news is, nothing's broken. The bad news is you've got one heck of a contusion. It'll heal over time with rest. And keep doing what you're doing with cold packs and heat," he said, turning to me now, his smile still plastered on his face.

"Thanks." *I literally just cost myself a thousand dollars to map out CCTV cameras.* "I'll do that."

"We'll get your discharge papers ready to go and have you on your way."

"All right," I said, sliding from the table. He shook my hand and I returned the gesture. Part of me wished Doctor Twofeathers would be my treating doctor, but life just wasn't that convenient.

Six years later, or so it seemed, I finally received my paperwork and they let me go. I hit the parking lot, at about dusk, and paused when an ambulance pulled up to the entrance, accompanied by two police cars. Sirens blared until the cars came to a halt. I kept my distance, and watched as they unloaded the vehicle with the elderly woman on a stretcher. My heart gave a squeeze when a man, who I assumed was her husband, exited with her while holding her hand. He cooed soft phrases to her while the EMTs wheeled her inside.

When the commotion died down, I turned away and headed down the sidewalk to the bus stop a few yards away. A car door closed, and I turned in time to see one of the cops exiting the vehicle. Right away, I recognized Zara. She didn't seem to notice me while she looked upward, her nose turned toward the sky as if taking in the scent of the fresh autumn breeze. A second later, her gaze snapped in my direction, and she looked right at me. It startled me so completely that I jumped with her quick movement. She leaned into the car, said something to whoever sat in the passenger seat, then headed toward me.

I gulped when I saw the way her shoulders bulked up under the weight of her uniform and vest. She had one hand resting on her belt by her service weapon when she approached. If I didn't know her, my heart would've pounded even harder than it already was.

"What are you doing out here?" she asked right away.

"Just leaving. You look really scary right now," I confessed, gripping my purse tighter. Her eyes scanned the area around us, and I could've sworn I saw the same creepy greenish shimmer in the darkness that I had a few nights ago.

"Sorry," she said, coming to stand unusually close to me. She continued looking around before finally meeting my gaze. "Are you okay?"

"I had my arm checked. It was still hurting."

"What'd they say?"

"Just a bad bruise. Is everything okay? You're acting funny."

"Did you drive here?"

"Bus."

"I'm off shift in five. I can take you home," she said, her hand falling to the small of my back when she nodded toward the police cars. "C'mon."

"I'm okay taking the bus, really," I told her, but moved with her anyway.

"I'd prefer to take you," she said, glancing around us again like the boogie man was about to jump out and scream at us.

"Zara, I—"

"I'd feel better if I took you, okay?" she said, looking back to me with the same soft expression of the woman that cared for me on her sofa after I nearly died.

"Yeah. Okay," I agreed. Relief seemed to melt over her and she nodded toward the car. Her partner, the same cop who stood with her on the first day that I met her, now leaned against the patrol car.

"What's the deal, Weston?"

"I'm taking Makayla home. Can you catch a ride with the chief?"

"No prob," he said, glancing between the two of us. "You good?"

"We're fine," she said, though she walked me to the passenger side of the car and opened the door. I wasn't sure if her chivalry belonged to her natural character, or out of whatever motivated her to keep extra close to me.

"Thanks," I said as I slid inside the vehicle. Zara came around the driver's side, turning over the engine as we buckled up. "This is my second ride in a cop car in forty-eight hours. I'm beginning to get suspicious."

"We like to keep our citizens safe." She shifted the gears, and we were out of there in no time.

The only sound belonged to the hum of the tires on the pavement for several minutes on the short journey toward the center of town. Zara kept her focus forward, but eventually she glanced at me when she caught me watching her.

"So...is something going on around here? Because I really could've taken the bus."

"It's late and this town has some tourists who've proven to be assholes. They've been picked up for harassing women at night who are unaccompanied," she said, though it didn't seem like the whole story.

"Is that unusual? I mean, I'm from Salt Lake City. Guys harassing girls in the streets isn't exactly unique," I said while fiddling with my purse in my lap.

"It is for here. And there's been one report of a sexual assault. So, if you can avoid it, please don't walk around at night alone for awhile," she said, pulling up to the front of the closed storefront. She parked half on the sidewalk without skipping a beat. I laughed a little, gesturing to the way she angled the car right in front of the *No Parking* sign.

"Really?"

"I do what I want, okay?" She chuckled, unbuckling herself. "I'll walk you up."

"You really don't have to…"

"I'm going to though."

"Pushy. Jeez." I rolled my eyes and we exited together.

I led her around to the side entrance of the building, and up the single flight of stairs to my loft. She stood one step down from me while I unlocked the door, and again I caught her looking around as if waiting for something. Once we headed inside, her odd behavior quelled some.

"Can I get you a drink or something?" I tossed my purse on the countertop in the kitchen, and motioned to the stools near it.

"I'm okay. This is a cute little place," she said, glancing around before taking a seat. "It smells like sage."

"It's from the shop below. I think my apartment is the most spiritually cleansed place in the whole city," I said, taking out a beer from the fridge and offering her one. "You're off duty now."

She cocked a brow at me, then snatched the bottle. "Thanks."

I swiveled to grab the bottle opener from the drawer, but when I turned back to her, she was already taking a swig. "Um...how'd you?"

"Magic." She flipped the bottle cap to me and I laughed, catching it after an ungraceful fumble.

"Liar." I popped the cap on mine, and sipped it right after. "Are you a beer drinker?"

"Not really. But if I do drink, I usually choose it. Wine seems a little dainty for me."

"Me too. It feels like I should be sitting down to a fancy dinner while wearing a skimpy dress. Beer is underwear booze," I said, lifting it in a mock toast. "Cheers."

"Underwear booze?" She laughed, clinking her bottle against mine.

"Yup. You can drink it in your underwear and no one gives a fuck. Wine is dress booze."

"You are an oddball, Makayla Parker. The oddest one in the bunch. But I don't hate it." She took a heavy draw on her drink, then glanced to the window where one of the street lights shined in. "You have a decent view of the town from here," she commented.

"It helps when I'm feeling particularly nosey," I said, leaning on the counter facing her.

"Good thing you live here then." She chuckled, and downed the rest of her beer. "I should get the patrol car back. Promise you'll stay in tonight?"

"Yes, boss." I saluted her and clicked my heels together once. She shook her head at me and stood.

"That's a pretty sophisticated rig you got there." Zara pointed at my computer set up. "That where you do your law-breaking?"

"Only when cops aren't in my apartment."

"Uh huh…" She chuckled, and I walked with her to the front door. "Catch you around."

"For some reason, that sounded like a promise."

She tossed me one of her half-smiles and said, "Night."

"G'night."

CHAPTER FOUR

"How long do you think it'll take?" Ian asked me while crunching on a pizza crust. The two of us stood over my computers, watching the screen scrolling.

"I scanned the IP address ranges, got the camera models, and the Wi-Fi names. Shouldn't be too long."

"And the password crack?"

"It's running."

"Are we gonna get arrested?" he asked, glancing at me while he reached for another slice.

"Probably not in this town."

"How'd I end up helping you with this?" He dropped down into the desk chair and spun it in a circle while eating.

"Don't puke on my gear. And I coaxed you with your name sharing mine in the byline, remember?"

"Oh yeah. That's low, Mack. Even for you."

"I want this story."

"Is it really that important?"

"Something's going on around here, Ian. I'm not the only one that noticed. You were the one who wrote that story about the club that opened downtown. Ever since those metal-head-goths showed up, strange things have been happening," I said, taking a seat beside him. "People disappearing, hospitals exploding. And what about that teenager who vanished, and returned like six months later? Her parents told people that she tried to bite them."

"She was high on PCP, Mack. People do crazy shit while drugged up. As for the club?" He shrugged. "Weird kinks aren't unusual in the city. Someone saw a market in this town and capitalized on it. Not that strange. I did the story on it after all."

"Still. I feel like something is going on."

"Or you're paranoid. Same thing."

"Come on. Give me the benefit of the doubt."

"I am." He motioned to the computers. "Aiding and abetting a felony and all."

I sighed while shooting him a glare. Just when I was about to run my mouth, the monitors screeched to a halt and a green blinking box appeared in the center. "Shit, look."

"Dude, you got in."

"Of course I did." I nudged my way to the center of the console. "Move over."

"Beast." He grumbled while I plugged away at the keys. Ian loomed over my shoulder so close that I could feel his body heat.

"I can smell your breath. Get away from me."

"Come on! Just get in already." He flailed, motioning toward the screen.

"Gross. Keep your penis away from me." I shoved him and he laughed.

"Just shut up and figure it out," he bellowed, pushing me right back.

"Hold on. I got—I got it. Shit." Images from the hospital appeared on both monitors. Patients and staff bustled about, completely unaware that another party looked in on them.

"That's a live feed. Get the recordings."

"Working on it. And….there." I hit the enter key harder

than I should. Sure enough, the screens shifted to the date in question. "That's the receptionist I interviewed there," I said, pointing her out at the desk.

"That must be Doctor Twofeathers there. With the long hair." Ian tapped on the screen. "Who is she talking to?"

"Not sure. A patient maybe?"

"Zoom in. Is there sound?"

"On it. No sound." I panned the image until it focused on the tiny woman that stood facing the doctor. She appeared like she just dropped off the ski slopes in her fluffy jacket and boots. "She looks young."

"I've seen her before..." Ian drummed his fingers on the desk while he considered the images.

"Where?"

"Not sure—wait." He flipped his phone out of his pocket and grew quiet while I attempted to make out what the woman said to the doctor.

"She's saying something about the doctor owing her something. A chair?" I leaned back. "Well, that makes no sense."

"Found her." He turned his phone around to show me. "She's the owner of the club downtown." Sure enough, her picture appeared on a document Ian used for his article that identified the new owner.

"Well...that's strangely convenient. Lilly Fairborne. She looks young."

"Why would the doctor owe a club owner a chair? Maybe she ruined it during a kink session or something," postulated Ian. It made me laugh at him.

"That's ridiculous. Are you sure that's her name? It sounds fake."

"It could be. Maybe a pseudonym," he said, shrugging as we both turned back to watching the video. I recorded the clip of Lilly and Doctor Twofeathers until they moved off screen. A few minutes later, the camera cut out.

"That must've been the explosion," I told him. "Cut the

power or the lines."

"Probably. So what's your next step, Nancy Drew?" He yawned, leaning back in his chair again.

"Well, if Lilly Fairborne was the last person seen talking to the doctor before she was kidnapped, we're going to wander, ever so delicately, into the club owned by Ms. Fairborne." I tapped my fingers against my bottom lip.

"First, you need to change your clothes. Argyle sweaters and Oxford heels aren't going to cut it." He pinched the end of his nose, pretending that I stunk.

"Ian! I *so* don't dress like that." I did.

He sighed, pretending to faint. "Fine. Cardigans and Oxfords."

"I hate you." I shoved his shoulder. "Fine. I'll change. Are you coming with me?"

"Fuck no. I've got a reputation to keep up."

"Jerk."

It took me about an hour to get ready. However, due to my lack of edgy fashion choices, I decided on picking out all of my black clothes from the closet and rearranging them. Black jeans, a black button-down shirt, and a pair of my best stilettos did the trick. Ian convinced me to leave my hair down, and with a splash of black eyeliner, I toed the line of *edgy*.

"Just barely. You'll pass," he assured.

I considered walking, but at the last moment, called a cab to drop me off a block from the establishment. At nearly eleven at night, my heels clicked as I headed down the busier street toward the club. Music boomed, and the bass made the ground vibrate under my feet as I neared the queue of people waiting to get in. Twice on the walk, I noticed police cars patrolling the area. They slowed to a roll every time they crossed in front of the club, then picked up again soon after. All the while, I pondered why the owner of a club would confront a doctor at her place of work. What could she have possibly wanted with Doctor Twofeathers that couldn't wait? More importantly, if Lilly Fairborne was behind the kidnapping, what was the motive?

When I took my place at the end of the line, the drunken chatter of the people in front of me unnerved me some. I hadn't been to a club or a bar like this in years. I gripped my phone in my palm, glancing down at the text from Ian.

You in?
Not yet.
Keep it cool, Parker.
You doubt my skills?
I do, in fact.
Asshole.

I smirked, slipping my phone in the back pocket of my jeans. The woman in front of me turned slightly, her black hair, pale skin, and raging red lipstick had her fitting right in with the rest of the patrons in gothic dress. She lifted a slender brow at me, onyx gaze flickering over me once.

"Haven't seen you here before," she said, her voice husky. She wore a shiny black corset on top of her pleather pants and platform heels. "You alone?"

I shrugged. "Figured I'd check it out. Sounds like you're a regular."

"I am. What's your name, honey?" She turned fully now, her arms folded over her middle.

"Sarah," I answered straightaway. "You?"

"You can call me Bronwyn," she said, smiling broadly. In the glare from the streetlight, something flashed in her mouth, resembling the stud of a pierced tongue.

"All right. Then what can you call me?"

"How about Astrid. It suits you." Her endless grin remained and the stillness in her demeanor brought me pause.

"Does it?" I tilted my head, crossing my arms over my middle when a chill ran up my spine.

"'Divinely beautiful.' Astrid suits you." She reached out, dragging her fingernail along the back of my hand.

A shudder raced up my spine, coupled with a sudden aversion to the closeness of this woman. My tongue tingled the same way it did before a horrible wretch. For some reason, this flawlessly beautiful woman creeped me out. I pulled my hand away, taking half a step back.

"Come inside and sit with us," she said, gesturing to the door when she and the man that accompanied her moved to the front of the line.

I made to open my mouth, but something firm and heavy bashed into my side, sending me into a wobbly step forward. Bronwyn leaned away, as if whatever rushed me in the darkness belonged to an orchestration of hideousness. Her face contorted, and she recoiled, moving quickly toward the bouncer who waved her entry into the club. Someone grabbed my arm, and yanked me right off the sidewalk.

"Let me go!" I pushed at the hand wrapped around me, until I recognized the squelch of the police radio.

"Be quiet and keep walking," Zara muttered, but the grip she had on my wrist nearly snapped it in two.

"You're *hurting* me." I gasped, my shoes clacking obnoxiously on the pavement. She dragged me half way down the road to the spot where the cab dropped me off. Once the music from the club faded, she loosened her grip. "Jesus, Zara."

"You can't be here," she said, her teeth clenched and her eyes wide with something I couldn't quite distinguish. Anger or fear—it was a tossup. "We need to go."

"What are you doing? You blew my cover. I'm trying to—"

"No," was all she said before tugging me toward the cruiser parked a few yards away. She pulled open the back door and forced me inside, her hand on top of my head. Images of my last arrest flashed through my mind's eye. I sent an aggravated punch into the back seat of the car after she closed the door. She jumped into the driver's seat, and tore out of there like the buildings around us prepared to fall.

"What the fuck is going on? You can't just...*arrest* me for nothing!" I protested, and she said nothing the entire way back to the center of town.

Once we drove into the well-lit area of the business district, she pulled into the parking lot of the grocery store and parked the car. Her left hand gripped the steering wheel, and her chest rose and fell as she appeared to try to calm her breathing. I sat there, staring at her and fearing her next response. In time, she ran her fingers through the loose strands of her ponytail and turned in her seat. She opened the window in the center of the cruiser, her eyes darting all over my face as if searching for something.

"What's the matter with you? Are you stalking me or something?" I asked, huffing out my frustration at being left in the dark.

"Look at me," she said, her face close to the open window.

"I am," I responded, meeting her gaze. She stared at me for the briefest moment, and finally, her shoulders relaxed. With her tension fading, so did mine. "What's going on?"

"You can't go to that club, Makayla. It's not safe. No one there is safe to be around."

"Why? What happened there?" I leaned forward in my seat. "Is it like a mob-owned thing or something?"

"No, but it's dangerous," she said, her expression softening from the fierce law enforcement agent, to the woman that I shared breakfast with not that long ago.

"Does Doctor Twofeathers have anything to do with it? Because something tells me that she does."

"You need to stop this. Whatever you're doing, it has to stop. Story or not. You can't." She paused, pursing her lips. "You can't do this anymore."

"And you can't tell me what to do." I crossed my arms over my chest, flopping back against the seat of the car. "Nor can you keep me locked up back here forever."

"No. But if it gets you to listen to me, I'll do it for

now."

"I *know* that doctor has something to do with the owner of that club, Zara. I saw the video. I *know* she was the last person to talk to her before she got taken," I blurted out, fighting the urge to throw a much larger fit. "Either you tell me what's going on between Lilly Fairborne and Doctor Twofeathers, or I'm going to walk into that club the minute you're not looking and find out myse—"

"What video?" Her brow furrowed. "What video did you see?"

I whipped my phone out of my pocket, poked the screen through the prompts, and pulled up the portion of the video that I clipped earlier. Her eyes widened as she watched, then, without a word, she turned around, shifted the car into drive, and pulled out of the parking lot.

"Where are we going?"

"Somewhere safe." She drove us away from town, into the darkness where streetlights didn't light the way anymore.

"You're a cop. I thought *you* keep people safe."

"I do." She closed the window with a snap and I couldn't hear anything she said when she flicked her phone to her ear. I gave her seat a swift kick, but she didn't even bother to look at me in the rearview mirror.

～～

"How long are you going to hold me hostage here?" I asked while sitting at Zara's kitchen table. She'd removed her vest and work shirt, before brewing a pot of coffee. She brought two mugs to the table, now wearing only her pants, boots, and a white tank top. With her tension, the defined muscles of her arms became more pronounced.

"Until I figure out what to do with you."

"Who'd you call from the car?"

She dropped her head in her hands, groaning quietly. "Makayla. You ask more questions than anyone I've ever met."

"I think I have reason to when a police officer kidnaps

me!" I banged my hand on the table then winced when I remembered my elbow. Zara looked up, her gaze flickering to my arm.

"Still hurt?"

"Not really." I rolled up my sleeve and bent it a few times. "I expected it to though." She paused, her brow wrinkling as she gazed at my arm. "What?"

"It's almost gone."

"Yeah. It was just a bruise." I shrugged then fixed my sleeve. "Now, back to the story at hand. Why am I a hostage?"

"Because you inserted yourself into an active police investigation. Until it's over, you have to stay here," she said, way too succinct for my liking.

"I have a job and a life. I can't just *stay here* until you think it's safe for me to leave." Again, I thumped my hand on the table and she frowned.

"None of that matters right now."

"To me it does. What exactly have I walked into, Zara?"

"I can't tell you that right now. But you have to trust me…"

"I don't…even know you," I admitted, lifting the coffee mug to hold it between my palms.

"I don't know you either," she said, leaning her elbow on the table. Her gaze flickered from the mug in my hands to the place where my shirt hung exceptionally low against my cleavage. Right away, she shifted her weight and lifted her mug to take a sip.

"Did you just check out my tits?" I laughed, swatting the table again to get her attention.

"No," she said, her expression falling, but a blush melted over her cheeks.

"You absolutely did." I rolled my eyes at her. "Or else you wouldn't be blushing."

She kept her gaze to the floor, and her cheeks only grew redder. "It's the outfit."

"Uh huh…right. Wait, are you the sexual predator that

you warned me about? Is this coffee roofied?" I held it at arm's length, scowling.

"If I wanted to roofie you, I could've poisoned your eggs," she said, smirking when she glanced at me again.

"Huh..." I considered her words, and shook my head. "I'm still kidnapped though."

"For now," she said, sighing some. "I didn't mean to...you know."

"Don't worry about it. I was checking out your guns when you took your shirt off anyway," I admitted.

She looked down at her gear belt, and her hand fell to her service weapon. "It's a *Glock*."

I chuckled, shaking my head. "Not that gun," I said, flexing my bicep like the feeble thing I was. "These guns."

"Oh." She laughed, shrugging a little. The pink tinge in her cheeks remained steadfast through our banter.

"Okay. Fun is over. I'm back to being pissed at you." I slouched in my chair, and returned to grumbling about being held captive.

"It's late. You can take the bed if you want," she said after some time. "I'm fine on the sofa."

"Why? So you can make sure I don't sneak out?"

"Partially." She tugged the ponytail holder from her hair and I watched as it tumbled over her shoulders. "Please don't sneak out. These woods aren't safe at night either."

"I need clothes, Zara. Money. I have nothing but my phone."

"Tomorrow after work, I'll take you to your place to pick up a few things. Okay?"

"Fine." I let out an exasperated sigh then stood. "I can take the sofa."

"No, really. It's fine. I have some work to finish up anyway." She motioned for me to follow her to the bedroom.

Her room, similar to the rest of the cabin, held quaint furnishings, pretty wall tapestries in Southwestern design, and a neatly made bed with loads of fluffy pillows. Even though I didn't know Zara, or understand anything that'd happened tonight, something about this room appealed to me. It brought of sense of comfort, and familiarity that I couldn't explain. I glanced over my shoulder at her, then pointed to the windows set higher up than usual on the walls.

"Aren't you worried that I might climb out?"

"Not really. I'm pretty sure you're still concerned about being eaten by wolves in the forest. After all, they can see in the dark." She smiled cheekily, pulling the door shut on her way out. "Night."

"Night...jerk."

〰️

"You're where?" Ian asked, his voice booming through the phone. "Is that even on a map?"

"I don't know, but just pick me up at the bottom. It's a dirt road," I said while frowning at the ridiculous heels by the front door. "Actually, just come up as far as you can. I'm not going to make it far in these shoes."

"Mack, what the fuck have you gotten yourself into?"

"I don't know, but hurry up. I've been here for like two days already."

"I'm coming. Just get out of there."

"I am." I hung up, pocketed the phone, and decided to brave the wild barefoot for the time being.

In the mid-morning autumn sun, dew dampened the grass and my pants all the way to my knees. Zara's property, beautiful in its natural expanse, overlooked the Rockies in the distance as well as the huge lake a few meters away. A cool breeze crossed my path, sweeping my hair across my face in violent lashes. Despite the beauty, I worried about the wolves in the woods. My last encounter occurred during the day time, and it wasn't a friendly meet and greet. I hoped that sticking to the same path that Zara and Steve took to and from her cabin would help get me out of there faster. Anxiety tightened my chest as I clutched my phone and waited impatiently for Ian to arrive.

I must've stood on that dirt road for half an hour before the crunch of tires approached. I gripped my shirt, shivering as my thoughts began to wander. Only when I saw Ian's SUV appear around the corner did any relief flood me. I rushed to him, threw open the passenger side door, and hopped inside.

"Did you hook up with someone last night, girl?" He stared at me, wide-eyed.

"No! I wore this to the club." I flailed my hands in his face. "Less talking, more driving."

"Bossy bitch," he muttered, which earned him a punch in the shoulder. "Ow!"

"Shut up and drive." I turned on the heat and aimed the vent right at me. "I'm freezing."

"It's like fifty degrees."

"Thanks for rescuing me."

"Yeah, well, I'm earning that byline."

Ian dropped me off at home, and my first foray into comfort was to drown myself in a long, hot shower. While the water massaged the worry from my system, my mind wandered to Zara. Why did she care if I was *safe* or not? Clearly, she had no idea what it meant to be a reporter. I wouldn't always be just a small town reporter. If I broke a few good stories, I could possibly get a job in a bigger city. For now, I liked what I did here. And it paid the bills. Sort of.

In the few years since leaving Salt Lake, Ian was the only somewhat-friend that I had. Second to him, Zara remained the most casual contact I'd made outside of work. Even so, it seemed one-sided at best. And I didn't even have her number.

After dressing in reasonable attire, I dropped down on my bed, setting my computer in my lap to check on some of the other CCTV footage. To my surprise, all of the data disappeared from my drive, save for the tidbits that I'd recorded. I gave up, frustrated by the whole situation. I tossed my computer back on the desk and dropped into the pillows. I closed my eyes, letting out a deep breath. Maybe Zara was right about this story. Was it even worth it? No one else seemed to care about what happened at the hospital and the reconstruction of the damaged spots already started. Was any of this worth it?

As fatigue pressed in on me, old thoughts from darker places pushed me away from the light that the rush of work brought me. My extreme focus on reporting blocked out any intrusive thoughts that attempted to pierce my consciousness. In that, I thought about the *family* I left behind in Salt Lake. None of them cared to protect me from some unknown danger. None of them cared to protect me at all.

I must've fallen asleep for awhile because when I opened my eyes again, darkness swallowed my room save for the nightlight in the kitchen. My back ached from the odd position I'd fallen asleep in. So instead of turning over, I rolled into the desk chair and flipped open my laptop. Part of me ached to write the story I'd spent days on, but a larger part of me couldn't give a shit about it. Instead, I checked my email and clicked through some of the missed work emails from yesterday.

Commotion outside my window startled me. Something metal rattled in the street. I leaned over the desk to see a woman, dressed in dark clothes, with long hair, kicking an empty can down the street. With her arms outstretched and laughing, she appeared to be speaking to someone. I watched for a moment, until she kicked the can so hard that it smashed into a nearby light post. Under the streetlight, I could just make out her features. Black hair, pale skin, red lipstick.

"What the hell?" I muttered.

"Hey!" the muffled voice of someone called out. "What do you think you're doing?" Even through the closed window, I heard a man's shout. From the building across the street, the man, wearing a soiled apron, rushed across the road, shouting profanities at the woman who then kicked the can at a car parked just below my window. It shot across the sidewalk so fast that the velocity of it shattered the windshield. I covered my mouth, watching as the man approached her, waving an angry hand in her face. He had a phone in the palm of the other, as he threatened to call the police. My heart pounded in my chest, and I snatched my phone from the desk.

The woman laughed at him, reaching forward and poking him in the shoulder. He pushed her hand away. In the middle of the street, the two of them faced off in a heated, but inaudible battle. I hesitated, my thumb on the keypad ready to dial 911, then the woman seemed to calm down.

"You're crazy!" the man shouted when she moved so close to him that her torso touched his chest. One hand snaked up the side of his body, almost seductively. In a swift motion, she snatched the phone out of his hand, crushed it in her palm, then grabbed him by the throat. He choked, smacking at her arm in desperation.

A gasp left me and I pressed the call button, standing up from my chair now. My entire body shook with the adrenaline that coursed through me. The woman lifted the man, his toes nearly leaving the ground, then in a swift blur, she shrieked and slammed her face against his shoulder. I started, dropping my phone and stumbling backward. My eyes trained on the incident in the street. Who else saw this? Did anyone call for help? Were they acting out some sort of scene?

When the woman leaned back, a rush of darkness flowed down the front of the man's white apron. It trickled, then sprayed across the woman's feet. She laughed, releasing him. He fell to the ground, clawing at the pavement in a frantic attempt to escape.

"Nine-one-one, what's your emergency?" the distant voice of the operator asked. "Hello?" I couldn't move. Couldn't speak.

The woman in the street stepped over the man. He twitched, clutching at his throat. She ignored him. She paused, gazing toward the sky as if expecting a rare meteor shower. In the glow of the streetlight, I saw the same darkness that covered the man's clothes dripping down her chin. Her eyes, wide and wild in their own right, looked up at nothing and everything at the same time. She spun in a circle, smiling like a twisted, vacant, psychopath with the grin of a comic book clown.

I clutched my chest, gasping for breath. The woman turned, her head shifting in a stop-motion, bird-like tilt before she screamed and crouched to the ground. A second later, she leapt into the air, disappearing for a blink until her form smacked against my window, perched on the ledge in a feline crouch. She looked right at me, blood dripping down her face, and smiled.

Two pearlescent beads pressed against her bottom lip before she lashed her tongue across them. The fangs belonged to a hell-born beast.

I screamed, tumbling backward over my chair and landing in a heap. When I looked back to the window, the only thing she left in her wake was a heart drawn in blood on the window pane.

CHAPTER FIVE

"She's in shock," someone said.

"Is she delirious?" Steve's familiar voice burst through my consciousness and I tried to move toward the sound. "Dammit, Parker. I liked this one," he said.

Feet bound up the stairs at a heated pace. "Move," demanded Zara and the sound of her voice brought a strange experience to my awareness. Indigo mist swirled in front of my eyes, clearing away the darkness. I sat on the floor, an EMT perched beside me, while Steve and Officer Lightfoot looked on. The purplish fog wiggled between them when they stepped aside. Zara appeared at the other end of the tendrils. The moment she dropped to her knees in front of me, the colors faded and reality crashed down on me in an instant. Overheated palms touched the sides of my face and tears tumbled from my eyes.

"I should've listened to you," I told her through a sob. "I'm sorry."

"It's okay. You're okay," Zara cooed, her thumbs stroking my cheeks. Heat radiated from her, like she'd been struck with a dangerous fever. Her body burned against me when I moved closer, crying softly as she hugged me. "You're okay."

The room around us paused, and when I calmed down,

I leaned back to see everyone staring at me. Zara remained close, holding my hand while Steve, Lightfoot, and the EMT looked on. Steve wore a surprised expression, then shared a glance with Zara.

"Come," said Zara, gently tugging me up to stand.

"Did he die?" I wiped my eyes with my sleeve.

"He did," answered Steve, his voice soft.

"He didn't deserve to die like that." I choked on a sob and Zara rubbed my back.

"Can you all give us a minute?" asked Zara, her lips pursing after. Steve squeezed her shoulder before stepping out with the others. Lightfoot and the EMT left, and Steve remained at the top of the stairs, standing guard like a soldier.

I looked back to Zara, noting that she wasn't wearing her work uniform. She was back in the leather-on-leather getup she wore when she found me in the woods.

"Let's get some of your things packed and head back to the cabin," she said, her voice soft. I nodded, sniffling again before glancing around the room.

Zara moved to the closet, pulling it open and waiting for me to join her. Together, we grabbed one of my duffle bags and began tossing in my clothes. A few pairs of shoes followed, and I grabbed the case with all my important documents. The desk area, in shambles under the window with the bloody heart, had me avoiding it at all costs.

"Anything else you need?"

"I don't know where my phone is," I croaked, sniffling again.

"Steve has it." She zipped the bag, and tossed it over her shoulder. "Let's go."

I handed Steve my keys on the way out. Instead of heading out to the front of the building where all the law enforcement investigated, he brought us through the side entrance of Imogene's shop. Inside, the thick smell of sage and leather overwhelmed me. The familiarity calmed me and I let Zara lead the way.

In the center of the room, Imogene stood beside a man nearly twice the girth of Steve. His copper skin and long, braided salt-and-pepper hair, made him a standout among everyone else. He looked nothing like his clean-cut brother. Hank, who I met only once in passing, loomed over the group gathered in the shop. Imogene hurried over to me, holding her hands out in a maternal manner.

"Oh, Miss Parker, are you alright?" she asked, giving my arms a squeeze.

"I'm okay," I said, glancing to the front window of her shop. In the street, a white sheet covered the body of the man murdered by the... "Mister Olsen isn't."

"No, he's not, love." She looked from me to Zara. "Are you taking her?"

"I am." Zara nodded, glancing from Imogene to Hank. I noticed she kept her gaze averted from both of them. "Is it okay with him?"

"Of course," Imogene answered, lifting her hand to place it on Zara's cheek. She flinched at first, but Imogene remained unmoving until Zara met her gaze. "Of course."

Questions swam in my brain. How did Imogene know Zara well enough to function as they just did? Why wasn't Zara dressed for work like she was when I last saw her? And why was Hank here? A non-cop appearing to be leading the course of action, despite his position.

"You can't drive though," Imogene said, releasing Zara's cheek then glancing at me.

"I know."

"Why not?" I asked, looking between them. Neither of them answered.

"Come on back here." Imogene led us to the back room of the shop, closing the door behind us.

"You'll have to trust me for a minute, okay?" Zara asked, holding her arms out to me.

"Okay..." I moved beside her, our faces awkwardly close. Again, the heat of her body engulfed me and the flash of the purple mist wavered between us. "I think I'm hallucinating," I admitted, and tears swelled again, choking me up.

"Hold on to me, and close your eyes." Zara hugged me, and I sobbed quietly against her shoulder. "Promise me that you won't open your eyes, Makayla."

"Okay." I sniffled, squeezing her tighter when I closed my eyes. "I won't."

"Say that you promise." Her arms wrapped around me, her chin resting on my shoulder. One arm gripped my middle firmly, the other held my face against her neck.

"I promise," I said, nodding against her. "I promise."

Something jerked me around the middle, like the sudden lurch of an escalating rollercoaster. I squeezed Zara as a whipping wind lapped at my hair and hers, forcing it to lash against my arms. A gasp left me when my body felt suddenly weightless, like lifting my feet up in a pool. Before it scared me too much, the gentle clunk of wooden floorboards met my sneakers. The wind stopped, and Zara rubbed my back.

"Okay," she said. "Are you dizzy?"

"A little." I leaned back, blinking my eyes open. My heart skipped a beat when I recognized her cabin. I cupped my hands over my mouth and sobbed. "I think I'm going crazy."

"You're okay." She set my bag down by the hearth. "Sit with me; come on."

Zara urged me to the sofa, wrapping a blanket around my shoulders. I leaned against her, tucking my knees up to my chest.

"I want to sleep. I just want to sleep," I confessed, dropping my head on my legs.

"Then sleep. You're safe here." She kept her arm around me, her hand on my head. "Just sleep."

"Don't leave me here." I sniffled, closing my eyes and allowing the heavy hand of sleep to drag me under. The smooth, rocking comfort of unconsciousness lured me into its grasp, and before long, everything came to a stop.

Daylight streaming on my face woke me the next day. The crackling fire in the hearth was the first thing I saw when I opened my eyes. On Zara's couch, cradled in the comfort of soft pillows and cozy blankets, I didn't want to move. A glass clinked in the kitchen and I saw her there, moving gracefully through whatever she was doing. With her hair down, it reached to the top of the loose-fitting jeans she wore. Even in her floppy sweater, the definition in her lithe body held my attention. Of course, in times of distress, I'd distract myself by staring at beautiful women. I dropped my head back down on the pillow, and allowed the chastising inner monologue to continue.

Zara must've noticed my consciousness because a moment later, she came to sit beside me, her hip by my knees. She placed her hand on the blanket above my midsection. It took me some time to meet her gaze as guilt weighed in on me. If I'd listened to her, none of this would've happened. She offered me a soft smile, patting the blanket gently.

"You okay?" she asked, her voice soft.

"Yeah." I nodded, sighing with it. "I'm sorry I left. I should've just...I don't know. Listened to you. If I had, then I wouldn't have seen a—" I stopped myself, and corrected. "A murder."

"What did you see, Makayla?"

"You'll think I'm crazy."

"I won't." She patted the blanket again when I looked away.

"What are the cops saying happened?"

"That there was a brawl in the restaurant and someone slashed the owner's throat. Does that differ from what you were going to say?" Her question and her tone were equally delicate.

"Yes." The burn of oncoming tears had me swallowing them down.

"Tell me," she implored, scooting closer so that I was

forced to look at her. The heat of her burned against my side, and when she placed her hand on top of mine, it became clear how hot her skin felt to me.

"You're hot," I said, starting a moment later when I realized what came out of my mouth. "I mean, you feel hot. Like you have a fever. I mean, not that you're not hot, because you are but I mean, your body is hot— *No!* I mean—"

"Easy." Zara laughed, shaking her head. "I understand what you mean. I've always burned a little hot. My mom always said so."

"Well, it's true." I nodded, settling back into the pillows again.

She nodded, but returned to the question of origin, "What did you see?"

"Promise you won't think I'm crazy?"

"I promise," she said, waiting patiently for me to explain.

"This woman, I didn't know her or anything. Black hair, black clothes, and super pale. I heard her kicking a can around the street, so I looked out the window to see her doing that. That's when Mister Olsen came out. She kicked the can so hard that it hit a car and broke the windshield."

"I saw the broken windshield. What happened then?"

"She tore out his throat." I gulped, squeezing the blanket tight. "With her *teeth*. She jumped up in the air after. I couldn't see where she went. Then when I looked again, she was outside my window. With blood dripping down her face." I took a deep breath. "She had fangs, Zara. *Fangs*. Like a vampire from a bad Halloween movie. She was crazy. She was a fucking crazy *vampire*. And she screamed like a crazy banshee." A few stray tears made it down my cheeks. "I saw a vampire. Am I crazy?"

"No," she said, simply. "You're not crazy."

"And you, somehow, managed to get us from town to your house in two seconds. I really am. I'm losing my mind." I covered my face. "Maybe I need to start drinking earlier in the day."

Zara chuckled softly. "Well, don't do that."

"And you." I sat up a little. "Why were you wearing your *Xena Warrior Princess*, outfit when everyone had on their uniforms? Weren't you working?"

"I was," she said, shifting her weight beside me.

"And? Is that like your go-to outfit or something?"

"Hard to explain."

"Want to try?" I asked, lifting a brow at her.

Zara averted her gaze and toyed with a lose thread in the blanket. Eventually, she shook her head, declining my request. "Are you hungry? I can fix you something," she said, still looking away.

"I'm okay. Can we just watch a movie or something? Preferably something without monsters or mayhem," I asked, observing her for a moment when she nodded.

She continued to avert her eyes so I reached forward and squeezed her hand. When she looked back at me, her eyes gleaming in the morning light, she smiled. For the briefest moment, the misty waves of indigo appeared before my eyes again. They tugged at something in my chest, strangling my heart and making my stomach lurch. Like some sort of creepy smoke, it swayed between us. I gripped my shirt at the same time that Zara placed her hand on the base of her neck as if searching for a necklace.

"We can watch a movie," she said, her soft voice breaking the panic that rose at the emergence of another hallucination.

"Okay. Let's do that."

We settled on the sofa together, and she turned the television on above the mantle. She clicked the remote a few times until the streaming video system appeared. It took us a good five minutes, but we settled on a *dramedy* series rather than a movie.

Over the next few days, this became our routine. The occasional meal or shower interrupted our binge sessions. Other than those instances, that's how we spent our time.

At the end of the fifth day, I emerged from the shower, and found Zara standing by the front door, pulling on a pair of hiking boots. She wore jeans and a fitted red flannel shirt. Her hair remained lose. Nervousness clenched my stomach when I saw her about to leave.

"Where are you going?"

"Nowhere. Meet me out here when you're dressed," she said, nodding to the towel I gripped around my middle.

"Okay…" I made off to her room, dressed quickly in jeans and a sweatshirt, and tied on my usual sneakers. A quick comb through my hair and I returned to her in the living room.

"Ready?" She opened the front door and waved me to follow.

"Where are we going?" I moved to her. Admitting to the anxiety that accompanied leaving the house wasn't something I was ready to do.

"For a walk. We've been inside almost a week. And it's a really nice day."

"Are there wolves out there?" I pointed to the open door.

Zara chuckled. "Not right now."

"Are there vampires?"

"Not in the daylight."

"Zombies?"

"Definitely not."

"Ghosts?" My eyes widened. "*Dragons?*"

"Dunno." She shrugged. "We'll just have to risk it," she said, smiling and holding her hand to me. "Come on."

Reluctantly, I took her hand and she tugged me out the door.

Cool autumn air rushed us when we made it onto the front porch. The only sound belonged to the rustling of the trees. Orange, yellow, and reds flecked the leaves, and a light layer of them crunched beneath our feet as we headed toward the woods. I stuck close to Zara, watching as she stopped for a moment to pick up a carved walking stick from beside a tree. Stained in a dark color, it appeared somewhat antique.

"Did you make that?" I asked, gesturing to it.

"No. My friend did. He makes all sorts of wood and bone carvings to sell at Imogene's shop," she said, ducking us through some low-hanging branches.

"Oh. I've seen some of those. Pretty nice."

"They are."

"Where are we going?"

"Nowhere special." Zara glanced back at me when I fell a few paces behind. "Am I going too fast?"

"No." I laughed, shaking my head. "Well, a little. Your legs are longer."

"Not by much." She smiled, slowing her pace as we climbed a small incline.

Twigs and branches snapped under my feet, but Zara's steps weren't as loud. We must've carried on for a good twenty minutes before we approached the babbling stream. Zara paused, crouching down beside a bit of plant life. I joined her, and she pointed to a pretty purple wildflower.

"It's a Marsh Violet," she said, a soft smile curving her lips while she poked it.

I watched her, leaning my elbow on my knee as an upsurge of emotion swelled in my chest. In this light, under the umbrella of the autumn foliage, Zara's beauty shined. Strong cheekbones, a perfect jaw line, and an athletic body that awakened parts of me that I kept at bay over the years. She was the epitome of strength and elegance at the same time.

"It's very beautiful," I told her, but I wasn't talking about the flower. In my mind's eye, a flash of the indigo mist struck me. This time, the tug in my chest brought a swell of emotion with it. She looked at me, her green eyes twinkling with the reflection of the water. Before I could stop myself, I reached forward and stroked a lock of her hair.

"They're my favorite," she said, holding my gaze for

only a moment before she stood.

"Good to know. I love Asters. All the bright colors they grow." I joined her as we followed the flow of the water. "What's your favorite color?"

"My favorite?" She glanced over her shoulder at me. "Indigo. Mainly because I can't decide between blue and purple." My heart skipped a beat when she said that, and immediately I thought about my hallucinations. I kept quiet about it though. "What about you?" she asked.

"Me? Hmm. So many. I like all colors, but if I had to pick one, probably magenta."

"Magenta? That's different."

"Mainly because I can't decide between pink and red." I grinned at her and she laughed.

"Well, if I can favor indigo, you can favor magenta."

"I'm glad we settled that." I chuckled, nudging her with my elbow. "How come you haven't offered another explanation for my vampire sighting?"

"Sometimes there isn't another explanation," she said, her pace slowing.

My phone chirped in my pocket and I pulled it out to see a text from Ian. A picture of a front page news article from The Salt Lake Gazette reported on a *Murder In A Small Town*. I rolled my eyes, pausing to text him back.

"Everything okay?" Zara asked.

"Just Ian. A Salt Lake paper scooped his story about the murder. He's pissed."

"Oh. Is he mad that you're not spending time with him?" Zara poked at the ground with the edge of her walking stick. Again, her gaze averted.

"Why would he be mad?" I pocketed my phone and watched her.

She shrugged. "He's not a demanding guy?"

"I mean, he could be?" My brow narrowed with confusion. "He just mostly annoys me. Does he come across as demanding? Wait—have you met him?"

"No. I mean, boyfriends can be that way, right?"

"*Boyfriend?*" I nearly choked and laughed at the same time. "He's *not* my boyfriend."

"Oh," she said, glancing at me with widened eyes. "Sorry."

"It's okay."

We started walking again, both of my hands in my back pockets while I pondered the situation. Neither of us said anything for awhile, until the woods grew so thick that the daylight dimmed. Should I tell her? How could she not know? I thought I made it clear, but...

"Zara?" I called out, stopping beside a thick bush covered in berries. She turned around, gripping the walking stick tighter. I crossed my arms over my middle, waiting for her to look at me. Eventually, she offered me a fleeting glance. "Did you...I mean, you know I'm gay, right?" Her gaze locked on mine suddenly, and the power of it nearly knocked me over. "Ian's not my boyfriend because I'm gay. Not for any other reason."

Silence hung thick for a moment before she said, "I didn't know."

"Well, I am. Just...to be clear."

She nodded, pursing her lips for a moment. I gave her time, hoping she'd say something else, but without warning, she jumped in front of me, shoving me behind her. A low growl sounded from somewhere, and I glanced around, until it seemed to come from in front of me. I grabbed on to Zara's arm that she held out to block my path.

From behind the berry bush, an enormous white tiger slid into view, silent and graceful. Crystal blue eyes stared us down, and heavily whiskered lips curled back in a roarish growl. The fur between its shoulders bristled. I started, my entire body shaking when my nails dug into Zara's arm.

"Do you...do you see that?" I cried.

"Yes," Zara answered.

The tiger stood there, staring at us, its gaze locked on

Zara's. It seemed to sniff the air around us, before settling down. It leaned back on its haunches, but this time Zara jolted.

"Don't," she said, holding her hand up to the tiger. "Don't. Just go. We're fine." I could've sworn I saw the tiger's brow wrinkle. "Please go." Zara's voice cracked. "Please," she pleaded, but the tiger didn't budge.

"Zara," a man's voice called out. To our right, a nearly-naked man approached. Flawlessly bronze skin, long hair, and clad in a loincloth, he approached the tiger and ran his fingers through its fur. "You okay?"

"We're fine, Mal," answered Zara, though I noticed she dropped her gaze when the man approached. "She's human."

"I know. We didn't recognize her." The man glanced at me. "I'm Mal. This is Vanessa." He gestured to the tiger.

I stood there, frozen while latched onto Zara's arm. I couldn't tear my eyes away from the tiger. She blinked at me twice, then winked. I smiled faintly, despite the trembling that I couldn't control. The tiger stood, moving right past Zara and bumping my hip with her giant head. I stumbled and Zara kept her arm around me.

"Her name's Makayla," Zara told them.

"Nice to meet you." Mal nodded to me, offering me a gentle smile.

"You, too," I managed to croak while watching the tiger. I held my hand to her, with extreme caution, and after only a brief pause, she nuzzled it with her cheek, lifting herself from the ground like a domestic feline. I glanced to Zara. She motioned to Mal, nodding faintly while he stood there, his arms crossed over his chest. They looked like they were talking to each other though neither of them actually said anything.

I returned my attention to the tiger. Purrs radiated from her, sounding more like growls until I felt the vibration under my palm. Even if all of this was some sort of fucked up dream, I would never forget touching a rare, majestic animal like a white tiger. Eventually, she opened her mouth, taking my hand between her teeth. It took my breath away for a moment. She didn't bite me. The rough lick she offered my fingers made me shudder. Without much warning, she let me go, turned to Mal, then padded off at a lazy gait back into the woods.

"We'll leave you be." Mal glanced from the tiger to Zara. "Be safe."

"Thanks."

We watched as Mal headed off, and I lost sight of him after a short while. Zara turned around to face me now. I just couldn't hold it together anymore. Tears streamed down my cheeks, and I swallowed down any sound my throat threatened to make.

"Tigers in Utah?" I swiped at my eyes. "You talked to it. You talked to that wolf, too."

"Makayla." Zara's face contorted with what appeared to be pain. "I'm sorry. I'm sorry about all of this."

"I'm just going to radically accept the fact that I'm going crazy." I laughed through my tears, shaking my head. "Wolves, vampires, tigers. What else?" I tossed my arms out in front of me. "I'm beginning to wonder about the dragons."

"There's no dragons," she said, appearing somewhat resigned. "At least not anymore."

"Shit." I turned my eyes to the sky and drew a deep inhale. "And you called me a human."

"I didn't—"

"I heard you tell that man that I was human. Don't even pretend." My legs wobbled under me and I sat down on the moss-covered log near us.

Zara's brow wrinkled as if perplexed. When I didn't press the matter, she sat down beside me, holding the walking stick between her knees. We must've sat there for a good ten minutes, unspeaking, with me sniffling on and off. In time, my tears subsided. She kept her eyes trained on her hands in her lap. It broke my heart, whenever I saw her pull away and fall into silence. I didn't understand it at all. Even after spending all this time with her, she tumbled away into something I couldn't comprehend.

Again, the indigo smoke wriggled between us like snakes freshly released from captivity. This time, instead of meeting it with fear and denial, I paid attention. I inhaled deeply, the fragrance of wet, fallen leaves, and the sweet scent of cinnamon and apples mixed in with it. Freshly washed linens, shampoo, and sage tangled in the undercurrent. The more I focused on the mist, the color, and the fragrance, the clearer Zara became to me. Her hair, a natural mix of tawny and honey, the freckles over the bridge of her nose, and her lips, pink even with her moderate tan, became an overwhelming sight. The more relaxed I became, the more she seemed to tense. She sat there, her fingers clenched against her knees, with her chest rising and falling in heavier than usual breaths. Something tugged me from the front, urging me to move toward her, at the same time that something pushed me from the back. The swirling mist began to settle into a long, solid, braided lure.

I leaned forward, and tucked Zara's hair behind her ear. She tensed, her shoulders broadening, though she didn't move. The mist seemed to like this, the indigo lapping at Zara, sending ripples down the rope. I repeated the gesture, stroking her hair and allowing my fingers to run through the length of it. Only then did she look at me, her pupils vast pools of ebony. My heart leapt in my chest, sending tingles of delicious warmth from my fingers to my toes.

"Do you feel that?" I whispered, as if making a sound would break the trance. She nodded, her eyes welling up and glistening. "What is it?" When she didn't answer me, I scooted closer, giving in to the sensations that spiraled through my insides. Part of it belonged to comfort, the other a fragment of desire that made my mouth water. Heat burned between us. Zara's form searing against mine.

This time, I dragged my knuckle down her cheek, then allowed my hand to wander over her shoulder, down her arm, and to her wrist. The minute my fingers wrapped around her, the skin to skin contact sent a shockwave of something through me. A burst of sensation raced over my skin, spreading through my veins like a shot of venom. Goosebumps coated my flesh, and whatever the mist became, jerked harshly inside me. Zara jumped, and tears fell from her cheeks to my hand.

"Zara..." I placed my palm against her cheek. At that point, I lost all control of myself, leaning in and capturing her in a kiss. She froze for the briefest second, before her lips moved with mine. My entire body swelled with something so powerful, so complete that I never wanted it to end. The connection between us lurched, and Zara cried out, pulling away from me.

"I can't," she said, her voice suddenly husky. "I can't."

My breath left me in heavy pants. "Zara—"

"You're human," she whispered, her hands cupping over her mouth. "I'll hurt you."

"That's the second time you've called me human. Of course I'm *human*. So are you."

"No." She shook her head, clenching her teeth suddenly. "We have to go." She stood up, grabbing the walking stick. "Let's go. Right now."

"Zara, I—"

"No more talking." Huskiness faded to a more guttural sound, and she pointed ahead. "Walk."

"But—"

"Just go!" She tossed the walking stick like a javelin, letting out an aggravated shout. The stick hit a tree so hard that a loud *crack* echoed when it wedged itself into the bark. The trunk split around it, parting like the ground during an earthquake.

"Holy shit. Okay. *Okay!*" I hurried in front of her and, with varied amounts of shock bubbling through me, we made our way back to the cabin.

CHAPTER SIX

Zara didn't speak to me for the rest of the day or through the night. The next morning, she didn't even come out of her room. I waited her out, knowing she'd eventually emerge for something to eat. I still hadn't processed any of the events that'd happened. Wolves, tigers, vampires, and purplish hallucinations. Someone must've been feeding me a heavy load of toxic mushrooms to trip this badly. Maybe the vampire actually attacked me and I was in the hospital, lying there in a coma dreaming all of this up.

Of one thing I was certain, however, that kissing Zara was the best thing I'd ever felt. I was sure of that much.

When the sun began to set again, and Zara still hadn't come out, I'd had enough of the tantrum and knocked on her door. She didn't answer so I turned the knob to find that it wasn't locked. I pushed it open, and peeked inside. Zara lay on the bed, still clad in the same clothes from our hike, and hugged a pillow to her chest while resting on her side. Her legs shifted when I entered so I knew she was awake. She ignored me, which only egged me on more. I stepped over the clothes that appeared carelessly tossed to the floor, as well as the broken chair beside them, then joined her on the bed. She stared straight ahead without acknowledging me at all.

I gave her a moment, but her stubbornness rang true. The only evidence of life belonged to the tear that slipped down her cheek.

"I'm sorry," I whispered, lying down beside her so that she was forced to see me. "I didn't mean to upset you."

Silence.

"Zara, if you're not into girls, I'll understand, but please just—"

"I am," she croaked, sniffling a little. "Please go away."

"I can't. You banned me from leaving this house. And frankly, after the last week, I'm afraid a dragon will swoop out of the sky and eat me."

She smirked, her gaze flickering to meet mine. "It might."

"I have no idea if you're joking or not anymore." I smiled, reaching forward and caressing her cheek. Softness melted over her face, and a sudden solace seemed to find her. This time, the purplish smoke flowed from the tip of my finger, and wrapped around Zara's entire being. When her body began to relax, she pushed my hand away and rolled over, turning her back to me which made the mist disappear.

"I can see it, you know. Whatever it is. That purple smoke. I've been seeing it since the night of the vampire attack," I confessed, because what the hell did it matter at this point. "I know you can, too." When she didn't respond, I sat up, climbed over her, and straddled her middle. "Fine. You won't talk to me then I'm gonna sit here until you do. Or until I have to pee. Whichever comes first." Still, she didn't move so I bounced on her. "Zara. Look. At. Me."

"Stop that," she muttered, shoving the pillow at me.

"Nope." I snatched it and bopped her in the head. "I can be stubborn, too." And so, I kept on bashing her with the pillow. Her hair fluttered with each strike, until she yanked it from me and threw it across the room. I laughed hard, then bounced on her a few more times until she rolled onto her back beneath me. Bouncing in that position would only bring on the awkward, so I resolved to just sitting on her. "Hey, girl…"

"Hey." She smirked up at me, though she didn't quite meet my gaze.

"So, uh…you into girls? Because I'm into you." I leaned down, planting my hands on the bed on either side of her head to hold myself up. She laughed then and I watched as her hands seemed to melt beside her, falling beside her shoulders.

"That's the worst pickup line I've ever heard."

"Good. I wasn't trying very hard," I said, chuckling softly while watching her. Her hands rested on the pillow, and her body under me dissolved to a malleable puddle. She seemed to relax into it for the briefest moment, until the lurch in my chest gave a great tug. Indigo burst into my mind's eye again, interrupting the playfulness. I didn't get a chance to react because Zara did first. She closed her eyes, and held her breath as if expecting a blow.

"Do you remember when you brought me here for the first time?" I asked. She nodded, but remained unmoving. "And I said how secluded this place was. You told me that 'someone like you does best away from others.' Remember?"

"It's true," she whispered.

"I think that's a lie. Know why?"

When the strange feeling in my chest faded, Zara opened her eyes. "Why?"

"Because for someone who thinks she's better off hiding in the remote forests of Utah, you sure seem to follow me around a lot. And don't give me the *right place, right time* thing. I believed it the first time, but not the rest."

"Not everything has a higher meaning."

"You don't believe that, Zara, and you know it. Now tell me. That woman who kidnapped Doctor Twofeathers, she was a vampire, right? And not just any vampire. A really bad one. Because if she wasn't really bad, something tells me you wouldn't've tried so hard to keep me away. And all these people wouldn't be patrolling the woods around here. Including that crazy huge tiger that probably belongs in China, not America. Is any of this correct?"

"You can't go write any articles on this, Makayla. You know that. They'll lock you up," she said, her fingers twitched as if she fought the desire to move.

"You mean like you tried to do?" I cocked a brow at her. "Zara, I'm already aware that my life as I knew it is over. I haven't been to work in a week. A *vampire* knows where I live, and I'm pretty sure it wants me dead. There's only two pieces of the puzzle left."

"What are they?"

"Why do I keep seeing indigo smoke every time I get close to you? And the fact that you keep calling me human. Only a non-human would call a human a human," I postulated, tilting my head and letting my hair tumble forward. "So...hey girl."

Zara laughed again, her body bouncing under me with it. "Hey..."

"Are you a vampire?"

"No." She scowled, scrunching up her face.

"Dragon?"

She chuckled. "No."

"Zombie?"

"No."

"Fairy?"

"Depending on the day."

"Ha. Ghost?"

"No." She smiled while she watched me, and the indigo smoke flowed smoothly between us while I distracted her with the silly guessing game.

"Ghoul?"

"No way." Again she grimaced.

"Troll?" I perked up and leaned down to sniff her.

"Nah. You smell too nice to be a troll. Wait— *Gremlin*? Should I pour some water on you and feed you after midnight?"

"Those aren't real." She waved me off.

"Wait! Oh my God. You're an *alien*." I thudded my hands on the bed. "An extraterrestrial? A Grey? Reptilian?"

"That's just ridiculous." She huffed, squinting at me.

"What? Undead vampires are real, but aliens can't be? Now that's some messed up logic."

"No, it's not," she said, chuckling faintly.

"It is. Sasquatch?"

"No." She smiled up at me, though her expression appeared more sad than lighthearted. "Something you shouldn't be this close to."

"It feels good to be close to you. Why wouldn't I want that?"

"Because I could hurt you…"

"I don't believe that." I reached over and brushed her hair from her forehead, then ran my finger down her cheek. "I don't believe it at all." Just like before, I claimed her mouth with mine.

She didn't hesitate as much this time and I caressed her face, keeping her in the kiss longer. The thrashing feeling in my torso settled to a contented thrum. Any fear that lingered about the loss of my life and job, faded in the sacred space we shared. Zara stroked my hair, finally unlocking from her frozen position beneath me. However, when my tongue poked her mouth, she ended the kiss and leaned back. In her pretty eyes, a flash of red flickered in her pupils. I started, watching for it to appear again. She didn't move, her gaze locked on mine, and the limbal ring around her iris turned bright red. A similar circle appeared around her pupils. I inhaled sharply, as I locked eyes with someone, *something* else for the briefest moment. When she blinked, the red faded back to her cool greens.

She smiled, not seeming to notice the change. I placed my palm against her cheek and rolled off her. We both turned on our sides to face each other. Our lower halves pressed together, and I continued to watch as the indigo mist skated around us. I tickled my nails up and down her arm, and felt her stomach flip-flop against mine. Her eyes followed the spirals of the smoke as it wove around the places where our flesh touched.

"What is that?" I asked, finally.

"Something complicated," she offered. "You're the only one who's ever seen it."

"Maybe I'm the only one who's supposed to." I laced my fingers with hers and curled her hand against my chest. Tears pooled in her eyes, though they didn't fall. She pursed her lips for a moment.

"Wolf," she croaked.

"Wolf?" I pressed my lips to her knuckles.

"I'm...a wolf."

"You're a wolf—like a werewolf?" My eyes widened, mainly because I hadn't even considered that. "Like the mythical sworn enemy of a vampire?"

"Yes. Just you knowing any of this could kill you."

"Let me tell you something about me, Zara," I said, still holding on to her hand. "Nothing would've stopped me from getting that story about the hospital. Nothing. Without your intervention, I would probably already be dead. Or undead, respectively."

"Don't even say that," she cried out, yanking me closer. "Don't even."

"Okay, okay." Fear shot through me, but it didn't feel like it belonged to me. "I won't. I'm sorry."

"You can't tell anyone any of this. No one. Not Ian or your family. No one. Promise that, Makayla." She jerked my hand again. "Promise."

"I promise, okay?" I placed my free hand on her cheek. "I won't tell them. Besides, my family doesn't believe in gay people. I don't think we have anything to worry about when it comes to matters of the preternatural."

"What do you mean?"

"They're radical Evangelicals who live in Salt Lake City. When I was a teenager, they sent me off to conversion camps twice. I turned eighteen in the last one, signed myself out, and never saw them again. That was a decade ago at least." I glanced to the full moon that peeked in on us through the open window. "I've never told anyone that."

"That's horrible. Have they ever tried to reach out to you?"

"No. They made it pretty clear that their beliefs were more important than me." I shrugged, rolling off the bits of shame that came with the confession. "What about your family?"

"Hard to explain. Wolves have—"

"Packs. Is that the same for you?"

"Yeah." She quieted for a moment, looking over my shoulder then back to me. "It's not the same for everyone though. I never knew my father. My mom was a Breeder, and father was the wolf."

"Breeder?" My brow crinkled with the question. "What's that?"

"It's a non-Changer that carries the werewolf gene. Like human, but with their own kind of magic. They're immune to the delirium that seeing a werewolf change causes, immune to all human diseases, they live longer lives just like Changers. We don't live super long, but many can live happy lives well-over one hundred years old with slower body deterioration. They can birth children that can be Breeders or Changers. Some of them have magic that can heal others, or sense things. Breeders support the Changers. We're nothing without them."

"Do they birth...like, animals?"

"No. If someone is a Changer, it happens around puberty. You're just a regular kid until then. Maybe a little stronger, or their senses are keener. Firstings are traumatic sometimes. When you're barely a teenager and all of a sudden you're turning into a werecreature with no control over yourself," she explained. For the first time, Zara spoke to me candidly. Without restraint or stopping herself.

"Was it like that for you?" I asked, returning to stroking her arm. From knuckles to elbow, over and over, and watching as the indigo continued to move around us. Everything about Zara calmed when I touched her like this. The more the smoke wove us together, the more relaxed she grew.

"A little." She nodded. "But I grew up in a big pack so it was easier to control."

"You're not in a big pack now?"

She shook her head. "I'm not in any."

"Why not?"

"The last one didn't treat me very well. I've stayed by myself since then. When Mal and Caden left the big pack, too, they came here under Hank's Sept. I ran into Mal last year and he said I would be safe here, and no one would bother me. He was right. So I stay here. And I have a job."

"What's a Sept?"

"It's a larger grouping of smaller packs under one Leader. There are dozens of Septs in the country, and thousands of packs under them. It's a lot about territory," she explained.

"Is there like one big head honcho like a president?"

She shook her head. "No. Sept leaders are the highest up. They used to meet in big forums once a year. Now there's a mailing list."

"Technology even changes the Changers, eh?" I snickered and she smiled. My ease at this conversation surprised me. Maybe because I was dreaming.

"Guess so."

"When you said your old pack didn't treat you well, did they hurt you?" I placed my hand on her cheek.

"Sometimes. They were very traditional and didn't think that wolves mating with same-sex partners helped contribute to the continuation of our species. So they tried to get me to mate with male Breeders and I wouldn't. At first it was just like dating, but then they tried assigning me really dominant Changer partners and it got scary. They figure feral-borns were better than none. So I left." Her gaze dropped from mine again.

"Wait, wait...mating like sex?" I stopped her because nothing she said made any sense to me at that point.

"No." She looked at me again. "I didn't explain that well. Mating is a term for like marriage, I guess? Changers and Breeders are supposed to pair. Though sometimes Changers and Changers will or Breeders and Breeders. As long as continuing the bloodlines were possible, it was okay. Being gay won't do that no matter what."

"So when you didn't connect to male Breeders, they tried forcing you to be with Changers?"

"Yeah. Dominant ones who could overpower me. Dominance is a spectrum among wolves. Supremely dominant like Hank and Caden. All the way down to submissive, like me. Submissive is more uncommon, because submissive wolves don't rely on a pack to keep themselves in control. But we're more vulnerable alone to being overrun by unhealthy dominants." She paused, and gave my hand a squeeze. "I'm sorry. It's confusing."

"Only a little. I think I understand. So they brought you into the Sept here to protect you? Because as long as you're part of something larger, you're less at risk. Right?"

She nodded. "Yeah."

"And it's bad that I'm a human because if I see you, or anyone change, I could go crazy? And I could get sick and die. Or not live as long?" I asked, tilting my head as I listened to her.

"It's harder to form mate bonds with humans because they don't have innate magic, and most of them end of getting killed by their partners or losing their minds when they see them change. It's horrible." She pursed her lips, and her eyes flecked with tears again. "Breeders have magics that help them withstand some of the damages that come from being mated to a werewolf. Humans don't have that. I could hurt you. I could kill you. I could make you insane. Just you knowing this, my old pack would've killed you if the information itself didn't make you insane."

"That's not going to happen, okay?" I urged her into a hug, and to my surprise, she let me. "I'm already crazy. Maybe it makes me immune."

She laughed a bit, and her hand snaked around my middle, holding me almost possessively. "Maybe. Or maybe you're unusually open-minded."

"I always have been. My life taught me to be accepting of others, no matter what. I can't afford to let my beliefs, or disbeliefs, hurt others. I've seen what that does." I kissed her cheek and she nodded a little. "If you find out someone is a Changer at puberty, how do you find out if they're a Breeder?"

"Sometimes they have marks or glyphs that give hints about their bloodline. Some Changers have gifts that can sense a species," she answered, rolling on to her back again. I moved with her this time, resting my head on her shoulder and placing my arm on her chest.

"And it's all about genetics? You can't get bit and turn into a werewolf?"

"Nope. Doesn't work like that. All genetics. Only a vampire's bite, as unnatural as it is, turns humans or Breeders into monsters. Of all the werecreatures out there, vampires are the only ones that thrive in death."

"So there are other species of Changers?" My eyes widened at the thought. "Like werebunnies?"

She laughed, nodding while she gazed down at me. "Wererabbits, weresharks, weretigers, werebears—"

"Weretigers?" I leaned up on my elbow. "That tiger in the woods?"

"Oh yeah." She nodded. "And she's the most dominant creature I've ever met. But she doesn't misuse it, from what I know anyway."

"Wow." I settled back down against her. "So now that I

know this, I'm a target. Right?"

"Yeah." Her lips pressed my forehead. "But not in this Sept. They'll keep you safe. After all, you've been living in our territory since you moved here. Imogene is Hank's wife, and therefore, the second highest in charge of the Sept. And she's your landlord."

"Whoa. And they have a ton of kids."

"Most of which are dominant changers. One of which nearly ate you in the woods a few weeks ago."

"That was... Oh wow."

"Yeah." She turned to me suddenly, pulling her knees up to curl with mine. I held her there and she held me, only then did the sheer pressure of her strength make itself clear. Her body burned, raging with heat against mine. It nearly made me sweat.

"I'll sleep in here tonight," I said, running my fingers through her hair. "If you promise to get up tomorrow and eat something."

She nodded, but I wasn't letting her get away with it that easily.

"Say you promise."

"I promise," she said, chuckling with me as we settled down together.

Despite the information given to me that night, a fragment of myself still believed I must be in the hospital while in a coma. How could any of this be real? Vampires, werecreatures, an underground society even larger than human life. It couldn't possibly be true. I'd asked Zara a million questions that night, but one still remained unanswered. What was the purple smoke, and why did it continue to haunt me every time she was close to me? I know she saw it, too. But was that part of the alleged delirium that humans got from seeing these creatures? Maybe I was already delirious when all of this started anyway.

"Don't you have to go back to work?" I asked Zara as

we spent time together by the lake the next evening. She perched herself on top of a smooth stone formation that squared off like the perfect nature-made bench. In her leather-on-leather outfit, and barefoot, she seemed impervious to the cold breeze that fluttered off the lake. Even in multiple layers, and a knitted hat, the cold still sent shivers through me every so often. I spent the time skipping stones across the top of the water, while she watched. Every time I failed, and the stone plunked into the water, she laughed.

"Eventually," she answered. "What'd your boss say when you called him?"

"He wished my dying mother a speedy recovery," I said, chuckling after. "Ian's suspicious though."

"Of course. Your *boyfriend*."

"Uck. Don't even." I scowled and the rock I threw hit right into the water. She grinned at her victory and I stuck my tongue out at her.

The next rock I skipped had a more successful journey across the lake. I tossed a few more, then as I wound myself up for another skip, a rock skimmed its way toward me, landing at my feet.

"What the heck? Did you see that?"

"Hmm?" She drew her gaze from the tree line back to me. "What?"

"A rock came flying at me—hey!" A second one hit my boot. Zara hopped up right away, her arm slinking around my middle as we both looked across the lake for the culprit. I couldn't see anything, but Zara's nostrils flared.

"It's getting dark. Let's head back," she said, still holding on to me.

"Is something there?"

"Nothing I can sense, which is concerning enough." Another rock skipped across the water and came to rest at our feet. Zara urged me away, looking over her shoulder as we headed back to the cabin.

She locked up behind us, then dropped down to sit on

the sofa. She watched me as I unbundled myself from my jacket, scarf, and hat. "Do your supernatural genes make you withstand the cold?"

"Yes." She laughed, but I could tell she focused on something else.

"What are you doing?" I slipped out of my boots and approached her.

"Telling Mal about the stones in the lake," she said, holding her hand to me. She expected me to sit beside her, but instead, I took her hand and straddled her thighs, settling in her lap. The indigo mist immediately returned, and it fluttered against my lips as if offering me a clandestine kiss. In response, I leaned in and brushed my lips against hers. Zara's body surged beneath me, her fingers lacing with mine as she squeezed.

"Sometimes your silence scares me," I told her. "Did you know that?"

A soft sound escaped her throat like the very beginnings of a growl. "I didn't."

"Do you want this?" I brought her hands to my chest, kissing her knuckles. "Do you want me?"

"More than anything," she said, her voice husky and guttural. Again, that reddish hue twisted around her eyes. I watched as her presence tilted away, from soft-spoken Zara to something stronger, hungrier. The smoke tightened to a braid again between us, and snapped like a whip as she grabbed my hips, jerking me toward her. A gasp left me before my lips met hers, and desire burst through me, tingling down my legs then settling between them. Again, the rope snapped and Zara gripped my rear.

Zara and I hadn't known each other long. Our intense time together, coupled with something greater, something more spiritual it seemed, urged me to her. I craved her presence, her closeness, and her touch.

I tossed my head back and a moan escaped me while I basked in the pleasure that her lips brought against my neck. My fingers tangled in her hair, holding her to me as swells of want tormented my core. She raked her teeth over my shoulder, and I released her, tearing my shirt off. I grabbed her face, and kissed her hard, forcing my tongue between her lips. I wanted her more than anything in that moment. Hunger tangled with lust, weaving circles around my heart. She moaned into my mouth, grabbed at the waist of my pants, and tugged them down.

"Zara." I gasped, ending our kiss when she dropped her face between my breasts. I held on to her shoulders when she moved down my body, nipping along my stomach. "My God." Pleasure swelled through me and she had barely touched me. She tipped me backward, her mouth an inch from my core. I arched toward her, my nails digging into her bare shoulders.

A growl left her at the same time that her nostrils flared. Under my fingers, something soft coated her muscled torso. Without thinking, I ran my hand over it, only then recognizing it as luscious fur. Zara tensed suddenly, grabbing me and spinning me away from her. She held me from behind, one arm around my middle, the other covering my eyes. A strangled cry left her.

"Don't look at me!" Her raspy shout freaked me out.

"Zara." I reached back, placing my palm against her face. "I'm okay. I'm fine."

"No," she cried, taking a few deep breaths. "She wants you. I can't."

"Who wants me?" I rubbed her arm, up and down the same way I had in bed. "Who?"

"My beast. She wants you."

"Okay." I hadn't a clue what she was talking about, but I forced myself to calm down so that she would, too. "What do you need?"

"I don't know." In time, her breathing slowed and she dropped her hand from my eyes. She hugged me from behind, and sniffled against my shoulder. "I'm sorry."

"I'm okay, Zar." I turned and kissed her cheek. Between her hold on me and my pants around my knees, I could hardly move. "Extremely horny, but okay."

She laughed a little, nodding against my neck. Her damp cheeks brought a stroke of sadness to my heart.

"I'm sorry."

"Don't be. Let me see you," I implored, turning in her lap. She released her hold on me so that I could. "What did you mean about your beast?"

"Human. Wolf. Beast." She held up three fingers. "Three parts of one."

"Werewolf." I nodded my understanding. "When your eyes turn red, does that mean the beast—"

"You saw my eyes turn red?" Zara's panic melted across her face, stealing its color.

"Yeah...a few times. Is that the beast?"

"Did you just see it now?"

"Yes. Why—"

"Oh my God." She started to cry, pulling me up to stand. "We have to go."

"What? Where!" I yanked up my pants and snatched my shirt from the floor. "Zara."

"We have to," she sobbed, heaving as she grabbed me. "Close your eyes. Don't look!"

"Okay!" I hugged her, hiding my face against her shoulder. "Okay."

A moment later, my feet left the ground.

CHAPTER SEVEN

My feet thunked on something wooden and Zara's grip loosened. In the darkness, the only thing I could see was the front door to a huge cabin. Zara knocked once, and the door swung open before she could knock a second time. In the doorway, a tall, lissome redhead stood, wearing nothing more than a skimpy green dress. She crossed her arms over her middle, lifted a brow, and waited.

"Whoa." I stared, and Zara elbowed me.

"Mal's sister. Is she here?" asked Zara.

"Why?" asked the redhead.

"I need to talk to her, Vanessa. Please?" Zara avoided her gaze until that moment.

"Vanessa? Wait...you're the tiger?"

"Yes, monkey." Vanessa's nostrils flared and a grin melted over her lips. "She smells of your sex." She looked to Zara then reached for me.

"Ness!" A voice called out from behind her. "Who are you talking to?"

"The submissive," she answered, turning her back to us and sauntering inside.

"Well, let them in. Jeez." A woman with black braided

hair, and wearing the absolutely bare minimum amount of clothing necessary to walk around in public, bounced her way over to us.

"Um...is this a brothel?" I asked Zara, my eyes widening of their own accord.

"What? Of course not." Zara urged me inside and shut the door.

"Only when Caden's home." The nearly-naked woman giggled, her hand held out to me. "Hi. I'm Xany."

"You're...what?" I shook her hand, my jaw hanging slack.

"We don't have time for pleasantries," Zara interrupted. "She's human and we were—"

"Having some yummy sex," announced Vanessa from her perch on the arm of the sofa.

Zara glared then looked back to Xany. "She saw my eyes. I mean, I nearly changed."

"I'm fine," I said, glancing between the three of them.

"But she's human and she saw it," Zara said, panic still lacing her tones. "Can you check her?"

"You betcha, grouchy. Come inside." Xany's hand slid across Zara's shoulders, and I watched as she visibly relaxed. "Have a seat, human whose name I don't know." Xany pointed to one of the chairs at the kitchen table."

"Her name's Makayla," Zara answered for me.

"Mack is fine," I said, sitting down on one of the chairs. The cabin, almost three times the size of Zara's, had a golden glow to it. All of the modern conveniences coupled with the handmade furniture, gave it the perfect rugged and useful feel. Xany crouched in front of me, her breasts nearly touching my knees. She held up three fingers in front of my nose.

"How many do you see?"

"Um...three?"

"Okay, good. Now count to ten."

"This is silly...but fine." I abided by her request, and she giggled at me again.

"Now trick question...Bananas and peanut butter, or milk and cookies?" She snickered and glanced to Zara who stood by, wringing her hands together.

"Uh...milk and cookies. What kind of test is this?"

Xany grinned, patting my knees as she stood up. She approached Zara, taking her hands in hers. "Silly, if she was *loca* she wouldn't be walkin' and talkin'. She would be slobbering all over herself and staring out in lala land."

"But she...she saw my eyes."

"And I felt your fur, don't forget that," I added, which only made Zara freak out even more. Vanessa snickered, and made her way over to us. She slid up to sit on the table beside me, crossing her legs. Purring emanated from her chest, and my eyes widened when I stared at her. "Don't look at me like that."

"Why not? You smell yummy," crooned Vanessa.

"Zara." Xany pulled Zara's attention away from me and the crazy cat. "Did you ever think that maybe she was supposed to see those things?"

"No. She's already seen a vampire kill a human. It's put her at enough risk."

"Should've staked it." Xany made a stabbing gesture, and Zara flinched. "Easy. I'm teasin'."

"I'm just...worried. Are you sure she's okay?"

Vanessa grinned at me when I looked up at her. Her eyes, as emerald green as her dress, squinted as if she meant to say something.

"You're very creepy," I told her. It only made her smile more. She ran her fingernail down my cheek in a barely-there caress. I jerked away from her, edging my chair backward.

"Positive. But if you wanted proof, you can ask Caden when he gets back from patrol," Xany said, now placing her hand on Zara's cheek. "Cool?"

"Where's Mal?"

"Patrolling with Caden. Vanessa is babysitting us frail ones." Xany sighed dramatically.

"Vanessa, what are you doing?" A woman emerged from the back hall. Like Mal, she appeared clearly Native American, with long, layered hair that fell down her back. Her eyes, bright and golden, stood out against her copper skin. It took me a moment before I recognized her from the video I lifted from the hospital.

"Playing with the monkey," answered Vanessa, turning her attention to the woman. She lifted her chin, and the purrs rumbled louder.

"That's the second time you called me a monkey," I said.

"Hey NeeNee, tell grouchy here this one isn't a bumbling idiot." Xany gestured to me after releasing Zara.

"And just who are you?" Doctor Twofeathers asked, her eyes falling on me.

"Mack Parker, Fourth Co—I mean, just Mack Parker." I stood up, offering her my hand. Zara's hand fell to the small of my back, but she avoided Shawnee's gaze the same way she did with everyone else. "It's good to meet you, Doctor Twofeathers."

"She's grouchy's girlfriend." Xany jabbed her thumb in Zara's direction. "And grouchy thinks that she's gonna make her go crazy because she's human."

"You're human." Doctor Twofeathers' expression, tight and clinical as expected from a doctor, gave no hints that matched the inflection in her voice.

"I'm human. Should I get a T-shirt?" I released her hand and she glanced to Xany, her brow twitching once.

"Perhaps. A button might be more useful. You can call me Shawnee," she said.

"I like this one, NeeNee." Xany giggled, reaching over to give my hair a tug. "Can we keep her?"

"No. You can't." Zara frowned at Xany. Vanessa snickered, wrapping her arm around Shawnee's middle when she got close enough.

"She smells like sex. Can we watch them?" Vanessa crooned in Shawnee's ear. Despite the suggestive statement, Shawnee leaned into her and swatted her hand at the same time.

"*Tla*. Behave yourself, kitten."

"Aw, Nee. She's just happy to see other lesbians wandering around." Xany grinned like her announcement was the cutest thing in the world.

"Well, then. This has been an interesting visit," I said, turning to Zara when she pulled me into a hug.

"I'm sorry," she whispered.

"It's okay. You don't need to keep apologizing for being who you are," I told her, rubbing her back in slow circles. I glanced over to the doctor, who offered me a gentle smile.

"Zara's afraid to love her because she's human," Xany announced, bouncing on her tiptoes.

"You love who you love," said Shawnee, her hand falling to the center of her chest when she glanced to Vanessa. Vanessa nuzzled her cheek, then wrapped her arms around her shoulders from behind.

"Mate bonds don't discriminate as much as you'd think." Vanessa's profound statement had me looking at her in a different light for a minute.

"I don't know anything about mate bonds," I said, leaning back to look at Zara.

"You'll know it when you see it," said Vanessa. "And when you feel it. Shawnee's is green."

"Green?" My eyes widened and I looked up at Zara. "Is that what the smoke is?"

She hesitated, then offered me a faint nod. Her eyes welled up again and I cupped her face, stroking her cheeks.

"I can feel it." A smile curved my lips, and I tilted my head while I watched her. "Am I your soul mate?"

"Yeah," Zara said, sniffling with her confession.

"Aww." Xany clapped once, giggling as she bounced up and down beside us. "They're so cute. Not like you two." She glared at Shawnee and Vanessa. "So dramatic and serious all the time."

Vanessa growled at Xany and Shawnee elbowed her.

"Let's go home," I said, hugging Zara again. "I won't look." She nodded, wrapping her arms around me.

"Thanks," she muttered to Xany.

"Anytime."

My feet left the ground again, but this time, when the familiar fragrance of Zara's cabin returned, she lifted me, keeping me in the tight embrace. I kissed her cheek, then leaned back to look at her.

"Why didn't you tell me the misty rope was a mate bond, Zara? I've been seeing it for weeks. The first time was the night of the vampire attack, when you ran in to make sure I was okay."

"I don't know," she said, she ran her thumbs over my cheeks. "It took me awhile to understand it, too. And then I didn't want to get my hopes up too high."

"Because I'm human and it's harder to form a mate bond?"

"Yeah. I'm sor—"

I put my finger over her lips. "Nope. No more apologies allowed. Ever."

"But—"

"Nope." I laughed, keeping my finger over her mouth. "Promise no more apologies unless you actually hurt me, like saying something mean during an argument or forcing me to eat boiled spinach."

"Okay." She chuckled, kissing my finger. "I promise."

"I can't believe you took me to that crazy house with all those crazy women. Also, do you *know* what kind of restraint I had to muster up to not ask Doctor Twofeathers a million questions?"

Zara toted me back over to the sofa. Instead of sitting in her lap, we lay down together facing each other. "I could tell. Her cat would've shut you down pretty quickly."

"Her cat looked like she was about to have a *lick* at *my* cat," I teased.

Zara laughed, swatting my arm. "Oh my God."

"Do you know how long it's been?" I flopped onto my back and sighed dramatically. "This one time, I was so close, but the sexy wolf I was playing with panicked."

"Kay, you're ridiculous," she said, though she hadn't stopped grinning. "How can you accept all of this so easily?"

"Kay? Is that my new nickname?" I wagged my brows at her when she gazed down at me.

"It's more suiting than Mack."

"You think so?"

"I do. Everyone calls you Mack. I want to call you something different."

"You can call me whatever you want, babe." I grinned that time and her cheeks reddened with a blush. "And thus, she was donned *babe*." I tapped her nose and she pretended to bite my finger. "Can you tell me more about mate bonds?"

"Do you see it now?" she asked, her hand falling to the center of my chest.

"I see it always when we're close together. But I think I'm getting used to it because it doesn't draw my attention as much. I feel it though. Like..." I paused to think about it. "Like this tunnel that connects me to you. And our feelings go back and forth in it."

"Yeah." She nodded, blinking away the emotions that made her eyes appear misty. "Exactly like that. Humans don't usually see it, or experience it like that. At least they're not supposed to."

"Maybe I'm different. Maybe I'm stronger because we're supposed to be together."

"I hope so." She inhaled deeply. "Mate bonds are supposed to be Gaia's greatest gift to wolves. Because wolves are her greatest warriors, our bonds are particularly strong. Pack bonds, Sept bonds, mate bonds. Our connections are what make us whole. But the mate bond, that's the most personal one. Most wolves only get one for their whole lives. Even in death, the bond remains."

"And you...picked me for yours?" My heart thumped in my chest with the uprising of emotion that accompanied it.

"I think...it picked you for me. Because it knew that you were—"

"Your soul mate." I smiled when I said it, brushing my thumb over her bottom lip. "You're mine. Even if you did call me *nosey* the first second you met me."

She laughed hard, leaning down to kiss me, for the first time, of her own initiation. This time, when the indigo braid of mist snapped between us, I knew exactly what it was. I melted under her, allowing her to lead the make out session that followed. Tenderness laced our movements, but when our connection strengthened, and my desire to please her rose, she ended the kiss.

"Can I hold you tonight?" she asked, gathering me against her chest as she pulled a blanket from the back of the sofa.

"You can hold me every night if you wanted."

We curled up together, and grew quiet. Zara rested her head on my chest, her gaze fixed ahead as she appeared to listen to my heartbeat. I stroked her hair, and after a few minutes, she drifted to sleep.

Despite the situation, things appeared somewhat clearer than they had the night before. Even if I was actually in a coma, I didn't want to wake up from it. After being alone for so long, and unloved for even longer, Zara filled all the gaps I needed, and I reveled in her presence always.

〰〰

"Kay?" Zara called out before she hurried out of her room. My stomach lurched, as if something yanked me from behind. I turned to see her skidding to a halt. She wore only a pair of basketball shorts and a tank top, and she appeared rushed like she'd just jumped out of bed.

"I'm here. What's wrong?" I asked, meeting her half way in the living room.

"Nothing. I thought you left," she said, her hands falling to my waist as she let out of a soft breath.

"Just making you breakfast." I reached up and smoothed down her hair, then laced my fingers behind her neck. "Do you like pancakes?"

"I like everything." She smiled, her body relaxing against me. "You're so beautiful," she said, her voice quiet.

"Not like you, Miss Muscles for Days." I rubbed her biceps and she flexed automatically.

She chuckled, her cheeks flushing. "I didn't mean to say that out loud."

"Well, you did." I grinned, leaning in to kiss her. She ran her finger down my cheek when I leaned back. "Also, we need to get groceries."

"I'll call the market. They'll deliver."

"Really? Do you always do that?"

She nodded, tucking her hair behind her ear. "I don't like...crowded places."

"When you're a cop, do you feel differently?" I tilted my head, watching as she melted away from me into the silence that stole her sometimes. Again, she nodded. "Tell me how it's different."

"I'm more in control. People see me as someone with power, even if it's not real."

"You don't have power regularly, as yourself? Only as Officer Weston?"

"Yeah," she said, a sad smile curving her lips.

"Know where you'll always have power?" I took both of her hands in mine. She shook her head. "With me. With us. You'll always have a voice with me, Zara. Always. I'll always hear you."

I didn't expect her emotional response to that sentiment. Tears welled in her eyes and she nodded, leaning her forehead against mine. The indigo mist, which I now knew belonged to the beginnings of our mate bond, thumped and pulsed inside me. In a way, it seemed like a second heart, nestled against my original.

"I'm really glad that you were nosey," she said, sniffling after. "Otherwise I wouldn't have met you."

"Yeah, baby. Me too." I kissed her gently, then took her hand. "Come eat something. You didn't yesterday and something tells me that wolves are supposed to eat way more than you do."

She chuckled, but allowed me to lead her to the kitchen. We sat together at the table, and I fixed her a heap of pancakes with fresh blueberries.

"Syrup or whipped cream?" I asked while pouring both of us coffee.

"Um...whipped cream. Did you make it?"

"I did." I grinned as I scooped a glob of it on her plate.

"So...you can cook?" Her whole face lit up with the question. I laughed, offering her a cheeky grin.

"I can cook. Not just breakfast foods and sandwiches, either." I took a bite of my food and she did the same. "How about this? I'll make a shopping list, and call up the grocery place. Then I'll fix you dinner, but won't tell you what I'm making so it'll be a surprise."

"I like that idea," she said, wagging her brows as she pulled her fork from her lips. "I know it might be strange, but I really like that you're here. I know it wasn't your choice to be here, but just know that I like it."

"It wasn't at first, I admit. But it is now, Zara. Normally, living so closely with someone I was just getting to know would be unusual. With you, it isn't like that. It's different. A little scary sometimes, but not bad. For the first time, I feel like I have something to wake up for that isn't a news story."

"Right back at you."

We settled into our meal, sharing honest conversations that were quite new to me. They weren't about work, or casual pleasantries, rather, I learned about Zara, and who she was as a person. One day, I hoped to learn who she was as a wolf as well. I filled Zara's plate three times and she ate every bite.

While we cleared the table, Zara froze, her hand falling to my back. "Mal's coming."

"What?" I rinsed off my hands in the water, and she pointed to the front door.

Half a second later, he appeared. Literally *appeared* out of nowhere in front of the sofa. This time, however, he wore actual clothes.

"Holy shit." I gripped my chest, gasping at the hulking sight of him. Zara panicked, her face ashen when she wrapped her arm around my waist.

"Seeing me bend won't make her crazy," Mal assured her. "I should've knocked though. Sorry."

"It's okay," I said, linking my elbow with Zara's. "She's worried for me."

"I can see that." Mal nodded, though he looked to Zara, as if waiting for her to calm down. She did, after a moment, though she kept her eyes low. "Zara? I'm your friend."

"Yeah," she said, meeting his gaze finally. "Sorry."

"Apologizing is outlawed." He smiled gently, gesturing to the table. "May I join you both?"

"Yes," I said, but he waited.

"Yeah, of course," answered Zara.

"Is that what it's called when you zip around magically? Bending?" I asked, sitting in Zara's lap when she urged me to.

"It is." Mal nodded. "My sister told me the two of you came for a visit."

"We did. You've got crazy nearly-naked sexy women in your house," I blurted out. He chuckled and Zara grinned, leaning her chin on my shoulder.

"Now you know why I live there," he said, pausing after for a moment. "I can feel your worry, Zara. Hank knows you'll only talk to me."

"I knew there was a reason for your visit," she said, her hand pressing my stomach.

"Why won't you talk to Hank?" I asked, turning in her lap so that I could see both of them. "You talk to Steve."

"He's different," she said, her eyes trained on Mal.

"Like you."

"But also your boss, so it creates challenges." He smirked and she nodded. "No one is going to take Makayla away from you. Human or not."

"Is that how you feel about the pack? Or Sept, is it?" I glanced between them.

"Sept," Zara answered, though she brushed her lips across my shoulder, ignoring my question.

"Do you, Zara?" I pressed, stroking her arms and tickling with my fingernails. My stomach lurched and the swirly indigo mist returned around us. It made me smile. "I'll take that as a yes."

"Take what?" asked Mal, his brow wrinkling.

"The pretty purplish smoke that she wraps me in when she wants me closer," I said, exposing some of the things I'd learned about our bond. Zara's eyes widened a bit and she looked to Mal.

"You can see the preliminary bond?" He narrowed his eyes, as a perplexed expression smoothed his features.

"Preliminary?" Again, I looked between them.

"The mate bond has two forms, preliminary when it's just forming, and permanent after bonding," he explained, with a comfortable ease.

"Bonding? What's that—" My eyes widened when Zara blanched. "Oh." I smiled at her, poking at her cheeks. "Don't be shy. Mal knows how girls get it on."

He chuckled, leaning back in his chair with a wide grin. "Oh yeah. Sure do."

"Gross. Don't get a boner in the kitchen." I pretended to gag, and finally Zara laughed.

"One thing your girl's got, Zar. She's not shy." Mal wagged his brows, continuing to laugh.

"Nope. Not shy." I turned to Zara, tucking her hair behind her ears while she swapped from pale to blushing. "But she is."

"Am not," she whispered, though she smirked at her own lie.

"Are too." I grinned, nipping her bottom lip. "So you mean to tell me the mate bond gets stronger?"

"So much stronger," answered Mal. "It's Gaia's greatest gift after all."

"I like the sound of that," I said, still attempting to coax Zara out of her quietness. She looked up at me and smiled. "No one's taking me away, baby."

"I know," she said, finally giving me a squeeze. "But I don't want to hurt you either. The last time..." She shook her head.

"What happened?" asked Mal.

"We were messing around and I saw her eyes turn red. And felt her fur. That's why we went to see Xany and the crazy cat lady," I told him.

"You know..." He leaned his elbows on the table. "My mate said something about that..."

"What'd she say?" asked Zara. Again, with her nervousness, the smoke spun faster around us.

"She questioned if your mate was fully human. She said that humans could, and should, have reactions to even small shifts such as eyes or fur. It should, at least, scare them or cause them panic. But there are some humans that are enlightened or gifted, or enchanted. Like witches, for example. They're still human, but they're immune to the delirium because of their open-minded beliefs. The same has been said for human shaman, and spiritual folks. Like the Dalai Lama," he explained, gesturing to me. "Any of that ring true to you?"

"Not that I know of." I shrugged.

"The cat seemed to hover closer to her," Zara added, glancing between us. "Cats are attracted to magic."

"And Vanessa is just the type to keep information like that to herself unless directly asked." He shook his head. "I'll ask her. Also, Zara, Caden can tell. He has a gift that he can sense bloodlines—"

"No." She waved her hand, offering a resounding refusal. "Not Caden."

"Why not?" I asked, returning to rubbing her arm.

"Caden's the son of the Alpha of my old pack. No. I don't trust him," she said, squeezing me to her.

"Zar, you don't trust any dominant wolf. Alpha's son or not." Mal gestured to her.

"You're dominant. I trust you," she retorted.

"Because our friendship is two-sided." Mal drew his attention from Zara to me. "For feral wolves, being around a submissive wolf helps calm their beasts. Zara is the only submissive in our entire Sept."

"What's feral mean?" I asked Zara, nudging her chin so that she looked at me.

"It means closer to the beast," she said. "Some are closer to the human, some wolf, some beast."

"And closer to the beast, means closer to falling under the control of the beast who seeks what a beast seeks. Survival, food, sex, anger," Mal continued.

"What are you closest to?" I asked Zara.

"Wolf," she answered, glancing to Mal who nodded.

"A lone wolf, but one who desires a pack of her own," he said. With caution, he held out his hand, palm up, to both of us. "Start with Makayla. You will feel stronger, Zar. Submissive does not imply weak, as you've been taught. Submissive equates to peaceful."

I put my hand in Mal's, and every bit of Zara tensed beneath me. "You said you trust him. So, I do, too." Mal shook my hand and I chuckled. "Your turn."

He held his hand out to Zara, holding her gaze for a moment before dropping it. To me, it appeared as a gesture of respect. Slowly, as if he were amping up to trick her, she reached out and shook his hand. He released her, and they shared a smile.

CHAPTER EIGHT

Heavy rain beat down on the cabin as a thunderstorm raged overhead. The windows rattled with the strength of each boom. I scurried out of the shower, a towel around me, in time to see Zara lighting a fire and some candles.

"We might lose power," she said. "Storm is a bit ragey."

"I think I nearly got electrocuted in there," I said, taking a deep breath. "And I might've shaved off critical body parts."

"Silly." Zara chuckled, standing up to place two lit candles on the hearth.

"Also, I might be out of clothes. I should probably do laundry."

"I'm not complaining." She grabbed me around the waist, tugging me to her. I squeaked, gripping the towel tighter.

"I'm shy! You can't see me naked yet!"

Zara chuckled, brushing her lips over my neck. "You smell good."

"Don't eat me, wolfie." I nipped her cheek and felt her lips smile against my skin. "I have an idea."

"What's that?" Gruffness laced her tone, and it sent shivers of enjoyment down my spine.

"First, let's turn the lights off and get some blankets and pillows by the fireplace," I said, nibbling her chin.

"Okay," she said, breaking away from me with a curious expression lightening her features. She watched me out of the corner of her eye while gathering up the pillows. "You're up to something."

"I am." I laughed, flicking off the lights and leaving us in only the glow of the fire and candles. I grabbed all the blankets from the sofa and together, we made a nest on the carpet by the hearth. "C'mere." I wiggled my fingers at her and she stepped in front of me, taking my hand. "Can you see in the dark?"

"Yes. But not the same as seeing in the light. Not as finely detailed," she said, her hand clammy in mine.

"Okay. Good." I leaned in, pressing my lips to hers as I let my towel fall off. Her body tensed with her nerves as I guided her hand to my stomach. "I noticed that when our skin touches, it feels so warm and amazing. Without any expectations, let's lie here together."

"What if I...what if I shift?"

"It's dark. I can't really see you well. We already know I'm fine if I see your eyes and if I touch your fur." I paused, smiling because I could almost feel her eyes on me.

"You're beautiful," she said, her hand sliding down the curve of my hip and confirming my suspicion.

"So are you, Zara." I caressed her cheek with my thumb. "Let me feel you."

Without speaking, her shadowed figure moved as she slipped out of her clothes. First her pants then her top, which she tossed aside. When she stood in front of me again, I stepped closer, allowing my breasts to graze against hers. Sparks burst through me, but it was Zara who gasped. I took her hand again, after finding it, and tugged her down to the blankets. Stiffness marred her movements until we both lay down together.

"Can I hold you?" she asked, her voice soft.

"Of course, baby. You never ever have to ask that," I assured her.

Her hands fell to my waist, and she guided me so that my back was against her front, turning me into a little spoon. Our bodies fit together like the perfect lock and key. Zara sighed against my ear, and I felt her relax behind me. In the darkness, I couldn't see the indigo mist, but I sure felt it wrapping me in comfort and security. My skin warmed against hers, like the very essence of her mirrored a heated blanket. Every inch of me was sensitive with life and alertness. My nipples hardened, my stomach ached with desire, and the burn between my thighs wouldn't stay hidden for long.

Zara's breathing against my neck picked up, and she brushed my hair aside to kiss along my neck and shoulder. Her breasts poked against my back and I could feel the same firm quality to her nipples. She pulled me to her, hugging me close and with less reserve than before. The mate bond, even though preliminary according to Mal, thrummed happily in my chest. I imagined it opening and closing like it had a pulse of its own.

Thunder continued to rumble around us, and lightning occasionally flickered in the windows. The raging storm outside matched my desire inside. Zara's hands grew braver, and she ran them over the curves of my middle at first. In time, she caressed my hips and thighs, as if tracing the image of me and burning it into her mind.

"What does it feel like for you?" I asked breathlessly as my heart thumped with excitement.

"So good," she whispered, nuzzling my neck. "I've never felt like this."

"Me either." I reached back to place my hand on her cheek. "It's like...I'm supposed to be here."

"Me too. We are." She kissed the palm of my hand, while her exploration of my body grew even braver. Both of her hands caressed my breasts a few times before she offered me a gentle squeeze. It made me giggle and she snickered softly. "Like that?"

"I like all of what you do to me." I bit my bottom lip in an attempt to hold on to myself.

"I don't trust myself with you yet," she admitted. "After last time."

"I know, baby."

"But...can I...I mean..." She grew quiet, her lips against my shoulder.

"Can you what, Zar?" I turned my head a little, nudging her cheek with my chin.

"Touch you. I want to touch you so bad," she burst forth, her fingers poking my abdomen when she tensed.

"Yes. All of me is for you. You can touch me. I want you to. I always want you to," I whispered against her cheek. Again, her tension faded and she nodded against me.

Thunder clapped louder than before and it made me jump. Zara held me closer until the long rumble passed. She kissed my neck and shoulder, alternating between that and the occasional flick of her tongue. Her fingers wandered down my stomach, circling around my navel, until she traveled to the apex of my thighs. My belly fluttered, and I took a deep in-breath as my knees lulled apart, inviting her affection like a submissive bow.

Her body burned so hot against me, searing the memory of her into my skin. She stroked my inner thighs with such care that it had the essence of delicate feathering. Slow, and with caution, she slid her hand between my legs. A single finger parted me, while others tickled my folds. My body lurched toward her hand as my mouth dropped open in a silent gasp. It was more than just a touch. The exhilaration that such a simple pleasure brought raced through me, deep and fierce, almost to the point of release.

"Zara." I sucked in my breath, arching toward her hand.

"You're so... You're amazing," she said, breathless against my ear. A shudder raced through me as she pet me, like I was made of the most delicate glass. "That okay?"

"Yes. God." I clenched my teeth, fingers digging into her arm. My body twitched and writhed under her touch as pleasure built in my core. It raced down to my toes, curling them and the muscles in my legs began to quake. "Zara, I—" My eyelashes fluttered against her cheek and a moan escaped me as my body trembled, threatening to break as her fingers slipped all over me. Just knowing how wet I was, that she could feel it, and that she caused it, brought a jolt of excitement. Zara circled my clit, flicking and massaging in just the right way. "Oh!" I gasped as my hips lifted toward her hand. "Zara!"

Her movements quickened as I cried out. My body exploded, unfolding in the most luscious release of my life. Pleasure wracked my core, lashing at me like a thousand lapping tongues. Our mate bond thrashed, inside and out, circling my pussy and flooding me with ecstasy caused only by Zara. She held me in it, moving harshly back and forth while using her knee to keep my legs parted. Shouts escaped my throat as my body sunk under the longest, deepest orgasm I'd ever experienced. My mind emptied, hips bucked, and when I finally crashed back to the floor, I could hardly breathe.

It took me ages to calm down. I turned in her arms and she gathered me in a hug. Between us, our bond swelled then cooled to harmonious ripples, offering the sensation that we floated along together over the rocking comfort of water. Zara kissed me, her lips soft and warm like the rest of her. Instead of agitated like last time, she seemed content and relaxed as she rubbed my back. Her chest rose and fell in long, calm intervals. She floated with me, on the sea of blissful contentment. We didn't need to share words, because we spoke to each other in a different way.

∿∿
∿∿

"Can I tell you a thing?" I asked Zara as we hiked back down the rocky slope we'd spent all day climbing. She led the way a protective pace in front of me. In her cargo pants, boots, and purple flannel shirt, her very essence screamed comfort. Unlike me, she didn't carry a pack or any gear. Only her long, dense walking stick. A new one, since the old one still stuck out of a tree somewhere.

"Always," she said, glancing over her shoulder at me. In the late afternoon, the storm clouds that rolled in over the mountaintops blocked out the sun. The plunging temperature sent a shiver down my spine.

"I think I can feel how much you enjoy being out here," I said, skidding on a stone. "Whoa." Zara caught me around the waist without missing a beat and I ended up beside her.

"Got you," she said, brushing her lips over my cheek. "What makes you say you can feel it?"

"Because before I met you, I wouldn't be caught dead climbing a mountain for no reason. Or letting my hair get rained on. Or wearing these horribly unfashionable shoes." I held out my foot and she laughed, a full laugh this time, not her usual stifled one.

"Those cute little heels aren't going to cut it out here, princess." She swatted my rump and we continued our trek, both of us chuckling.

"Uh huh… Go ahead. Try to pretend you didn't like those heels. Part of the reason I annoyed you all that time was because you *liked* me. Admit it." I poked at her a million times like a childish fool. She squirmed, swatting at me before grabbing me around the neck, albeit gently.

"Not true at all. Not a word of it," she said, grinning as she wrestled with my wriggling form. She stopped when I lost my footing and opted to link my arm with hers. "Walk carefully before you tumble down the cliff."

I laughed, leaning my head on her shoulder. "You'll catch me."

"Wolves are fast, but we can't fly."

"Speaking of. I have a question—"

"You? A *question*?" She stared at me, her mouth wide with mock shock.

"Zara!" I cracked up, giving her playful shove that didn't move her a millimeter. "Did you just tease me? Oh my God, you teased me."

"I'd been working up to it for awhile." She chuckled, a smile parting her lips. It made my insides leap with happiness.

"Well, it was a good one." I poked her nose and she snapped at my finger, pretending to bite it. I squeaked. "Fresh!"

"Only with tasty women like you," she said, her smile perpetual. Zara's voice, her real voice, emerged in our more playful moments when we were alone. Every time someone visited her, she'd fall into silence again for hours or days. The more time we spent together, the louder she became. For that, I was grateful.

"How do you know I'm tasty when we haven't gotten that far yet?" I wriggled my way in front of her once we made it back to flatter land. She smiled, her hand sliding across my waist as we stood facing each other. The cold breeze from the lake made her hair flutter against her cheek. I leaned in, kissing her gently as the wind began to whip at us. We settled against each other, Zara's body burning against me even though my jacket acted as a barrier. Her skin didn't feel even the slightest bit chilled.

By the time we surfaced, the clouds thickened and the sun set behind them, dimming the landscape. Zara kept her arm around me as we moved toward the trail beside the lake. "It's getting dark. We better head back."

"Are there takeout places that deliver out here?" I asked, leaning my head on her shoulder again. "I need pizza. Or Chinese."

"No, but have you forgotten I can pick it up in twenty seconds?" She wagged her brows at me. "Hank's son, Henry, when he was younger, he used to work for the pizza place in town. He could bend and would make deliveries to all the Sept members during his shift. It was awesome. The only time I didn't mind someone appearing on my doorstep."

"Aw, that sounds perfect. No one else does that now?"

"Not yet. I'm sure his next kid to learn to bend will."

"Hmm. Too bad. So pizza or Chinese, babe?" I stroked her arm as we walked together, my boots crunching on the rocky path. Zara barely made a sound.

"Chinese. I'm in the mood for some ribs," she said. "Like forty ribs."

I laughed, and imagined a plate filled with that many ribs.

As we neared the place where the trail forked, one leading to Zara's, the other to Mal's, we headed in our appropriate direction. A few paces into our journey home, a rock skipped across our paths, colliding with a nearby tree. Zara's gaze shot in the direction of it faster than mine. Her pace slowed, and her nostrils flared as she appeared to take in our surroundings. In the dim light, the greenish color flashed in her pupils just like every other time when she attempted to see in the dark. At least now I knew what it was.

Again, another rock skipped across the low-lying grass, this time landing at our feet. We looked down at it, Zara's arm outstretched in front of me. Flat and wet, like the perfect skipping stones that I'd used not that long ago. At the same time, we both turned our attention to the lake. In the very center, small waves rolled in a vast ring as if something disturbed it from beneath. The ripples moved closer to the shoreline at a tempered pace. Zara gripped my elbow, tugging me backward.

"Let's go. Now," she urged, nudging me forward.

"What is that?"

"I don't know. I can't smell anything. But that's not normal." We hurried away from the lake, my feet shuffling in order to keep up with Zara. We didn't get far before a splash sounded behind us. I swung around, scanning the water. Zara's pace morphed from hurried to urgent in a heartbeat.

"*Run.*" She squeezed my arm, and we bolted. My legs reacted to her command before my mind had a chance to process it. My heart slammed in my chest, and Zara wrestled my backpack from my shoulders. She tossed it, and with a lighter load, I ran faster. Whatever we fled from made both of us react, even though I hadn't a clue what we tried to escape. I trusted Zara, and thereby trusted her warning.

In the distance, something screamed a nasty, blood-curdling sound that brought a bash of fear to my heart. There was no mistaking that scream. Images of the vampire perched outside my window, with blood dripping from its chin, raced through my mind.

"It's here!" I shouted, but Zara's growl behind me only forced me on. I couldn't breathe, both out of fear and anticipation.

Water rained down on us in a splash as if someone dumped a bucket from the trees. I looked up in time to see a giant bird dropping from the sky. It screeched and screamed like something tortured it. Only, it wasn't a bird at all.

Zara shoved me so hard that I tumbled forward, skidding across the dirt and slamming into a tree stump. I gasped, crying out as I tried to scramble to my feet. My nails dug into the ground, pulling me forward until I found my footing. A few yards away, the black figure dropped out of the sky again. Zara brandished her walking stick like a baseball bat. She swung, and a *crack* echoed around us. The vampire cried out, landing on the ground in a horrible gray and black mound between us.

Her clothes, the same as last time, dripped water into a puddle around her. She shrieked, tossing her head back. The sound stabbed at my ears and I covered them, ducking down under the pressure. Zara didn't flinch as she stepped over the creature, sending her boot into its face. A horrible *squish* and *pop* followed the impact. When the creature turned to me, her skin, pale and bloated, hung from her skull. Nausea swirled in my gut. In the darkness, her eyes glowed a violent crimson.

Terror tore through me, and I screamed the moment she made to leap for me.

Zara caught the vampire around the throat, holding her in mid-air. The vampire thrashed, clawing at and tearing up Zara's shirt. She roared, her face contorting with pain. Her knuckles whitened and her forearm thickened along with the rest of her. I watched as her shirt disappeared, replaced by a shadow that melted over her body in a slow roll. It stretched, elongating and broadening her form at the same time. Bones popped, growls deepened, and her face molded into a long, sharp muzzle.

I stood there, frozen, watching, and lost in the thralls of undeniable fear. The sound of a shrieking monster overpowered my senses.

The vampire in Zara's hand, dwarfed by the breadth of her beast, screamed and tore at her hairy arm. Unlike before, its nails couldn't break the flesh which only enraged it more. She kicked, and gnashed her teeth, her attention focused on Zara. Fangs—pearly, horrible fangs—glimmered in what little light that surrounded us. They paled in comparison to Zara's enormous canines. The vampire's gray, waterlogged skin flopped from her arms and legs, hitting the ground in squishing slaps.

"*Goddamn leech*," growled the beast.

"*Astrid!*" The vampire screamed to the sky, ricocheting around us as if the sound belonged locked inside an eternal sarcophagus. I cried out, covering my ears again and stumbling over the tree stump to land on my ass.

Zara's fingers wormed up the neck of the vampire until its entire face disappeared in her clawed hand. She tossed her head back, and let out a deep, rage-filled roar as she crushed the vampire's skull with barely the flex of a bicep. Blood gushed, splashing in a burst around her. It didn't stop the vampire from thrashing. Zara leaned back, threw the ragged body of the creature in the air, then tossed her walking stick with her other hand. Like before, the pointed end speared the vampire through the chest before it landed on the ground in a soggy, battered heap.

Just like that, silence plunged around us. My rapid breathing broke the lull as I struggled to tear my eyes away from the dead, *double-dead,* vampire on the ground. A shadow loomed over me, though it was the sound of puffing from a huge snout that made me look up. An inch from my face with hot, bated breath that blew my hair from my face, the black nose of a canine stared me down. I gawked, locking gazes with the familiar red eyes that I saw twice before.

"Are you okay?" I asked on a whisper.

Zara's beast nodded once, bumping its muzzle against my forehead. The second our skin touched, the red eyes faded to green and the beast melted away. Fur withdrew, muscles shrank, and the nearly three feet of height it had on me faded, leaving only my leather-clad mate kneeling in front of me. She froze at first, her eyes wide, before gasping.

"Kay!" she cried, reaching for me in a panic. I leapt into her arms and she grabbed me to her chest. "Oh no." She sobbed, breaking into a round of tremors.

"Zara! I'm okay. Easy, baby." I cupped her face in my hands, forcing her to look at me. "Zar, shh." I stroked her cheeks with my thumbs, brushing the tears away as they streamed her cheeks. My fear dissipated into concern for her. "I'm fine."

"No." She cried as if she already mourned my death. Her head fell back and a pained howl left her lips for the briefest moment.

"Zara, baby. I'm right here. Look at me." I placed my hand on her chest, drawing her attention to the spot where I experienced our mate bond whenever it tugged or pushed. She sucked in her breath, holding it for a moment when her gaze dropped back to mine. I nodded, encouraging the calm moment. This time, the dark didn't prevent me from seeing the swirling, floating waves of indigo that wrapped around us. Zara's shoulders relaxed, her fingers encircling my wrist.

"Kay…"

"Hey, girl," I teased, looking her up and down. "Nice outfit." I chuckled and she shared a tense smile.

"How are you okay?" she asked, pulling me into her arms.

"I don't know, but I am." I hugged her, squeezing tight as we melted into our embrace. All we could do was breathe and hold each other.

"You must move from here," a smooth, soothing voice came out of nowhere. I jumped, gripping on to Zara when we both looked up. Beside us, the towering sight of a Native American woman loomed over us. A beaded tunic hung down around her jean-covered thighs, and well-worn leather moccasins rose to her knees. Black hair met her waist, with a single gray streak in the front. Had she fallen out of a history book and landed here, misplaced in time? Her ethereal presence unnerved me until she crouched down, and a familiar pair of amber eyes bore into me. "Zara, we must."

"Okay," Zara responded finally. She urged me to my feet, though her grip on me remained firm.

"There is much taint, young ones." The woman waved for us to move away, ushering us from the trail. "Come, quickly."

"Where are we going? Who are you?" I pressed, though I went with Zara as she followed the woman into the woods and closer to the stream.

"Anadaya," the woman answered without much explanation. I couldn't tell if it was her name or a phrase right off the bat.

Zara pulled me into the icy water without giving me a second of warning. I squealed, sucking in my breath and shivering right away. "*Zara.*"

"We have to wash off," she said, accepting a wooden

bucket that Anadaya offered her.

"Your mate first," she instructed. Why Zara listened to her without question freaked me out, I had to admit.

Zara scooped up a bucket of water and poured it right on my head. "Zar!"

"Shh." Zara laughed a bit, repeating the gesture a few times until Anadaya instructed her to switch. This time, the stranger took the bucket and poured it over Zara. When she stepped closer to us, I couldn't make out the way she muttered under her breath.

"Good," said Anadaya, taking the bucket and setting it down. "We must get her warm."

"She needs to see Xany right now. Can we take her?" Zara asked as she helped me out of the water. My teeth chattered so I stayed close to her, reveling in the heat that radiated from her body.

"Makayla is well." Anadaya placed her hand on top of my head, though her gaze remained on Zara.

"She saw me change. *Please*. She has to," Zara begged, wrapping her arms around me again.

"I will bring Loud Mouth to you. Come now." Anadaya pointed in the direction of Zara's cabin. Zara heeded her, and we walked the short way back home.

My mind spun, lungs squeezed, and heart pounded as I replayed the events of the evening. How the hell did that vampire find me all the way out here? How long had it been living in that lake? Was it there the last time I skipped rocks across it? It must've been *weeks*.

Anadaya lit a fire in the hearth while Zara brought me a towel and a change of clothes to the bedroom. I chattered my way through drying off and dressing. Zara threw a thick blanket over my shoulders, and only then did warmth return to my core.

By the time we returned to the living room, not only had the strange woman built a fire, she'd also prepared mugs of hot tea.

"Come sit," she implored, gesturing to the blankets in

front of the fire. "Must get her warm, Zara, yes?"

"Yes. I will." Zara moved behind me, her legs on either side as she hugged me in the blanket.

"I'm okay," I said, accepting the cup of tea from the woman. "Thanks."

"I will fetch Loud One," Anadaya said, her gaze on Zara. "If you wish."

"Please. Just in case," Zara answered

"I will return." Anadaya offered me a gentle smile, glanced to the front door, then vanished.

"Who was that?" I asked, turning a bit so that I could see Zara.

"Another lone wolf. She's Doctor Twofeathers' mother," explained Zara.

"Is she submissive, too?" I sipped my tea, keeping my eyes on her. Zara pet my hair, then rubbed my back to warm me up.

"Ana?" She scoffed, shaking her head. "No way. She's incredibly dominant."

"But...why do you talk to her and not Hank or Caden?"

"Lone wolves are different. We understand each other. She's also a woman, so that helps."

"Sounds like your last pack really sucked more than I thought it did," I said, nuzzling her cheek with my forehead.

"It did." She hugged me, and I leaned into the warmth of her.

"And what's a leech, by the way?" I asked, meeting her gaze.

"Leech? Where'd you hear that?" She cocked a brow at me.

"When you were killing it. You said, 'Goddamn leech.' Is that an expression?"

"It's a term we use for vampires. They're bloodsucking parasites, just like actual leeches." Zara's eyes widened and she placed her hand on my cheek. "Was I in beast form?"

"Yes."

"Baby, I can't speak English in beast form..."
"But I heard you say it..."
"I don't unders—"
Before we could finish our conversation, Anadaya returned with Xany and the doctor from the other night. Xany bounded over to us, dropping to her knees. "Hiya. Miss me?" She giggled, her breasts bouncing with her quick movements.

"Um...not particularly," I said, which only made her laugh more. I drew my gaze from her to the two women who loomed over us, noting their resemblance. Both quiet, stoic almost, and their piercing amber eyes made me feel like they could see into my soul.

"Were they hurt?" asked Doctor Twofeathers, her attention on Anadaya.

"*Tla*," she answered, in a language I didn't understand.

"She saw me change. For real this time," Zara told Xany, drawing my attention back to them. "But she seems okay..."

"No one's explained why Xany shows up when I see Zara change," I said, looking between them.

"Xany has a gift that can heal the mind, or soothe it. And she can tell if you have delirium," explained Zara. "She's the only one who can do it. Probably the only one most of us know about."

"Which is why it's a secret," said the doctor as she approached. She crouched down beside me, her elbow resting on her knee. Something about her calmness and steady handling of herself unnerved me. She offered me a polite smile, then looked to Zara. "Permission to examine your mate?"

Zara nodded, though she gulped afterward and her gaze flickered to Anadaya.

"She's only letting you because you're Mal's mate," I told the doctor, then turned to Xany. "And you out of pure necessity. Even if you are Mal's sister. Because Caden's your mate." Zara hadn't ever said any of these things aloud. For some reason, unbeknownst to me as to why, I spoke for her.

"Ya think?" teased Xany, while shifting around to kneel behind me when Zara leaned back. "I'm gonna hug you for a hot minute."

"Okay." I chuckled and let Xany do her thing. Zara watched, her expression blank, though the way her lips pressed together and how our mate bond flailed all over, I could tell she wasn't very happy about it.

"Makayla, how are you feeling?" asked the doctor. "Any pain or discomfort?"

"Only from you all staring at me. That's pretty uncomfortable."

Xany giggled up a storm behind me, and finally let me go. "She's fine on my end. No feeble-mindedness. But this one over here is all wonky." She jabbed her thumb in Zara's direction. Zara frowned, though didn't respond.

"Well...good." I looked back to Doctor Twofeathers. "And what do you think of me, Doc?"

"I think that you're a good fit for Zara." She placed her hand on my head, and a slow-moving warmth trickled over me as if she poured a vat of hot tub water over my shoulders. "And you can call me Shawnee."

"She is a good fit for me," Zara spoke up. "Like you are for Mal."

"I am." Shawnee released me, looking to Zara. "Are you all right?"

Zara nodded, moving behind me again now that Xany and Shawnee backed off. She settled with her knees around me, her arm protectively, or possessively around my middle.

"You're warm," I told her, leaning into her. I glanced to Xany and Anadaya who held each other's gaze. Anadaya appeared stoic and calm, but Xany gestured like she carried on a full conversation. Her mouth never moved.

"Are you?" Shawnee lifted her hand, moving toward Zara's head. Every inch of her tensed behind me.

"Permission to touch you."

"I'm fine. You don't have to," said Zara, her chin falling to my shoulder.

"Let her check you, baby..." I nuzzled her cheek with mine. "Just in case." Shawnee met my gaze, her lips curling into a kind smile. For some reason, she carried a usually calming presence.

Zara hesitated, then offered her a nod. With caution, Shawnee placed her hand on Zara's head. Her expression remained steady. As quickly as her assessment began, it ended. Shawnee leaned back, both elbows on her knees as she crouched beside us.

"Zara, I really wish you'd allow Caden to meet Makayla," she said.

"*No.*" Zara's chest rumbled behind me, and her fingers dug into my hip.

"As someone who's been in bad packs before with psychopathic dominants, I can honestly say that Caden isn't like that. And not anything like his father." Shawnee glanced between us. "Mal and I could be there."

"No," repeated Zara. "Thank you for your help, but no."

"Does she have any glyphs at least?" Shawnee stood, though her eyes fell on me.

"She doesn't." Zara gave me a squeeze again. "Thank you for your help."

"If you change your mind, let me know." Shawnee joined the others while they continued not-talking talking. They remained that way for sometime while Zara helped me warm up by the fire. By the time I finished half my tea, the chill had left me.

After a few pleasantries, we bid our helpers goodbye and they disappeared beside the front door, the same way they'd arrived. Zara continued her hold on me despite the empty house. I stroked her arm, turning my head to kiss her neck.

"What's the matter?" I asked, noting her tension.

"They're outside." Her arms tightened around me.

"Who?"

"Everyone."

"Well, a vampire just tried to kill us after spending a long period of time in the lake," I reminded her. "Her name was Bronwyn."

Zara's eyes widened. "How'd you know her name?"

"She told me at the club before you rescued me. And she named me Astrid. Remember?"

"I didn't know that." She cupped my face, her hands burning with heat. "Learning the name of a vampire is like learning the name of a demon. When it names you, it intends to turn you."

"Well, good thing you saved me." I pressed my lips to hers briefly, before leaning back. "And now I've seen you change. We know it won't make me crazy."

"I never...wanted you to see me like that." Her gaze dropped to the space between us. I leaned forward, pressing my forehead to hers.

"To be fair, I didn't take much of it in, on account of the vampire trying to eat my face."

Zara let out a small laugh, and brushed her lips against mine.

"And to be equally fair, your beast is beautiful and so are you. I'm getting to know both of you better," I confessed, stroking the side of her neck. "I already know your wolf."

"How?" She nuzzled her nose against mine.

"When you're extra quiet, and when we're walking in the woods, that's when I know your wolf."

"Kay, humans don't talk like you... They're—"

"I don't care what I am. I talk like myself."

Zara's attention snapped to the front door, and a growl rumbled in her chest. Her fingers dug into my hip so hard that I winced. A knock sounded, which only made her growl more.

"Zara, I'm not here to hurt ya, but we need a chat, ay?"

a deep, raspy voice called out.

"Who's that?" I whispered, wrapping my arms around her neck when she made to stand.

"No," she answered the man behind the door. We stood together, though she kept quite a hold on me. "It's Hank."

"Zara, please?" That time I recognized the voice.

"It's Steve," I said, and she nodded.

"We won't come in without an invitation. We just really need more information about the leech," Steve continued.

"You can come in. No one else," answered Zara. Her eyes glared at the door, but the rumble in her chest never ceased. When I noticed her shoulders relax a smidge, she said, "And Mal."

The doorknob turned, and Steve entered, wearing his usual police uniform. On the stairs behind him, Hank stood beside Imogene. She waved at me and I returned her smile. After Steve, a shadowy wolf trotted in. In the dim light of the fire, his beautiful ebony coat shimmered when he came to rest at our feet. He chuffed, sitting back on his haunches like an oversized dog waiting for a treat.

"Whoa." My stomach lurched with a mix of excitement and nerves. "Is that Mal?"

"Yep," answered Steve. He shut the door then sat down on the sofa, as relaxed as ever. "No one's going to take Miss Parker away, Zar. I promise."

"The vampire was after her." Zara's grip on me remained steadfast while she recounted the series of events to Steve. Mal nudged his head against my hip, drawing my attention to him.

"Can I pat you?" I asked him. He nodded his wolfy head, and it made me giggle nervously. I reached my hand down, and he sniffed it once, then rubbed his face against my knuckles. With caution, I turned my hand over and ran my fingers through his fur.

The softness mixed with the rugged nature of fur that belonged to a wolf, enthralled me. I broke away from Zara while she spoke with Steve, and knelt down on the floor in front of Mal. He lifted his lips, as if to snarl, though it appeared more like a smile. I laughed when he nudged me with his head, his cool, wet nose against my shoulder. His breath puffed against me, soothing me in the same way that my old family dog used to. We called him Shark, for no reason at all.

Zara's hand on my shoulder drew me away from Mal and I looked up at her. Concern tightened her features, so I gave her hand a squeeze.

Mal closed his eyes, and I watched as the wolf's body began to change. His bones snapped and popped, contorting his form and elongating his limbs. I held my breath, and before I could release it, Mal stood before us, clad in only a loincloth.

"Show off," muttered Steve. He glanced to Zara and gestured to me. "She doesn't even flinch, Zar. That's why Caden wants to get a whiff of her. What if she's a Breeder?"

"We're fine how we are." Zara gripped my hand, and I stood up to embrace her.

"I'm afraid we're not going to be able to keep my brother away forever, Zar. You're a part of our Sept and your mate has been targeted by a leech. Possibly more than just the one," Steve said, a mild sigh accompanying it.

"Is that just a nice way of warning us that Hank's coming in?" I asked. Zara's grip on my elbow tightened and she pulled me away from them. "Easy, baby."

"No," she said, backing the two of us into the kitchen. There wasn't anywhere to go so we ended up tucked against the side of the fridge and cabinet. Zara's fear blasted from her, overwhelming me and making my heart pound. Somehow, I could tell that it wasn't my emotions. All of my instincts told me that these people weren't a threat. Zara's history informed a different story. Fur bristled over her forearms and I saw flashes of red in her eyes.

"Zara." I pulled her to stand in front of me, our middles pressed together. I guided her hands to my waist, then clasped my fingers behind her neck. "Look at me." She did. "Only me. Don't look at them." Tears welled up in her eyes, and she trembled against me.

I heard the front door open, and the looming presence of Hank followed. Out of the corner of my eye, the three burly men stood without a sound.

"No one's going to hurt me," I told her, holding on to her shoulders. "No one's going to hurt you, or make you do anything you don't want to do. Do you trust me?"

She nodded, though a single tear slid down her cheek. No sounds escaped her, though the fur on her arms began to spread. She must've gained a few inches in height by the time it met her shoulders, because I couldn't reach her neck anymore. I placed my palms on her chest, skin to skin. Her eyes never left mine, though the agony of her distress rattled around inside me.

I had no idea what Hank or the other guys did when they walked through the house. The elusive Caden didn't join them, of that much I could tell.

"They're making sure we're safe here." I glanced to the living room when the three men returned, though Anadaya and Imogene followed along with them now.

"Young ones, you are safe." Anadaya's voice preceded her as she entered the kitchen. Again, the front door opened and we both glanced over to see the men by the door. Mal stood by the sofa, with Shawnee beside him. She placed her hand on his face, and he turned his head to kiss her palm. Imogene had her hand on Hank's shoulder, both of them watching us.

"I think it's time for everyone to go," I said, gripping Zara's hand as I turned to address the crowded living room. "If we're safe, then you all need to go."

"A'right, Miss Parker?" Hank's sharp, firm gaze landed on mine. His soft, aged face made him appear like a wise old grandfather. The energy of him, strong and unyielding, offered a stark contrast to his appearance.

"We're fine." I held his gaze, despite the strange pressure on my shoulders. It made my body feel heavy, and like it would take a lot of effort to move. "I can take care of Zara."

"It seems ya can," said Hank, his mouth twitching as if threatening a smile. "Ya got my number if ya need anything."

"I do?" His declaration surprised me.

"Aye. I've been ya landlord for a few years now, 'cept my wife does all that business." He wrapped his arm around Imogene's shoulders. She swatted his chest, chuckling.

"Mack, if you need anything, you can call me any time," she said, her voice much more relaxed than the rest of us. "Have a good night, ladies."

Through all the talk, Zara stood frozen beside me. She never looked away from me, never spoke a word. The tension in her shoulders faded only after everyone left, save for Anadaya. The fur on Zara faded and she shrunk back to her regular height, forcing my hands to slide over her shoulders.

"Young one." Anadaya placed her hand on Zara's head. She closed her eyes and leaned closer to me while Anadaya turned her attention to me. "If the beast takes over her, you must remind her to run. Yes?"

"Um...okay, yeah." I nodded, pulling Zara into a hug. She melted against me, her lips against my shoulder.

"She is our only submissive female in a vast Sept. And one of only three submissives. Honorable dominants are drawn to protect submissives. Of that you must understand." Anadaya kept her hand on Zara's head while she spoke. She didn't seem to mind it, which surprised me. "These things are important for you to know."

"Is that why they swarm here whenever there's an issue?" I asked.

"Yes. They cannot bear to feel her fear. To worry for

her safety. Submissive ones are great gifts as they help quell the violence of the more feral beasts. They balance the pack, the Sept." Anadaya seemed to speak in some sort of riddle.

"Is that why she and Mal are friends? He seems kinda beastly," I said, shrugging. Zara sniffle-laughed against my shoulder, and then I knew she'd returned to herself.

"Mal is quite feral, yes. Being near Zara soothes him. Their beasts have an understanding," answered Ana, offering me a soft smile. "I will go, but not far. The others will return to their territories." She dropped her hand to squeeze Zara's shoulder. "Yes?"

Zara nodded, glancing at Ana after.

"Alright. Rest and eat," she instructed, reaching over and nudging my chin. "You are a good mate."

"So is she." My confidence broadened with the compliment.

Anadaya left us, this time through the front door. When it clicked shut, Zara remained frozen against me. I wrapped her in a hug, pressing her head to my shoulder. Her arms wrapped around my middle, and I could've sworn I heard her heart pounding. We stood there together for awhile, until the rest of her calmed down.

Like before, in times of stress, she lost her voice.

When she finally leaned back to look at me, her eyes bloodshot from emotion, I took her hands, and walked backward through the house while tugging her with me. She didn't fight it. Every inch of her screamed exhaustion. I pulled her to the bedroom, and released her when we came to stand beside the bed.

She watched me as I undressed, tossing my sweats to the floor. Another tear trickled down her face, and she swiped at it.

"You, too. I'd attempt to undress you, but I have no idea how to untie all that leather." I grinned, reaching over and tucking her hair behind her ear.

She turned her head to the side, brushing her lips over

my wrist as the clothes faded from her body. In the faint light from the hall, I couldn't see much of her. I took her hand, climbed on the bed, tugging her along. Zara moved with me, until I urged her to lie down.

"This time I get to hold you," I said, sliding behind her to wrap my arms around her and spoon her body with mine. She hugged my arms after I pulled the blankets over us. "You're safe, Zara. I have you."

Again, no words, but she pressed her lips to my fingers. Our mate bond made itself known by fluttering and dancing between us. Zara's body relaxed when I saw hints of indigo mist weaving around us. My chest gave a great lurch with a mix of joy and worry. Zara curled up tighter against me, and I held her like that.

I didn't know all the details of what happened to Zara in her original pack. All I knew was that whatever it was, it stole away her confidence and trust in other people. I didn't understand what everyone's concern was over me being a Breeder or not. To me, it didn't matter. I might not have known Zara for very long, but the connection I felt with her spanned distances greater than I could ever imagine.

It was different, and ancient. In a way, it seemed like I'd been waiting for her my whole life. Like in some mystical way, we'd been reaching for each other this whole time. And now that we were together, that same ache continued to tumble around inside us, waiting for release. At first, I didn't understand it. After tonight, the picture became clearer and so did my role.

I'd spent my entire adult life as a voice for others. As a reporter, a journalist, a busy-body. More than anything, Zara needed a voice. And maybe, if I loved her enough, I could help her find it. Until then, I'd be the voice that she couldn't. I'd tell those dominants to get away from her if she couldn't. I would say no, when she fell under the spell of fear. I wouldn't let anyone take away her choices, even if that meant being the loudest one in the Sept.

CHAPTER NINE

Like the last time she was upset, Zara stayed in the bedroom all morning despite my attempts to cajole her into leaving. Instead, I took a quick shower, then fixed her a lunch that she wouldn't be able to resist. I'd learned pretty quickly that she preferred meatier meals.

I carried the tray filled with giant cheese steak sandwiches, fried potatoes, and iced tea into the room. At first, she didn't move, then I noticed her nostrils flare when she caught a whiff of it.

"That's right, wolfy. I brought the meat." I sat down on the bed, setting the tray between us. She opened her eyes, and watched as I lifted one of the sandwiches, taking a heaping bite. "Mmm. Want some?" I held it to her, and she leaned up on her elbow. Before she could make contact, I pulled it away to take another bite. "This one's mine. The rest are for you."

No matter how shut down she was, her wolf couldn't resist sustenance for long. She rolled to sit cross-legged, and helped herself to one of the rarer cooked sandwiches. Without much pause, she brought it to her lips and tore off a huge bite. Her brows flicked upward at me, and I smiled.

"Good?" I asked, nibbling on a potato. She nodded,

and devoured the first sandwich in record time. The second one lost its life slower than the first. Happiness bubbled through me, lightening my mood and it seemed to lift Zara's as well. She relaxed into eating, and eventually tried the potatoes and tea.

"Thanks," she said, eons later, her voice raspy from lack of use.

"Glad you like it." I grinned when her mouth curved into a smile around the bite of her third sandwich.

We ate quietly together while she devoured every last bite. She downed the tea, set the cup back on the tray, then melted against the fluffy pillows, her arm draped over her full belly. Unlike before, she appeared less tense. I finished my tea, then set the empty tray on the floor before crawling up to lay beside her.

"Better?" I asked, and she nodded. "What's your favorite thing to eat in the whole world?"

"Anything you make me." Zara smiled for the first time in days it seemed.

"Even if it's boiled spinach sprouts?" I scrunched up my face and she chuckled.

"Yup."

"Hmm…" I climbed over her lap, straddling her thighs. "Fine. Nothing but boiled spinach from this point on."

"I'll eat them," she said, her hands falling to my legs. "But you will starve."

I laughed, leaning forward to kiss the end of her nose. "You're right. I would."

"I'm sorry about the other day," she said, her gaze weary again. "You must think I'm weak and can't protect you."

"Quite the opposite, Zara. What I saw was a woman trying not to kill everyone around her, because their very presence threatened us. I don't think you're weak." I stroked her cheeks, nudging her chin up when her gaze flickered away. "I don't think you're weak at all. Submissive doesn't mean weak."

"How do you know?" Her expression darkened with the question, casting doubt over my portion of the conversation.

"Because I listen. Anadaya said submissives balance the Sept. To me, it meant that submissives are strong because they can control themselves, all parts of themselves, and can help others do it, too." I leaned down, pressing my lips to hers in a quick kiss. "Nothing says strength better than self-control. And physically, you're just as strong as the other wolves."

"She didn't say any of that..." Zara tucked my hair behind my ears, her thumbs then stroking my cheeks.

"Not directly. But it's what she meant." I leaned into her touch, and her body under me became more pliable. "Zara, whatever happened to you in your old pack...I don't believe it will happen here."

"You don't know that," she said, though she didn't tense up again like before. I pulled my shirt over my head, leaving me naked from the waist up. Zara's belly quivered against my thighs. She stroked my arms as I held myself over her, the heels of my hands pressing into the bed.

"You're right. I don't know it for sure, but I feel it. And it's not because of who I am, it's because of who you are. Mal told me about the bonds while you were sleeping. He said that when we have a full mate bond, I'll be able to feel the Sept like you do. Is that true?"

Her eyes lingered on my breasts while I poked at the leather lacing in the bodice of her top. She nodded her answer and the corner of her mouth twitched as if threatening a smile.

"So you can sense that they don't want to cause you harm, too?"

"It doesn't mean that they won't..."

"No, baby. There aren't any guarantees like that in life. But I'm the kind of person that gives other people the benefit of the doubt." I fiddled with the leather string that held her top on and huffed. "You know, you might as well be wearing armor."

Zara laughed, bouncing me a little when she did. "I have a question."

"Ask it." I continued to fiddle with her top, until it melted into her skin. I blinked a few times, hoping to catch a clearer glimpse of the effect.

"Before me, did you often tear your shirt off without much warning when in the presence of women?" Even though her eyes appeared tired and red-ringed from tears, her smile hadn't faded yet.

"Actually, no." I thought about her question, while caressing the curves of her abdominal muscles. Her nipples hardened under my attention and she quivered against my thighs. "Before you, I was much more modest. And to think, that was a little over a month ago."

"Modest?" She scoffed, folding her arms behind her head. The gesture made me shudder with excitement as I watched her body move with majestic deliberation. "You were an argyle sweater wearing prude."

"Zara!" I cracked up, slamming my hands on the bed beside her when I lunged forward. "That was *so* mean."

"It was *so* honest." She grinned, lifting her chin to me as if to initiate a nuzzle. "You like touching me."

"I do." I nodded, smiling as I leaned over her. "It feels good when we're close. I've never been someone who sits in laps or is overly affectionate. It's different with you…"

"Because I'm a wolf," she said, breaking stance to stroke the ends of my hair. "And you're my mate. Changers and Breeders thrive on physical contact. It's a gift from Gaia. The pleasure we feel, the intensity of the mate bond. It's one of Her greatest gifts."

"I think that's the longest, most honest thing you've said to me so far." I placed my palm between her breasts, resting on the spot where I felt our bond. "I'm not a Breeder though…"

"Everyone thinks you are. That's why they want you to meet Caden. They think you're a Lost One."

"Lost One?" I tilted my head, and she nodded.

"A cub, Changer or Breeder, who's been displaced. Alone. Our Sept takes in Lost Ones. They attract them somehow, too."

"Like you?" I lifted a brow at her, and her mouth twitched with her smirk.

"Somewhat. Yeah." She tucked my hair behind my ear, and I watched as her voice faded again.

"I like when you talk to me, Zara. I could listen to you all day. I'll always want to hear what you have to say. Understand?" I ran my thumb over her chin. She met my gaze before nodding.

"Steve wants me to go back to work," she said, without elaborating, per usual.

"Maybe you should. We killed the vampire that was after me. Maybe I should, too."

"You can't yet. One vampire after you means more. They don't travel alone. They live in nests and sometimes have a hive-mind. Until we find that leech's nest, you have to stay in the patrol area." Both of her hands fell to my hips with her fingers digging in some.

"Well, I won't go running off like last time. If you go to work, Zar, I'll stay here. You can trust that now." I sat up again, straddling her stomach like before. "I promise."

"I'll think about it," she said, sliding her hands up to fall on my waist.

"When we can roam free again, would you like to go out to dinner?" My bottom lip found its way between my teeth. I released it as soon as I noticed.

"Did you just ask me out?" Zara smiled straightaway. The more we talked, the brighter her expression grew, and the fatigue faded from her eyes.

"I do believe I did, yes." I grinned, taking her hands when she offered them. "Gonna answer me?"

Zara's fingers laced with mine as she laughed. "Yes. I'd like to go out to dinner with you."

"And a movie?" I wagged my brows at her and she

continued to chuckle.

"There's no theater in town."

"I know, but you have magic that can poof us to one." I bounced on her while squeezing her hands. "So...movie?"

"Yes." Her laughter rang out without any reserve, sending a leap of happiness to my heart. "Yes to a movie as well."

"Yay. And a hike together today?"

"Haven't you had enough of hikes after the last one ended in a vampiric assault?"

"What are the actual odds of that happening again?" I leaned down to kiss her quickly.

"High."

"I'll take my chances."

"Suit yourself."

〰️
〰️

"Why are you out here alone?" a sultry voice asked as I sat on Zara's front porch with a notebook in my lap. I scanned the area, though no one appeared. Worry leapt in my chest, and I pulled the blanket tighter around my shoulders.

"Who's asking?"

"Me." From around the corner of the cabin, the ethereal form of Vanessa appeared. In her usual green dress with her blazing red hair down to her waist, she stepped barefoot into the snowy grass.

"Are you able to turn invisible or something?"

"No. You're just a monkey." She shrugged, coming to pause at the bottom of the stairs.

"I don't know what that means, but it sounds pretty rude." I set my notebook down on the chair beside me.

"It *is* rude." Vanessa's unwavering posture spoke of a cocky confidence and allure that brought a sense of worry to my core. How would Zara act around her if she made even me shudder?

"You're a rude cat." I frowned at her, folding my arms in aggravation. "I think you do it on purpose."

"Perhaps." Purrs rattled in her chest while she flicked at some snow on the railing.

"Are you here to make sure I'm not dead?"

"Mal asked me to," she said, her gaze chronically on everything else except for me.

"Where is he?"

"Somewhere else." Again, she flicked more snow, glancing in my direction.

"Aren't your feet cold in the snow?" I gave her a once over. "And the rest of you?"

"Changers don't get cold, monkey," she said, taking a step up closer to me. I gulped down my nerves and fought the urge to sink in my chair.

"What are you doing?"

"Nothing that concerns you." Vanessa joined me on the porch, looming over me like a willowy tree of judgment.

"Vanessa," a sharp voice called out. I looked around her to see Doctor Twofeathers approaching. "Don't pick on her."

"But she's fun." Vanessa pouted, immediately turning away from me. The pressure on my shoulders dissipated, and I sat upright.

"She called me a monkey and is acting weird," I tattled like a child, huffing at Vanessa when she narrowed her eyes at me.

"Ness, really?" The doctor hopped up the steps, coming to land beside Vanessa. Unlike the cat, she wore appropriate clothes and boots for the weather. Her hand slid around Vanessa's middle and the sound of her purrs grew louder.

"Mal said to."

"Mal said to check on her. Not *scare* her." Doctor Twofeathers swatted Vanessa's arm. "Are you okay?" Her steely, amber gaze fell on me.

"Um... Yeah. Thanks, Doc." I nodded, glancing to the cat then back to her. "She's intense."

"She is. And Shawnee is fine," she said, offering me a

kind smile. Every bit of her screamed doctor, with a good bedside manner at least.

"I keep forgetting," I said, keeping my attention on her to avoid the troublemaking redhead.

"It's okay." Shawnee turned to Vanessa when she began to fidget. The inch of height the cat had on her was quite obvious. Vanessa leaned down, nuzzling Shawnee's neck. I watched as Shawnee hugged her, stroking her hair through it. "We'll leave in a minute, baby."

"Now," Vanessa muttered, her arms around the doctor.

"Let's talk a moment, then we can go. Okay?"

"Yes," answered Vanessa, stepping back afterward. They held hands, and Shawnee took a seat beside me. Vanessa lowered herself to the floor, her head falling in Shawnee's lap. Without skipping a beat, she ran her fingers through Vanessa's mane of red.

"Are you two...together?" I asked, watching them with a lurch of something tangling in my gut.

"We are," answered Shawnee.

"I thought you were Mal's mate..." Confusion crinkled my brow, and tightened my shoulders. "Zara said wolves are monogamous..."

"I'm not a wolf," Shawnee said, simply.

"Oh..."

"She has two mate bonds." Vanessa leaned her chin on Shawnee's knee.

"Is that like, bisexual?"

"I'm not really a fan of any label," Shawnee said. "I love them both. That's it." Her expression, soft and pensive at its very core, didn't change much with her declaration.

"I can understand that." I nodded, leaning back in my chair when the crazy cat calmed down while soothed by her mate.

"How are you doing out here alone?" Shawnee asked after a brief quiet.

"Good. Zara's only been back to work for a few days. I'm getting used to it." A smirk met my lips. "Did you know that all of this started because of you?"

"I'm aware." Shawnee's half-smile matched my own. "Did my poor choices ruin your life?"

"Well, I wouldn't say that. I never would've met Zara. Or found out about this unbelievable world of vampires and werecreatures." I laughed when I said it. "I'm still unsure if I'm dreaming."

"One day, you'll feel differently." In that moment, Shawnee's stillness mirrored her mother.

"You sound like Anadaya. She calls us *young ones*." I laughed a smidge at the notion.

"I hope one day I will truly be like my mother." Shawnee continued petting Vanessa's hair. The once intimidating werecat appeared subjugated by her touch, if not tamed.

Gravel crunched and we all looked up to see the police car pulling up the road. It rolled to a stop, and the passenger door flew open. Zara leapt from the vehicle, clad in her work blues, and bounded up the stairs. Steve emerged from the driver's side, appearing much more relaxed than Zara.

"What are you doing here?" Zara rounded on Vanessa, her eyes blazing. I stood to greet her, and she whipped me up into a hug. My feet left the ground as I wrapped my arms around her neck. Vanessa hissed beside us, her fingers digging into Shawnee's knee.

"I'm fine," I told Zara. Her grip on me resolute.

"Leave," demanded Zara.

Vanessa didn't budge from her spot beside Shawnee. She lifted her lip in a half-hearted snarl.

"They were checking on me, baby." I touched her face, urging her to look at me. Her body radiated heat, and I could've sworn I felt her heart pounding against my flesh.

"I don't want anyone near you," she spat, seething with rage. Her eyes flashed red, and I brushed my thumb over her bottom lip. She glared at Vanessa, who appeared mildly irritated by our existence. When she made to rise,

Zara's right hand flew to her hip where her fingers wrapped around the grip of her gun.

Vanessa rose from the floor without a sound or hesitation in her movement. She guided Shawnee behind her, and growled. "You better have silver bullets in there," Vanessa warned, her voice deep and husky.

"Ness." Shawnee held on to Vanessa's elbow.

"Hey!" Steve hurried up the steps, his hands held out between them. "Enough of this. Zara, come on now."

"Stop. *Stop*." I tossed myself in front of Zara, both of my hands on her chest. "Don't. Look at me." She met my gaze, her eyes flickering between hazel and red. "Creating enemies in the Sept isn't what we want to do. I'm fine. No one hurt me." My heart slammed in my ears as I cupped her face. "Zara."

She lowered her hand from her gun and gripped my wrists. With a shaky sigh, she leaned her forehead against mine. Her shoulders relaxed, and I pulled her into a hug. Zara lifted me again, higher than before, and urged my legs around her waist. I followed, latching on to her before she sat down in one of the chairs.

"C'mon, Ness. Let them be," Shawnee's soft words rang out.

"Are you sure she's submissive?" Vanessa no longer growled while she spoke, and her purrs returned.

"Submissive has many meanings, baby." Shawnee held Vanessa's hand as she led her away from the house.

"I don't like that monkey or her dog." Vanessa glanced over her shoulder at us as they crunched their way through the snow.

"Shh. C'mon." Shawnee thwapped Vanessa's hand as they headed off.

When they were out of our line of sight, I turned my attention back to Zara. Tears shimmered in her eyes and she pursed her lips together so firm that they nearly disappeared. Steve took a seat beside us, then reached over and squeezed Zara's shoulder.

"Easy there, Weston," he said. To my surprise, she didn't push him away.

"Zara, we need to talk about this." I brushed her bangs from her face. She shook her head, then pulled me back into a hug. I rubbed her back, glancing to Steve. "Can you give us some time alone?"

He nodded. "I'll check back later."

"Thanks." I slid from Zara's lap, taking her hand as I tugged her up to stand. "Come with me."

Zara followed without complaint. Steve returned to his vehicle, watching us before we entered the cabin. I closed the door behind us, then pointed to the sofa. "Over there with you."

"Kay…"

"Nope. Have a seat, please." I locked up then returned to her after she sat down. Every bit of her burned with anxiety. She wrung her hands and bounced her legs. I climbed into her lap again, which soothed her fidgeting. "Your gun is bruising my thigh."

"Sorry," she muttered. It took her a second to realize that my leg wasn't anywhere near her gun. Her gaze shot to mine. "Not funny."

"A little funny." I draped my arms over her shoulders. "We need to have a talk."

"I don't want to." Her hands fell to my waist.

"Then I want you to listen to me, baby. Okay?" When she nodded, I continued, "Zara, eventually, all of this will be over. I'll return to my job, you'll go back to your normal work schedule. We'll be apart sometimes." I watched as her expression fell from tense to sad, and tears welled in her eyes again. I stroked her cheeks while I spoke. "I have coworkers and friends in town. I'll be around other people. For this to work, you can't threaten to shoot or eat everyone who comes near me."

"I won't eat them," she said, smirking with it. "It's against the rules."

I flicked her nose. "You know what I mean. I

appreciate that you're protective of me, I do. A part of me doesn't want anyone near you either. I never ever want to see that fear in your eyes again." I cupped her cheeks in my palms, brushing my thumbs over her spattering of freckles. "There are limits to how much we can protect each other, and picking fights with an insane weretiger is one of them. Yeah?"

"Yeah." She sniffled, taking hold of my wrists.

"You have to trust me sometimes. Trust that I can keep myself safe. I've had a decent twenty-eight years so far." I smiled, leaning in to peck her on the lips. "Okay?"

"Okay." She blinked away the tears before they tumbled down her cheeks. "I'm sorry."

"You don't have to be sorry for caring about me. I understand your motivation. We just have to come up with ways that aren't based in fear."

Zara opened her mouth as if to say something a few times. She gave up and just closed her eyes. I kissed her forehead, then hugged her. Our mate bond rattled between us, settling to a quiet lull. Zara's inner pain and turmoil showed more every day. I wondered if I could even help her in the long run. What if my presence made her feel worse? I shook my head at myself, straightening my posture. I couldn't think like that. If all of this was truly meant to happen, our presence in each other's lives was as it should be.

"C'mon," I said, kissing her again quickly. "Let's eat something and then watch a movie."

"I'm going to shower first," she said in a tiny voice.

"Good. I'll get dinner started while you do that."

Zara hugged me when we stood, her arms firm around me. I rubbed her back and she swiped at her eyes as she pulled herself together. If it took me forever, I'd get her talking. At the very least, I got her to tolerate me and to listen without falling into anger or despair. That was a start.

CHAPTER TEN

Snow fell heavy and thick around the area over night. The white blanket over the land and trees brightened the inside of the cabin through the windows. It must've been a solid foot of snow at least. Zara sat on the sofa, gazing at the fire while wearing a cozy sweatshirt. I emerged from the shower, a towel wrapped around my middle, to the warmth of the sitting room. Zara's nostrils flared and she smiled at me, her bottom lip held between her teeth.

"Do I smell good?" I laughed at her reaction. She nodded, holding her hand to me. I took it and climbed into her lap again, straddling her thighs—our new favorite sitting position. Our bond gave a great leap in my chest, and the purple mist danced around us. My insides swelled with affection and lust, setting fire to the apex of my thighs.

Zara pulled the towel away, tossing it on the floor. *So beautiful.* Her voice carried an echo to it, and I blamed the effect on the snow piling around the house.

"You think so, do you?" I cupped her face, capturing her in a deep kiss. Her hands slid down my back, and gripped my rear. My gasp broke our connection, and heavy pants carried between us. Zara's lips, ruby with her arousal, brushed against mine. "Do you trust yourself with me yet?"

"Yes," she confessed. Again, she bit her lip, telling me that her affirmation wasn't as confident as it sounded.

I chuckled, leaning in to nibble her neck while I pulled her shirt up. Her body trembled under mine, though she allowed me to disrobe her. I chucked it on the sofa beside us, then cupped her ample breasts in my palms, my thumbs stroking her pert nipples.

"Then let me have you. No stopping me this time." I brushed my lips over hers. Hot breath left her in nervous puffs.

"Kay..." Her hands tickled up my back as hesitancy swallowed her.

"I'm going to pretend that you forgot the *O* that preceded the *Kay*." I slid down her body, kissing my way over her breasts to her navel. My fingers wrapped the waist of her sweatpants, and I gave them a harsh yank.

Zara's breath caught in her throat and her stomach muscles tightened. I kissed along the curves of her abs, while working her pants off her hips. She let me, leaving both of us naked. I met her gaze, her cheeks red and her eyes wide as she sat frozen, her hands gripping the sofa cushions. I stroked her thighs, from knee to hip, while kneeling on the floor between her legs.

Gaia, she's so beautiful, said Zara, her voice echoing again.

"You're beautiful and you don't even know it," I told her, gripping her hips and urging her toward me. The motion made her slouch and her thighs parted around me. Her body burned with heat. I ran my fingers over her lower stomach, barely grazing the top of her pussy as to gauge her reaction. "Trust me?"

She nodded, gnawing her bottom lip. Our bond gave a great leap and the excitement shot through me so sharp that I had to brace myself. Heat swelled between my thighs, and I held my breath to regain control. Zara's fingers dug into the pillows and a rumble formed in her chest. Desire coursed through me, tangled with lust and want. I held Zara's gaze as I dropped between her legs, claiming her with my tongue, for the first time, in a languid caress.

A growl made it to her throat, and she swallowed it down in a gulp. Her eyes, deep green with her hunger, pleaded with me. *Don't stop.*

I didn't plan to, regardless of her request. Her strong, muscled thighs parted further with my urging, and I moaned into her soaked core when I flicked my tongue over her clit. Zara's body lifted toward mine and she sucked in her breath. I fought the vocalization that threatened to leave my mouth as my own body throbbed with want. I'd never ever been so stimulated without being touched before. My mouth hungered for her, and my yearning to please her trumped everything else.

Fuck, Kay... Zara's hands fell into my hair, holding me to her. It didn't take much for her to lose herself in the long-awaited lashing. I wanted her this way for ages, and my insides screamed with excitement. She didn't make a sound while I flicked my tongue all over her until her body tensed, she gave my hair a yank, and sucked in her breath.

The bond inside me thrashed, bashing against my chest and setting off a rippling release of my own. I moaned against her flesh, until both of us settled down to heaving breathless heaps. Zara relaxed under me, her entire body releasing a wave of energy that seemed to hold her together. She closed her eyes, covering her face with her hands while she calmed down. Her bashfulness made me chuckle, and I climbed into her lap again. My thighs straddled hers and she burned against me like she'd caught a high fever. It warmed me both inside and out.

I poked her elbows, then tickled her a little. She smiled, dropping her hands to rest on my legs. "Hey, girl..."

"Hey," she said, laughing softly. Her gaze appeared cool and comfortable when it landed on mine. She continued to smile when she reached up and placed her hand against my cheek. I turned my face to kiss her palm as she stroked her thumb over my bottom lip. *Does she have any idea how much I love her? Is it possible to love someone so soon?* Again, her voice sounded like a distant echo. Only this time, I noticed her mouth didn't move.

"She does know it," I said, rubbing her forearm to keep her from moving away. Zara's eyes widened and her face turned red, which confirmed to me that I wasn't hearing voices confessing their affection for me.

"You...you heard that?" Zara gulped as if she swallowed down a great wretch.

I nodded. "And she loves you, too. It's not too soon."

"Makayla...I didn't mean to—"

"I don't know what you did, but I don't care. I love you. Even if you can throw your voice like a ventriloquist." I pressed my lips to hers in a tender kiss. She kept her hand on my face, though our bond tore up my insides like I'd suddenly come down with a case of intense palpitations.

You can hear me talk like this? Zara asked, in the same odd cave-like sound.

I ended our kiss to look at her. "Yeah. It sounds funny though. How are you doing it?"

You asked me about gifts a long time ago, remember? This is one of mine... Zara's mouth remained still, though her expression shifted as if she spoke aloud.

"What is it though? Like throwing your voice?"

No. I can talk in your mind. Except I didn't mean to. I'm sorry. Her expression fell slightly and I cupped her face in my hands. My eyes must've darted all over her face as I tried to understand hearing her without actually *hearing* her.

"Don't apologize. I like it. You sounded clearer that time."

Because you're aware of it. You can answer me back. Focus for a second. Don't move your lips. She placed her index finger against my mouth. *Think about what you want to say to me.*

I watched her and listened to my thrumming, eager

heartbeat. Connecting with her this way excited me in an unusual way. Sure, I'd seen a lot of strange shit in the past month or two, but I hadn't truly experienced it for myself. This was something different. I took a deep breath and focused on my thoughts. Nothing happened yet and I let out an annoyed sigh.

Keep trying. Look at me and project something, imagine it coming from the roof of your mouth and you're directing it at me like an arrow. Zara spoke more like this than she did with her actual voice. In a way, her inner voice sounded more confident. The strange echo attached to it faded as well. I took a deep breath and decided to try something ridiculous.

Your pussy is delicious.

Kay! Zara shouted in my head and laughed out loud at the same time.

"Of all things, that's what you heard?" I grinned. "Before that I said that I wanted ice cream for dinner."

That's so embarrassing. She shoved my shoulders playfully. *You're talking aloud. Try again.*

I scrunched up my face while I focused on asking her what she wanted for dinner. She watched me expectantly and her smile never ceased. Zara's excitement over accidentally sharing her gift radiated from her, lifting her mood almost as much as sex.

Why didn't you tell me you could telepath? Oh. I perked up. "I think I did it."

You did then moved your mouth again. She pressed her finger to my lips again. *I didn't tell you because humans don't respond well to magics. It happened by accident.*

You mean you accidentally told me you loved me? I smiled, biting her finger to keep myself from talking out loud.

Yes... She nodded, wiggling her finger a bit.

I accidentally love you, too. Everything about us has been an accident, in a good way.

She nodded again, pulling me into a hug. *Hearing your voice in my head is amazing. I do love you...on purpose, too.*

I know, baby. I melted into her embrace. *Is it easier for you to talk like this?*

A lot....

Do it more often.

I will.

~~~

The next morning, I stood in front of the mirror behind the door in Zara's bedroom, adjusting the button-down shirt that I tucked into my skirt. Zara watched me from the bed as she fastened her gear belt to her waist. Anxiety rattled around our bond, radiating from Zara's end mostly, and partially from mine.

"What if I can't stick to the dying family member tale?" I burst forth, looking at her over my shoulder in the mirror.

"You're a reporter. You're good at fabricating the truth," she said, offering me a playful smile.

"Very funny, wolfbutt." I swung around, cocking a brow at her with my hands on my hips.

Zara laughed, her eyes wandering over me from head to toe. Our bond gave a great tug, and the image of a widening indigo vortex flashed through my mind. It flooded me with a sense of affection that almost mirrored a hug from Zara. It made me smile.

"So...you like my outfit?" I flipped my hair, then spun in a theatrical circle for her. Zara gulped, nodding as her eyes wandered down my skirt then back up again.

"I nearly forgot how you used to look."

"And just how do I look?"

"Like a trendy, argyle-sweater wearing millennial who orders pumpkin spice lattes with her avocado toast," she said dryly, her mouth twitching as she fought a smirk.

"Zara!" I laughed, bounding over to her and landing a feeble punch on her arm. "That was so mean."

She burst out laughing and snatched me around the middle, grabbing me into a hug. I squealed, wrapping my arms around her neck.

You're beautiful, Kay... When her voice sounded echo-ish, I knew she'd inserted her thoughts into my head again.

So are you. I reached up and tucked her hair behind her ears. She hadn't pulled it into her work-ready ponytail yet. *I can feel your worry,* I told her.

Zara grew quiet, her forehead pressed against my cheek. She melted away from me the same way she had in the past when her fears got the better of her. I listened to her soft breaths against my neck while rubbing her back.

I don't want to be apart from you, she said, her voice strong in my mind. *I don't want to feel the distance. I've really loved being so close. I've never felt so soothed and safe before the way I am when we're together.*

Her words surprised me with her candid honesty. I leaned back, brushing my thumb over her bottom lip when she met my gaze. *I'm right here, love.* I placed my palm against her chest. *You can feel me now. I'll be right in the center of town, down the block from the police station.*

I know. It's not enough sometimes. What if someone bothers you or hurts you? Her fingers tightened on my waist.

You'll know right away and you can bend to me. Right? Zara had never ever been this open about her feelings before. My heart raced with my excitement over her sharing her inner dialogue.

I guess so. Are you going to go back to living in your apartment? She dropped her gaze when she asked.

Um...I haven't really thought about it. I nudged her chin so she'd look at me again.

Why not? I can't stop thinking about it... Her eyes shimmered with emerging emotions. Was this what she was like all the time on the inside? Worried? Insecure?

For how long have you been thinking about it?

A really long time. She shrugged. *Maybe since I killed the leech and thought you'd leave.*

Normally, I'd ask if we were traditional lesbian U-hauling and moving in on the second date. But being mates, it's different, isn't it? I tilted my head, awaiting her answer.

She nodded, her gaze flickering away for a moment. *I want you to live here with me...*

Are you officially asking me to move in? I smiled, shifting my weight in her lap.

Again, she nodded and our bond wiggled with her worry. *I am.*

Well...there's no pool or Jacuzzi... I tapped my lip and it made her smile. *I guess I could move in with the woman I love. The person who exists both inside me and out. And the one I can't stop thinking about pretty much ever.*

Zara chuckled, her eyes welling up for a moment. *I can put in a Jacuzzi.*

Then it's a done deal. I pulled her into a kiss, and her body melted against mine. *I love you, silly wolf.*

I love you, too, scrawny human. She let out a playful growl and nipped my lip when we parted.

We better go to work. I squirmed in her lap.

I can't wait to come home again, she said, smiling with her statement.

Me either.

∿

"How are things at home?" Ian asked me, his tone gentle, once I settled back at my desk. It took three seconds post-sitting in the chair before he rushed me. I set my hot coffee cup down before turning to him.

"Good. Mom got the transplant she needed and she's doing well now. Big turn around." I fought the smirk that threatened to accompany my lie.

"Well, that's great." He leaned his elbow on my desk. "So...tell me about your rosy cheeks," he said, looking me up and down. "And those keenly shaved legs."

"Ian. I hate you." I smashed my hand in his face and he laughed while attempting to bite me.

"So who's the girl?" He wagged his brows at me.

"None of your business..." I turned to my computer, and began going through the two months of work emails. No one else was in the small office that morning, so it gave Ian grounds to continue his line of questioning.

Snow fell in big fluffy balls outside the vast window that faced the street. Memories of the vampire murder that happened only a block or two away in front of my apartment plagued my thoughts. Christmas bows and twinkle lights adorned the light poles. Businesses decorated their doors with spirited wreaths, and in the town square, a group of people decorated the huge tree in the center.

"I can't believe it's almost Christmas," I said, glancing at Ian.

"Three weeks. Yep. You missed Friendsgiving this year," he said, poking my elbow. "Are you coming for Christmas?"

With no family in sight, since I'd been working at the paper, Ian invited me to the holiday festivities he threw with his friends. While they weren't my friends, per se, I did make a few solid connections with his group. "Um...probably not this year."

"You can bring your girlfriend." His wicked grin made me want to shove him off his rolling chair.

"Thanks, but I think we're doing something else together."

"So...who's the new lady? Do I know her?"

"Probably not." The more I thought of Zara, the more I felt the bond in my chest. It stretched and thinned, leaving me with a sense of longing. Mal called our mate bond preliminary and I wondered how we could tell when it was a full bond. Anxiety settled in my stomach and the distance from Zara overwhelmed me.

"Will I get to meet her sometime?" Ian pressed.

"Maybe." I sighed. "Can we talk later? I have about two-thousand emails and the chief wants me to get started on this editorial."

"Fine fine." He waved me off and rolled back to his desk. "But don't think I'm not coming back to this topic later."

"I don't doubt it."

I spent the better part of the morning attempting to work on my assignments, but the more I worked, the more my mind wandered to Zara. Over the last few weeks, when she'd gone off to work, worry didn't consume me the same way it threatened to at present. My mind wandered to places of origin, questioning my reality. Had I really experienced Zara? The vampires? Werewolves? What if I'd been sitting there that whole time, imagining up the entire situation?

I glanced to the clock on the wall that told me noon was just about an hour away. "I'm going to go to lunch early. I have some errands to run."

"Okay then." Ian glanced at me, his expression remaining quizzical.

Instead of errands, I headed to my apartment. Imogene's shop had quite a few people shopping when I walked by. I made my way up the stairs to my place and unlocked my door. The unused space smelled like a library to me. I attributed it to the shelf of books, and little else in my small world. I closed the door behind me, and took a long look around the place.

The small apartment served as my home ever since I left Salt Lake to seek safety and solitude in the tiny town where my *family* couldn't bother me. I made friends, found my career, and lived simply, never once noticing the peculiarities that surrounded me every day. There, alone again and sitting on my dusty bed, I could hardly believe the events that happened over the past two months. *My girlfriend is a werewolf. A vampire tried to kill me. Werewolves are everywhere. What the actual fuck?*

It seemed like I was outside my body, disoriented and dissociated from my former life. Had I just woken up today after a season in a coma? I reached up, touching my head to check for bumps or scars of any kind.

Kay, what are you doing? Zara's voice snapped me out of my meltdown.

"What?" I started, glancing to the door. My phone rang a second later and I swiped it from my pocket. Zara's name flashed on the screen and I answered it.

"Where are you?" she asked, her voice steady.

"In my apartment. Are you far away?" Tears welled in my eyes as the anxiety crashed down on me.

"Not very. I'll be right there. Don't leave."

"Okay." I hung up the phone and sniffled, wiping my eyes on the sleeve of my jacket. Panic continued to ricochet around inside me and my leg bounced as I waited for her. Was that call even real? I checked my phone's recent calls list and text messages. Zara's number appeared where it should.

My front door opened and a uniform-clad Zara entered. Her brow furrowed with concern as she hurried over to me. I stood and wrapped my arms around her as soon as she grabbed me. Zara's warm breath against my neck calmed me down and she stroked my back. Only then did the anxious bond settle in my chest again where the panic replaced it.

"Nothing felt real." I sobbed, squeezing her tightly. "It felt like I dreamt everything. That you weren't real. And the wolves and vampires were fake."

"It's okay. You're okay." Zara cradled my head to her shoulder. She kissed my cheek and rubbed my back in soothing circles. Eventually, I calmed down and leaned back to look at her.

"I'm sorry," I said, reaching up to stroke her cheek. Zara's expression smoothed as it usually did when she stopped speaking and hid her feelings away. Worry tightened my throat, until her voice poked into my mind.

I think you had a panic attack, she said, tucking a fallen strand of hair back around my ponytail.

I think I did, too. I nodded, fixating on the buttons of her work shirt while I fiddled with them. *It felt like nothing was real for a minute. That being back here confirmed that I hallucinated everything while I was in a coma or something.*

Do you often think like that?

Not much lately, but I did in the beginning. I took a deep breath. *I'm okay now.*

Everything is real, Kay. Everything. Maybe we should have Xany check you again...to make sure the delirium isn't slow or something.

Now I've made you worried. I chuckled and settled her collar on her shoulders while smoothing it out. *You badass sexy cop, you. I'm fine.*

Zara chuckled, leaning in and placing a gentle kiss on my forehead. *If you feel panic like that again, I'm taking you. And I'm not a sexy cop.*

Babe, you are the sexiest cop ever. Look at you. I smiled, resting my hands in the center of her chest. *How about we have dinner together tonight after work? Like at a restaurant.*

Like a date? Her eyes widened while she held onto my waist.

Yeah. I perked up. *Our first date. Kinda. At least the first date not at the cabin. What do you say?*

I'd do anything with you...

My heart skipped a beat and I smiled. *Ditto, babe. A date it is.*

I'll meet you at your office after my shift. Her cheeks tinged pink and I leaned in to kiss her.

Most excellent.

CHAPTER ELEVEN

"Does alcohol affect you?" I asked Zara while we sat across from each other. The cozy restaurant wasn't busy on a random weeknight. Twinkle lights lined the top of the walls, and shimmered in the dim light. Quiet music played in the background, though not enough to overwhelm.

"It can, but I have to drink like twenty glasses of wine to have the same impact that one would have on you," she said, lifting her glass of red in salute. "Better get a move on."

"Zara." I laughed and swatted her hand. "They gave you a giant portion. Do they, you know, *know*?"

"Here?" She nodded, gesturing to the waitress. "She's a Breeder in Baron's pack. The owner is someone in the Sept. I don't really know everyone that well. This is the place where everyone goes, though. It's safest."

"It's really nice." I smiled at her, leaning back in my chair while we waited for dessert to come out. "Spending time with you like this is really nice."

"It is and right back at you," she said, a blush meeting her cheeks. *Everything with you is.*

"I heard that." I grinned and reached across the table. She placed her hand in mine and I squeezed.

"I think I'm constantly connected to you so you get my accidental thoughts."

"Do we have a full mate bond or is it still what Mal said?"

"It's still preliminary, I think. I mean, I don't know what it's supposed to be like. I've never had one before and with a human, it could be different," she explained, drawing circles in the center of my palm. Shivers raced up my spine and settled to an achy burn in my belly. Heat rushed my face when I realized the arousal she caused in public.

"What if I wasn't human? What should I expect to feel?" I asked, clearing my throat.

Zara toyed with my fingernails and I continued to burn in my seat. "Um… well, the Sept and such. You would appear in the ranks and feel them. They'd feel you, too. Our bonds are sort of a matrix. We can sense each other more strongly."

"Our bond would be stronger?" I smirked at the waitress as she set down our dessert. My warm brownie with ice cream, and Zara's white chocolate cheesecake. "Thanks."

Zara waited until she was out of earshot to answer. "Much stronger. We wouldn't feel much distance from each other, from my understanding."

"I can't wait for that."

"Me too." She scooped a dainty forkful of dessert. "Like right now. I'd be able to feel your arousal, not just sense it." Zara's rosy lips curved into a playful grin.

"Zara!" I whisper-shouted. "You cannot."

"I can so. You like when I tickle you," she said, brushing her nails against my palm.

"I do." I pouted at her, crossing my legs then giving her hand a squeeze. "Tease."

Her laugh warmed my insides. I loved this side of Zara. Relaxed, playful, and confident. Her green eyes twinkled with mischief and it only made me love her more. "You know what's worse?"

"What?" I gulped down the bite of ice cream.

I can say all sorts of things in your head to make you squirm and there's nothing you can do about it. Zara's lips wrapped around her fork and she wagged her brows at me.

That's so evil! I squeaked and thwapped her knuckle with my spoon. *Will I ever be able to initiate this?*

She chuckled, and snatched my spoon away. *Eventually, maybe. It takes time.*

I reached for it and she jerked it away. *Hey.*

Come over here and get it.

Don't think I will? I slid under the table, ducking under it, then emerged on her side of the booth. Zara laughed, grabbing me into a hug.

You fold down so tiny, she said.

It comes in handy. I kissed her cheek then stole her spoon. *Yay.* I grabbed my dish across the table, and scooped up a bite. I held it to her and she smiled before accepting it.

Yum. Thank you.

Yummy like you. I leaned in then stopped. *Can I kiss you?*

Of course. Her brow furrowed.

Just checking. I pulled her into a kiss, stroking her cheek when her hand fell to my thigh. My insides burned and I ended the kiss before it got too far. "Let's go home."

"Okay." Zara nuzzled my cheek, and I felt her lips curve into a smile.

We finished our desserts in haste and Zara stole the check before I could. I waited until we hit the pavement outside the restaurant to lay into her about it.

"You broke the lesbian dating rule," I said, holding my elbow out to her. She linked her arm with mine and chuckled.

"And what rule is that?"

"I asked you out. I should've paid." I leaned my head on her shoulder. My heels clicked on the frozen sidewalk while she walked without a sound beside me. She turned her head and kissed my forehead.

"Rules are stupid. I do what I want."

I laughed and gave her arm a tug. More of Zara's personality began to emerge lately and it brought me great joy. "I agree." I pointed at the erected Christmas tree and the lights that adorned it. "What do you think of Christmas?"

She shrugged. "I'm not sure. As a kid, it was okay sometimes. Haven't celebrated in like a decade though," she said as we strolled to a stop. Zara's eyes glowed in the flickering white lights of the star-topped wonder. A plush red skirt, made up of some type of water-resistant fabric, lay spread beneath it. Small mounds of snow surrounded it, and the giant fake presents around its base. We stood there for a moment, taking in the sight.

"What do you think of it?" she asked, her voice soft.

"I think, under the right circumstances, I would love Christmas."

"You don't now?" Zara's eyes narrowed with concern as we turned to face each other. Zara held fast to my waist while I laced my gloved fingers behind her neck.

"Not much."

"How come?" She tilted her head. Under the night sky with twinkle lights in our midst, Zara's beauty shined, both in its gentility and feral nature. I stroked the back of her neck with my thumb, wishing I could toy with her pulled back hair.

"It often reminds me of my aloneness. When I was a kid and came out, my parents stopped inviting me to holidays. I lived in their house, but they told me to stay in my room. It reminds me of how unwanted I was because of who I am."

Our mate bond gave a great leap in my chest. Zara's anger inside matched the way her expression fell. "I'm sorry that they treated you that way, Makayla. You deserve better."

"You've given me better, Zar." I smiled when I cupped her face in my hands. "It's like I've waited my whole life for you."

"I've waited all of mine for you." She dropped her forehead against mine. Our breath brought puffs of white to the space between us while I melted under the luscious thrum of the bond in my center. Indigo wrapped around us again, as if the mist ached to melt us together. I closed my eyes, reveling in the warmth of us.

I wasn't sure how long we stayed that way before Zara edged us around the dark corner of the building. Before I knew it, the strange swirly feeling returned to my belly. When my feet hit the floor with a clunk and the scent of gardenias filled my nose, I knew we'd landed back at the cabin. I opened my eyes and Zara offered me a smile.

"I could get used to your teleporting."

Zara laughed, cupping my cheeks in her hot hands. "Bending, silly. Teleporting is something different."

"Same thing to me!" I grinned, leaning up to kiss her. "Ditch the gun so I can touch you properly."

"I plan to," she said, releasing the clasp of her gear belt. She set it on the coffee table, then nipped my cheek while I took off my coat. I grabbed her hand, tugging her with me as I walked backward.

"Come on."

"Where are we going?"

"For a bath."

"Together?" Zara's eyes widened and I nearly giggled.

"Never had a bath with a girl before?"

"I haven't…"

"Well then. You're in for a treat."

I led her through the bathroom, then turned on the faucet after plugging the tub. While it filled, I watched her standing there nervously. With Zara, I realized that I hardly ever stopped smiling. I undressed, ditching my panties last. She followed suit while I squeezed a bit of body wash under the flow of water to create some bubbles. Fragrant jasmine filled the room along with the steam. I stepped into the tub first, then held my hand for her.

"Come on, pretty." I wiggled my fingers at her.

Zara's hair tumbled down her back when she pulled out the hair tie, then accepted my gesture. We slid into the tub together and I sat with my back against the deeper part of the claw-foot tub. Zara settled between my legs, facing me as she attempted to figure out how to sit. With slow, cautious movements, she finally settled and I reached forward to stroke her face.

"Lay against me, baby."

Zara said nothing while she shifted around to lean back. I guided her against my chest, kissing her shoulder, and both of us seemed to sigh. Zara held on to my arms, her body a little tense at first. *Not used to this*, she said, her voice echoing in my mind

I can tell. I have you. I stroked her belly, up and down over her abs, and she quivered under my attention. It calmed her down and she laid her head on my shoulder.

The sound of the running water soothed me, and thereby, soothed Zara as we enjoyed the hot bubble bath together. My insides swelled with affection for her which offset the inner chastising I'd done for doubting her existence. Zara was like no other woman I'd ever met. And I had certainly not fallen in love with anyone before. Knowing her, feeling her the way I do, brought more happiness to my life than I ever thought possible.

Zara turned her head, kissing her way up my neck until she closed the gap between us. Our lips pressed together and her body burned hotter than the water. She settled after, her head resting on my shoulder with her palm in the space between my breasts. The water rose around us, warm and comforting with the fragrant bubbles. When it reached the edge, I used my foot to turn it off. Zara closed her eyes and I pressed my lips to her forehead while I held her. Even in the water, the indigo wove around us. It brought me almost as much comfort as the closeness with Zara.

In the quiet bathroom, with only the sounds of trickling

water, it mirrored the silence inside of me. Zara existed in the same space. She moved when I moved, and breathed in time with mine, as we choreographed our existence. Zara lived inside me and out, and our bond, as I imagined it, expanded from something straw-like to a vast, open siphon between our souls. I had no idea how our bond could've been labeled preliminary. To me, it seemed whole and complete.

The water around us grew cold and Zara stroked my shoulder when goose bumps plagued my skin. A shudder raced through me, hardening my nipples along with the chill. Zara smiled straightaway, sitting up in the water. She pulled the plug, then slipped an arm under my knees before lifting me right up. A small gasp left me with the sudden movement, and I wrapped my arms around her shoulders. She chuckled, and kissed my cheek.

"I won't drop you, baby," she said, then nodded toward the sink. "Grab those"

"Sometimes I forget you're strong." I snatched the towels on the way out.

"Sometimes I forget that you get cold." Zara toted me through the chilly house and into the bedroom. She set me down, then wrapped a towel around my shoulders. I tossed one over her head and she shook it off like a wet puppy. It made me laugh when she sputtered her hair out of her face.

"You're incredibly silly," I said, reaching up and cupping her face. I brushed my thumbs over her lips and she kissed each of them. "And incredibly beautiful."

"Says you." Zara pulled me to her, capturing me in a heated kiss at the same time our bond gave a great yank. She stole my breath and I grabbed a handful of her hair, keeping her in it. My body raged with want, and my heart filled with need that only Zara had ever been able to fill.

I pulled her toward the bed until the back of my knees collided with the mattress. Zara pursued me, urging me back on the bed then reclaiming my lips. I moaned against her, as she fell between my knees, her breasts pressing against mine. My fingers tangled in her hair, as my tongue probed her mouth. Rumbles stirred in her chest as her desire rose with mine. Our bond thrashed, and dampness rushed the apex of my thighs. I cried out, ending our kiss with it. Zara grabbed my hands, our fingers lacing against the pillows as her gaze locked on mine. Flecks of red mingled with her sparkling greens, and I gave her hands a squeeze.

Zara kissed me, this time too quick for me to catch her in it. She moved down my body, placing soft kisses on my chin, down my neck, then between my breasts. She paused over each nipple, offering them a teasing flick of her tongue. A sharp inhale followed the tingling warm that rattled down to my core, curling my toes and making me writhe beneath her. Zara smiled, biting her bottom lip as she moved down my body. Her gaze remained locked on mine.

I want you, her voice burst into my mind. *Taste you. Make you mine.*

"Zara." I gasped out her name, unable to focus enough to answer her telepathy.

She raked her teeth from my navel down to the top of my pussy, stopping right before her mouth met my clit. I cried out again, grabbing hold of the linens when she released my hands. She nudged my thighs apart, still her eyes on mine. *Mine.* She growled, then dragged her tongue over the full length of my slit. Rapture tangled with lust, causing my stomach to flutter and my hips to lift toward her. The connection between us flooded me with desire, almost as if it lapped at me the same way as Zara.

A second growl left her when she dropped down between my legs, and devoured me. She shoved her hands under my rear, squeezing tight as she held me to her. I nearly screamed as her tongue lashed at my saturated core, snaking around my folds like she knew every inch of me. Pleasure pulsed through me in volatile waves of deliciousness, threatening release at every peak. No one had ever taken me like this, moved me through passion of want in such a way that begged insanity. I moaned, squirmed, and bucked against her mouth. Her lips wrapped around my clit and my mouth fell open as my head thrashed on the pillow.

"Zara!" I cried out as I erupted against her mouth. Pleasure rushed me, curling my toes and arching my body as every muscle spasmed with release. My moans and shouts continued through the endless flicks of Zara's tongue as I came. Once, then twice, one after the other as she drove me up and down the most decadent rollercoaster of bliss I'd ever experienced. Sweat beaded my brow and my body remained on fire in endless waves of ecstasy.

When I calmed down to a puddle of breathless mush, Zara continued to lap at me, until she, too, relaxed and lowered me back to the bed. She dropped her head against my thigh, her eyes closed as her heavy breaths met my middle. I reached down, tangling my fingers in her hair as we tumbled into a sweet afterglow. Our bond thrummed between us, like the slow, rhythmic beat of a drum.

"My God," I said, once my breath returned. "Do that to me every day." Zara looked up at me, her smooth lips curved into a luscious smile. "Every day."

"I will," she said, using her thumb to stroke my soaked core. I shuddered under her affection, watching her as continued petting me. *She's delicious. And her pussy is almost as beautiful as she is.*

I laughed as my face burned with a blush. "*Zara.* I can hear your naughty thoughts."

"Oh my *God*," she burst forth, startling me as she shifted between my legs.

"What?" I leaned up on my elbows while she stared down at my center. "What? Am I bleeding or something?"

"Oh my God." She pushed me back, shoving my legs further apart, then rolling my labia through her fingers.

"Zara! You're freaking me out!" I nearly panicked and looked down at myself. No blood, no turning into a werewolf. "Am I giving birth or something?"

Zara fell quiet as she touched the spot on the right side of me, close to my clit. Tears welled in her eyes and I stared at her like she had absolutely lost it. Our bond lurched and thrashed with the intensity of her emotions.

"Baby, I know you're fond of my pussy, but what the heck?" I took hold of her hand, squeezing it in hope of getting her to answer me.

"You have a glyph," she croaked, sniffling through it. "You have one."

"I have a what?" I nearly freaked out, shooting upright to examine myself. Images of random bugs crawling on my skin came over me. I batted at myself as if trying to kill them.

"Here." She swatted my hands away. "Here." She pointed to the spot on the right side of my girly bits.

"It's just stretch marks or something. See what happens when I shave for you?"

"No." She swatted at me again, letting out a soft sob. Zara's words fell away as they always did when she grew emotional. I focused inward, attempting to urge myself into her thoughts. My efforts drew my attention to our bond as it flooded me with her feelings; relief and joy.

"Baby…" I cupped Zara's face, forcing her to look at me. Tears streamed down her cheeks, but she smiled through it. Green eyes twinkled as she cried, touching me all over as if she'd seen me for the first time. "I love you so much. And I have no idea what's going on." My breath left me in a gasp as Zara backed me down into the pillows. My feelings flourished with hers, overwhelming my senses.

Zara captured me in a heated kiss, more forcefully than she ever had, as if she wasn't afraid of breaking me anymore. Her lips seared mine, and the heat of her above me magnified. I grabbed a handful of her hair as her tongue danced with mine. She moved to straddle my thigh and I slid against her, fitting together like a perfect puzzle.

I love you, Kay. Zara's voice burst into my mind.

I know you do. I ran my hands up and down her back as we moved together, our bodies rocking in a way we hadn't done before. *But now you're not afraid to anymore.* Everything about her intentions, her thoughts and worries, flowed through me somehow as if the dam that she'd built so tightly around herself broke.

I can't hurt a Breeder. She ended our kiss, dropping her head against my shoulder. Her breath puffed against my neck. Whatever she meant, whatever meaning me being a Breeder held for her, seemed to unlock her from a sarcophagus of fear.

You wouldn't hurt me no matter what I am, baby. I ran my fingers through her hair and she leaned back to look at me. *Not you or your beast. Because you, Zara Weston, are one of Gaia's heroes. That much I've learned, and of that much I'm certain.*

Her lips pursed together as she surveyed me, until she offered me a solemn nod.

We melted together after that, tumbling together into the throes of lovemaking. Different from sex. Different from pleasing or soothing each other. For the first time, we met each other in the same place, filled with joy and love.

Zara's body writhed against mine, and we climbed the sharp mountain toward release together. Indigo smoke *bound* us together in a *sacred* circle, branding us as mates the same way a *glyph marked* a Breeder.

When we crossed the chasm of pleasure, erupting inside and out, our bond thrust open, flooding my senses with Zara. Her laugh, her smile. The first time I annoyed her at a crime scene. Her tears and pain. Fear of Caden and Hank, or any man who threatened to dominate her for their own selfish desires. Her possessiveness of me, and mine of her. The Christmas tree in the town square reflecting in her beautiful eyes. Everything all at once. So much. So fast. Images, sensations, smells, tastes. All of it.

Taking me, pulling and pushing, devouring my psyche while I hovered on the edge of ecstasy and insanity.

The weight of Zara's body crashed down on me, and the bed bounced with us. Both of us panted heavily while holding on to each other. Zara gasped and heaved, her forehead against mine as she trembled. I had a moment of quiet until she met my gaze. Visions immediately assaulted me, appearing in my mind like images on a movie screen. I saw Mal and his doctor mate. Xany and a man I didn't recognize. Steve and some of the other folks on the force. The waitress from our first official date. Children with black hair and copper skin. Wolves of all colors and sizes. A raging beast roaring in the woods. Imogene and finally Hank. At the center of everything, Hank's image, strong and bold, hung in the center like a giant spider hanging in his vast web.

I held on to Zara, choking on my breath as I tried to work through my experience. Every inch of me shook from adrenaline and the urge to run overcame me. To run and chase, devouring the exhilaration of freedom.

Everything came to a screeching halt and finally, Zara's presence returned. Vast and brazen, in her leather shorts and halter, with her hair fluttering in the wind. She looked at me in my mind, and right in front of me. I touched her face as her tears tumbled against my wet cheeks.

"Oh my God," I breathed out. "I feel you. And everything. *Everyone.*"

She nodded, sniffling as a soothing calm poured over us. Her arms shook as she lowered herself to the bed beside me. I rolled with her, the two of us unable to separate. Supernatural glue held our flesh together, or so it seemed. She reached for me, her palm against my cheek as she fought to keep her eyes open. My eyes grew heavy, my mind and body weakening, before darkness swallowed me, both of us, as our consciousness faded.

CHAPTER TWELVE

I sat by myself on the sofa, my legs folded under me and my eyes closed. I focused on the newfound business of my inner world. The indigo smoke that surrounded Zara and me wasn't there anymore. Instead, our bond appeared to me like a throbbing indigo life form that connected us like an eternal, flexing tube. It pulsed in rhythms like a heartbeat, and expanded and contracted like a lung. Our connection was a living, breathing part of us that completed me in every way. Any doubt, fear, or anxiety I ever had seemed soothed by it. The chronic solitude of my life was nothing more than a memory. In all my years on earth, I wasn't ever able to meditate. Now, every time I closed my eyes and focused inside myself, the grounded balance of a meditative state overcame me. It was all Zara. My Zara. She would never be anyone else's.

When I wandered beyond our bond, to the tendrils of an intricate vascular-like system, each route led to someone in the Sept. People I didn't know, but I could sense somehow. Like, I knew Mal was okay, and from him, smaller threads stretched to the system where he belonged. His pack, Zara explained, with the elusive Caden as the central point. Mal stood out strong because I knew him,

Zara told me, and as I met others, they would appear stronger as well. Oddly enough, I could tell who was a child and who was an adult. I kept my focus on Mal's web for a bit, then switched to the thick threads that bound me and Zara to the pride. At the center of everything, the white pulsating center, sat Hank. When I gave my attention to his connection, he felt closer to me, as if he just walked through the front door.

But it wasn't Hank's bond that changed. Mal's grew larger, brighter. In my mind's eye, I saw a clear image of his face and tell-tale smirk. His hand held tightly to the glowing figure beside him until I recognized his mate.

Be right there, I heard him say.

I started, gripping my chest as my eyes shot open. "Zara?" I called out. She closed the fridge door, a bucket of fried chicken tucked in the crux of her arm.

"Yeah, baby?"

"I did something..." I bit my lip as Mal's presence grew stronger. "I think I broke it."

"Broke what?" She joined me in the living room and set the chicken on the table.

"I dunno. Mal's bond feels funny and I heard his voice," I told her, wringing my hands together.

She chuckled, reaching forward to brush my hair from my shoulder. "You called him. He's coming over."

"I did what now?" My eyes widened.

Zara's eyes twinkled with amusement. "When you pay close attention to the bonds, you can call the Sept's attention to you. He's the one you know best. How'd you do it?"

"I don't know. I mean, I was looking at the bonds and stuff..." Anxiety rattled my insides, but diffused a moment later.

"Looking at it?" Zara's smile broadened and she took my hands in hers.

"Like how it looks inside me. Don't tease me!" I squeaked, giving her a yank. She laughed and pulled me into a hug.

"I'm not, silly." She rubbed my back at the same time she smooched my cheek. "I believe you."

A knock sounded on the front door and Zara nodded to it. "You have company."

"Accidental company!"

"I can hear you," Mal's muffled voice said from the other side of the door.

Zara's laughter continued as she stood to open the door. Mal's grin wasn't much different. His eyes fell on me right away while Zara greeted his mate.

"Don't tease me either," I said to him, flopping back on the cushions with a pout.

"I had to show up to check on the girl who has spent the last twenty minutes staring at me through a magical portal," he said, snatching a drumstick from the chicken bucket.

"He's kidding, Mack," offered Shawnee, swatting Mal upside the head. Zara shut the door behind them, then returned to me on the sofa. Without missing a beat, her arm snaked around my middle. My insides raged both from her contact and from the close quarters with the people in front of me.

"Slightly." Mal tore into a bite of chicken, then looked to Zara. "This was for me, right?"

"Yeah." Again, she laughed as she hugged me from behind. Since our connection became a full mate bond, Zara's unease faded some.

"Didn't you plan to take Zara on a run?" Shawnee asked Mal, a single eyebrow cocked at him.

"Right now?" Zara tensed behind me.

"Oh. Yeah." Mal started, then nodded toward the door while he chewed a mouthful of food. "Let's go."

Zara looked between us.

"I'll be okay. It's obvious the doctor wants to talk to me alone and they're trying to be shady about it," I said, kissing Zara's cheek. "I'll be fine."

"I don't want to." Her panic shot through me, and I turned to face her.

"I know. You can feel me now, remember? And just do the head talking thing," I told her. With that, she calmed down and looked to Mal.

"Are you tricking me?" she asked him, but released me to stand.

"I wouldn't do that." His solemn nod earned him a few brownie points in my book. Zara followed him to the rarely used back door off the kitchen that led to the small deck. With one last glance over her shoulder, she followed him out.

I don't like this, she said in my head.
I'll tell you everything she says and does.
Deal.

"Is this a Breeder initiation?" I asked Shawnee as she sat down on the edge of the coffee table in front of me.

"No." She chuckled. "Zara has a difficult time allowing anyone close to her and now, close to you. So, I've been solicited to share information with you."

"Why you? I mean, I don't mind, but why?" My mind wandered to my old article that I never finished, and the excuses that I passed to the Editor-in-Chief as to why I couldn't write it.

"Xany is threatening to her because of Caden, and Imogene because of Hank. Mal is the only person she gently trusts," explained Shawnee.

"Are you supposed to confirm my Breederdom?"

"A little." She smiled, a soft, warm smile that spoke of a gentle bedside manner. "Zara told Mal that you have a glyph when you formerly didn't. When we all felt you burst into the ranks of the Sept, and so strongly at that, they asked me to verify."

"Do you think I'm a witch?" I snickered at that.

"Well, maybe. Caden can scent bloodlines and usually is the one to confirm for the Sept. Out of respect for Zara's wishes, this is the compromise."

"Are Zara and I considered a pack?" I asked.

"A tiny one, but yes. Two mates are pack."

Are you okay? Zara's query brought me pause as I focused inward to answer.

She wants to verify that I'm a Breeder by seeing my glyph. She has no idea that she's asked to see my pussy. Does that freak you out?

A little.

Why did they ask you to leave?

Mal's trying to convince me to introduce you to Caden and Hank formerly.

"You're a terrible mind speaker. Your face changes and you gesture," Shawnee said, dragging my attention back to her. "Better work on that."

"Don't tease the newbie," I said, and she laughed.

What are you telling him? I asked Zara. My inner voice sounded distant with the effort to manage both.

No.

"So, you want to see my glyph?" I jumped right to the chase.

"That's the idea." Shawnee nodded. "Where is it?"

"Somewhere that you're not going to like." I paused, tapping my lip. "Or you might, depending on your preferences."

"What do you mean?" Shawnee leaned back.

"Zara found it when she was mouth deep in my nether region." I pointed to my pelvis.

Shawnee chuckled, shaking her head at me. "I've seen it all at this point. I won't touch you. I'll just look."

"Okay." I stood in front of her, tugging down my sweats before returning to my seat. I tugged my panties aside to show her. After seeing it a few times, it still looked like more of a three-line scar or stretch mark patch to me. "Can you see it?"

"I think you win the award for most unusually placed glyph." Shawnee looked on with a neutral expression, a pokerish doctor face that gave away no hints of her feelings about it. I wondered, that if she'd noticed something terminal in a patient, they wouldn't ever have a clue.

"Do you think it's one? It looks like nothing to me."

"You're very fair so it's lighter than usual. Did you ever notice it before?" She patted my hand which told me I could cover myself again.

"No. I mean, I only just shaved bare. Normally, I don't." I pulled my pants back up then dropped back on the sofa.

"Why did you?"

"Good first impressions for the woman I'd accidentally fallen for while she harbored me in witness protection?" I smirked. "Before Zara, it'd been a few years since I was with anyone."

"I understand." Shawnee gave my hand a squeeze when she moved to sit beside me on the sofa. "To me, that's a glyph. You've always felt like a Breeder to me."

"Do you have one?"

"I do." She pulled down the collar of her sweatshirt and showed me the upper part of her arm near her shoulder. Unlike mine, her glyph stood out a clear, dark bronze against her copper skin, and it had four lines instead of three.

"Yours is different."

"It is. My blood line is different. Most have three lines, some have four."

"Why did you think I was a Breeder?" I asked, pulling my knee to my chest.

Are you okay? Zara asked a second time.

I'm okay, baby. Shawnee is very kind to me.

I know...but still.

Worry wart.

Hey. I almost felt her smile.

"Because of how you've handled learning about all of this. It shocked you at first, but you settled right into it as if it was as natural as anything." She gestured between us, her movements deliberate and controlled.

"It is. It felt like everything just made sense about the world," I confessed. "Though for awhile, I thought I was in a coma and dreaming."

"Understandable. Have you ever gotten sick before? In your entire life?"

"Um...not really or terribly or anything. I haven't really thought about it."

"Colds? Flu? Chicken pox?"

"Nope. But I got vaccines. Why?" My brow furrowed as I leaned my chin on my knee.

"Breeders don't get human illnesses. And you won't need vaccines anymore. Frankly, don't get any vaccines anymore unless you talk to me about it. Stomach bugs?"

"Only from drinking too much in college."

For an instant, a flash of something crossed her expression, tightening it. "Do you still drink alcohol? Or use any drugs?"

"Sometimes I'll have a drink, but not like that. No drugs. Am I having a physical?"

Shawnee laughed softly. "A little. Do you have any questions?"

"Actually...I do. Did you know that you're the reason I'm here to begin with?" I grinned when I dropped that bomb. "I'm a reporter."

"I knew the latter, but not the former. Why?" She leaned back against the sofa, relaxing as if my interview was over.

"Because of everything that happened at the hospital. I was investigating the alleged incident when I learned you were kidnapped. I came out here to interview you and Zara found me wandering in Sept territory. The rest is history."

"That was pretty dangerous. You could've died." Her doctor poker face returned despite the serious nature of the reflection.

"A wolf nearly ate me," I affirmed.

"That was Hank's daughter." She laughed at that. "You were lucky. She's pretty snappy."

I shuddered at the thought of being nearly eaten by a wolf. "Can I ask you something?"

"Sure." Shawnee nodded, her legs crossed casually as she sat there. Everything about her screamed calmness and gentility, like she belonged gazing out over the ocean with her fingers grazing the surface of the sand.

"Why was that vampire after you? Why is she still?"

"It's a long story…"

"Give me the Twitter version."

"Twitter?" Shawnee's brow wrinkled in question.

"I mean the short version." I laughed a little. "A few sentences."

"Vampires are very possessive of their fledglings. Ileana believes that I gave the kill order to take out one of hers." Shawnee's succinct explanation left a lot to the imagination. The way she spoke, however, told me she knew how to spew out facts while not confirming anything either.

"Did you?"

"Technically, I agreed with the termination of her violent, out of control fledgling that killed people for the thrill of it," she said, her eyes narrowing in speculation. "You're a reporter. This is off the record."

"Trust me. My entire life is suddenly off the record." I perked when a sudden idea hit me. "Will you give me an exclusive interview? They blamed the hospital bombing on a domestic terrorist and said you were hurt during it. You can tell me your version of the story."

"Doesn't the news have to be the truth?"

"We can write it in code. Only the Sept will understand and humans will think it was exactly what the police claimed it was." I snatched my notebook from the coffee table.

"I'm not sure I'm comfortable with that. What about an exclusive interview about what the hospital is doing to rebuild and prevent future incidents?" She gestured in my direction. "It would still be an exclusive."

"Yeah. We can do that." I tapped my pen on the page.

"Has Hank attempted to turn you into the Sept's media consort?" she asked, offering me a smirk with it.

"I'm not anyone's consort." I smiled when I thought about it. "Except Zara's."

"The wolf's consort, huh." She reached over and patted my hand.

"Yeah." I smiled at the label and the affection. "I'm her consort."

"What's this like for you? How much of your life has changed?" Shawnee's question seemed more than just curious. She connected to it somehow, of that much I could tell.

"Zara is the love of my life. In such a short time." I leaned my head on my hand while watching her. "She's saved me from loneliness that I didn't even know plagued me until after I came here. And now, with our bond…" My hand fell to the center of my chest. "I feel *everything*. All of her. Connection, wholeness."

"It's amazing, isn't it?" A sparkling smile broke the controlled nature of Shawnee's expression. I watched as she touched the center of her chest the same way I had.

"It is. You hold two mate bonds?"

"I do."

"Are you Two-Spirit?"

"I am." Shawnee nodded, though her tension returned after a moment. It seemed to reveal itself anytime I asked her something somewhat personal.

I opened my mouth to say something, but before any words could leave my lips, a red and green blur appeared in front of the fireplace. I started, gripping my shirt as Vanessa's tall frame manifested on the rug by the fire. She crossed her arms over her chest, her eyes falling on Shawnee.

"Shit, you scared me." I huffed at her, but she ignored

me.

"Baby, what'd we say about knocking on the doors of Sept members when we visit?" Shawnee stood to greet her. Vanessa's lips curved into a plump pout.

Admitting that Vanessa's sex appeal radiated from her like sharp snaps of solar flares wasn't the easiest thing to do considering my recent matedom. I would have to be blind not to notice how she exuded sexual energy.

Shawnee chuckled when Vanessa continued to pout at her. "What is it?"

"You got to see her pussy glyph and I didn't." Vanessa's gaze flickered in my direction.

To say that I didn't expect to hear those words leave her lips was an understatement. I cracked up, shaking my head at her. "Well then."

"Ness." Shawnee laughed out her name. "I think it might be best to acknowledge Mack's presence and say hello first."

Vanessa looked at me, her brow narrowed, then glanced back to Shawnee. They held each other's gaze for a silent moment before Shawnee lifted one eyebrow then blinked twice. Vanessa turned to me finally and muttered, "Hi."

"Hey." I smirked, leaning back into the sofa with a pillow hugged to my chest. *Babe, you better come save me. That ginger-head cat is mad she didn't get a chance to see my glyph.*

Be right there.

"Let me see it." Vanessa turned to me, her eyes glinting with playfulness.

"Nope. Leave her be." Shawnee grabbed Vanessa by the waist and pulled her into her lap when she sat in the rocking chair by the fireplace. In that moment, I couldn't tell who had greater strength.

Zara and Mal returned a moment later with the former entering the back door first. Zara offered me a half-smile, her eyes red-ringed from tears. I hugged her to me, nuzzling her neck with my lips. "You okay?"

"Yeah." She nodded, giving me a squeeze.

"What's your assessment, love?" asked Mal as he messed up Vanessa's hair on the way by. He snatched up another drumstick, then sat on the arm of their chair. His gaze locked on Shawnee's and he brushed his finger over her cheek.

"My opinion remains unchanged." Shawnee leaned into his touch. "She's a Breeder."

My focus steadied on Zara until I knew she was truly okay. Her bond felt similar to her usual, despite her tearful expression. "I'm a Breeder."

"I can't believe it a little," she whispered, leaning her forehead against mine. I rubbed her back while nuzzling her, my gaze flickering to the trio on the rocking chair.

"They're pretty," said Vanessa, at the same time soft purrs entered the room. It filled the area around us with soothing waves of comfort.

"Very," affirmed Shawnee. "So are you." Vanessa smiled at her, then stroked her arm that lay across her lap. I thought I caught her fingers moving in a kneading fashion a few times.

"So why'd you make my girlfriend upset, Mal?" I asked when Zara leaned back, taking a swipe at her cheeks.

"We spoke about meeting Caden," he said, his simple answer leaving everything to the imagination.

"And?" I drew my gaze from him to Zara.

"No," she said, her attention on him. "Can you go away now?"

"Zara." I laughed uncomfortably. "That was a little rude."

Mal grinned, but I couldn't understand why Zara's slight made him happy. "Wow, Zar. That's a new side of you. Yes, I can go away. But I get to take these two pretty ladies with me. Does that kill your spirit a little?" Mal stood with the others and wrapped his arms around Shawnee and Vanessa.

"Not anymore." Zara hugged me. "Bye."

"Bye, girls." Shawnee chuckled then nudged Vanessa.

"Bye. I'll come see your pussy glyph later." She shot a grin in my direction.

"No she won't," said Shawnee while Mal continued laughing. "Bye."

I scrunched up my nose as I waved. "Bye." We watched them disappear as they took a few steps toward the front door, their image blurring then fading away. "I'm scared of that cat. She looks at me like she's going to eat me. Or worse, fuck me against the wall."

"She might." Zara nudged me to lie down on the sofa and I obliged, pulling her with me. She settled with her head on my shoulder and half of her draped over me. Her body burned so hot that I suddenly felt over dressed.

"Did you run with Mal?"

"A little."

"You're always super on fire after you run." I ran my hand up and down her back.

"Take off your clothes." She leaned up and tugged my shirt.

"I will, but only if you promise to talk to me about things, bossypants. Deal?" I cocked a brow at her. Her eyes twinkled while she watched me as if contemplating the bargain. "I shaved for you." I grinned, knowing that'd sell it. "Because I know you like to *see* me."

"Deal," she said, gulping down the rest of her sentence. Flutters of excitement tumbled through our bond and made me shiver. I pulled my shirt over my head, then wiggled out of my pants. Zara lay down on top of me again, though more on her side so she could look up at me. She tickled her fingers over my breasts, then laid her hand between them when we settled again.

"And no distracting me with sex," I warned as I pat her bent knee.

She nearly pouted. "Fine. What's your question?"

"Did Caden ever hurt you? I mean, you seem close with Mal and Caden and Mal are in the same pack, right?" I held her hand, kissing her knuckles while I waited for her to respond. It took her awhile, and silence fell around us. I waited, minutes, until I remembered our mental connection. *Tell me here.*

Caden never hurt me. She paused, her attention lingering on my fingers. *He saved me once. When one of the dominants forced me to kneel in front of him. I couldn't get up and he was going to put his dick in my face. Caden beat him up when he showed up. Mal, too. We all left that pack afterward.*

Then tell me why you're afraid of him, baby.

Because...because of how strong he is. That wolf was so much older than us. Twice Caden's size and he still took him out. If he can do that to him, who's to say he can't turn it around?

It sounds like he's chosen not to. And Hank, too. I waited for her to respond. She just nodded. *Zara, did they do more than bully you and push you around?*

What do you mean?

I gulped down the emotions that came with the question, *Did they rape you?*

No. Nothing like that. Zara started, meeting my gaze again. *There was incidents like that in the old Sept. Caden and Mal fought against a lot of it, then eventually we just left when it became too much to handle. Many people left.*

Well, I'm glad. You scared me a little thinking that happened to you.

Mal said his mate grew up in a pack like that. Her father hurt her badly...

You mean the doctor? My eyes widened and she nodded. *She seems so put-together and strong.*

Looks can be deceiving.

What if I told you that I wanted to meet Caden? How would you feel?

I'd tell you no.

But baby, you said he helps people.

You can't trust dominants like him or Hank. No matter what.

Zara. I cupped her face in my hands. *I love you so much. In my experience, I form opinions based on facts. We don't have any facts to prove Caden is worth distrusting.*

There are plenty. She frowned at me.

Prove it then. I poked her nose and she swatted at me.

Fine. I will. She huffed, then slid down my body until she lay between my knees. *But first, I have something I want to do.*

Shudders wracked my core, sending excited tingles to my fingers and toes. *What?*

Lick you until you come.

Zara! I laughed, squealing until the moment her mouth claimed me, and I melted under her delicious affection.

CHAPTER THIRTEEN

Zara positioned me on the bed, my head in the pillows with my knees digging into the mattress. She took me from behind, while I cried out and gasped for breath. We'd gone like this for the entire day, taking turns pleasing each other. Never in my life had I spent so much time in the thralls of ecstasy.

"Oh God," I cried as her tongue lashed at my pussy. "Zar!" I exploded against her, bucking my hips and pressing back to her mouth. A growl escaped her as she dove under me, grabbing my hips and continuing her assault on my clit. She lashed her tongue over every inch of me then diving inside as I clawed at the sheets, screaming out my pleasure as I came again. Zara's fingers dug into my rear even as I calmed down. My body sprawled out on top of her, and she lapped at me until I was a heaving mess.

She flicked my clit once more before sliding out from under me. I panted as I rolled onto my back, and she licked her lips while grinning. "I love doing that to you."

"Come over here." I grabbed at her, pulling her to me until she landed over my middle to straddle my stomach. She leaned down to kiss me, as I grabbed her hips. "Up here." I urged her forward and she obliged without hesitating.

Zara quivered as she knelt over my face. I eyed her soaked pussy, glistening above my face. Perfect folds, engorged nub, and waiting to be sucked. I devoured her. The gasping moans she emitted encouraged my siege upon her. I didn't care if my lust and hunger pushed her too quickly. She cried out, tossing her head back as her hair tumbled down her back. She tugged her own nipples and I bounced her. My submissive, passive Zara awoke with our affirmed mate bond, and out came a delicious, confident, sex-loving woman who I couldn't get enough of.

My tongue poked deep inside her, as I shook my head, manipulating her folds to my will. Her legs trembled around me, threatening the release that I knew she'd held on to for minutes at least. Abandon followed her, reckless and beautiful, as I stroked her taut stomach while sucking on her clit.

"Yes," she moaned, grinding her hips against my face. "*Kay.*" She gasped, and sharp, quick movements followed. She cried out when she came, coating my lips in her sweet nectar. I took her right through it, her legs twitching and shuddering as she panted heavily.

We collapsed together, a mess of sex and sweat. Zara buried her face against my neck while we struggled to catch our breath, both of us bumbling along in the afterglow. Our bond throbbed happily between us, wrapping us in perfect warmth. Nothing surpassed that feeling, and the amount of joy that bounced around inside me. Zara moved me to rest against her chest, pulling the blanket over both of us. Wrapped up with her, for the first time in my life, I knew what safe meant.

That night, like every night since I'd loved her, we fell asleep and my dreams filled with contentment.

The next morning, Zara watched me as she dressed while I fussed with my hair. This became our morning routine as we got ready for work.

"How do you even do that to your hair?" she asked, settling her gear belt around her waist. "You're not even looking at it."

I laughed, turning to her as I finished off the twisted braid, and tied the end of it. "Practice."

"And you look like Kara Danvers ready for her first day at CatCo Worldwide Media." She leaned back on her hands, watching me with a cocky smirk.

"Who's that?" I lowered my arms and tugged at the part of my button-down blouse that hung out beneath my sweater.

"Skinny pants, penny-loafers." She grinned now, holding her hands to me. "You sexy little nerd."

"Zara!" I laughed and bounced over to her, taking her hands. "Who's Kara Danvers?"

"Supergirl's alter ego. Didn't you read comics? Or watch the show at least?" She kissed my knuckles a few times before pulling me into her lap.

"Nope. Your gun is gonna bruise my hip." I wriggled about until I got comfy. "Want me to braid your hair?"

"The guys at work will tease me."

"So?" I gave her shoulder a sharp punch. "Tell them to fuck off. I'm gonna braid it." I slid from her lap until I wormed my way behind her. "A tight French braid will make you look *official*."

"Fine, fine." She waved me off, but let me do it.

I took my time running my fingers through her damp hair, then weaving it into the braid I desired. Her long, tawny hair slipped through my fingers like the finest silk. By the time I finished, the tied off end of her braid hung to the middle of her back. "There," I said, smooching her cheek. "Feel it."

Zara reached back and ran her fingers over the braid, her lips curving into a smile. "Thank you."

"Welcome, baby," I said. She tugged me back into her lap and kissed my shoulder. "Meet you at my apartment after work?"

She nodded. "Should be the last trip then you're all moved out."

"I know. Think we'll have enough space here for my stuff?" I bit my lip as she held my gaze.

"You mean your books. You mean enough space for your books," she teased, chuckling after.

"Yes!" I squeaked when she tickled my side. "I like my books."

"I know. And I like you so your books are always welcome." She patted my hip. "C'mon, Supergirl. Time for work."

I let out a dramatic sigh. "You mean no more hiding away in our den of sex and cuddles?"

"Hmm." She nuzzled her nose against my cheek. "Just a pause. We'll resume sex and cuddles this evening."

"I'm looking forward to *you*." I cupped her cheeks and pulled her into a kiss.

〰️

"Where are we going?" I asked Zara as I pulled on my sweater.

"To Mal's. The Sept is leading a siege on the leech nest this morning," she said, tucking her phone into her back pocket.

Nerves tightened my throat while I watched her. "Did they ask you to go with them?"

"Not this time. But they've asked us to gather in case something happens. Some folks are holed up at Barron's, and the rest of us will be at Mal's with Imogene and her kids," she explained. "It's safer in large numbers when things are going down."

"This feels scary. I feel really freaked out." I pulled my sweater tighter around my shoulders. "And I don't even know why."

"Our Sept bonds are a little crazy right now. You're probably picking up on that." Zara held her arms to me when she finished zipping her hoodie. I slid into her arms and she kissed my forehead. "You're okay. I have you."

"Will we have to fight vampires?" I stroked her cheek as she hugged me to her.

"Nope. Breeders have a different role for the most part. You'll see." Zara's grip tightened around me and my feet lifted from the floor.

Zara led me into Mal's cabin without knocking on the thick wooden door. In the vast cabin, Anadaya and Imogene sat together by the hearth with a bunch of kids in their midst. I recognized Imogene's youngest two, Cote and Isabelle, as they were with her almost all the time whenever I went down to pay rent. Behind them, two wolves slept peacefully on a blanket. They didn't stir when we entered.

My hand tightened on Zara's when a teenager approached.

"You're the new one," she said, folding her arms over her chest. Her moccasins rose to the knees of her jeans, and her purple sweatshirt stood out against her copper skin. When I met her gaze, a sense of heaviness fell around me. Eyes with depth like that didn't belong to a teenager.

"I um...I guess I am?"

"Where's your glyph? Let me see." Adia waved her fingers at me, her brow wrinkled with challenge.

"Adia…" Anadaya approached, her hand falling on the girl's shoulder. "That is not how we greet new Sept members."

"Or anyone," defended Zara, her hand tightening around mine.

"Dia *not* a Sept member." The girl pursed her lips when she looked up at Ana.

"You are so," I said, frowning at her. "And your bond is *really* annoying to deal with." Pointing it out made me pay attention to the connections I held with the people in the room. Adia's bond held an airy, swirling quality to it, with silver tendrils floating all over the place. Her brows lifted when she turned back to me, jutting her thumb in my direction.

"She be a weaver," she told Ana.

"I am aware." Anadaya placed her hand on Adia's shoulders and guided her away from us. "Leave them be."

"Fine." Adia grumbled her way over to the kitchen table and plopped down like an ornery brat.

"Mack," called Imogene from her perch on the carpet by the fire. "Come in, come in." She waved us over, a smile on her kind face.

I tugged Zara to her, noting the anxiety that rattled around my mate. "Hi, Gene."

"Hello there, loves." She stood, placing her hand on my cheek and Zara's at the same time. "We're sorry for dragging you out here."

"We understand," I said, glancing to Zara who seemed content to let me speak for her. Movement at my knees drew my attention downward and I watched as the two formerly sleeping wolves wove themselves between us. Both of them, a similar shade of gray-brown, seemed focused on Zara.

"Girls, be gentle," Gene said, running her fingers through their coats. "My daughters, Arielle and Silo."

"Arielle was the one who tried to eat me?" I asked as the familiar gaze of the wolf met mine.

"Did she?" Gene's eyes widened at the disclosure.

"Yes," answered Zara. Arielle stood on her hind legs and dropped her front paws on Zara's chest. Zara smiled and roughed up her face a little after releasing my hand. Arielle made a few noises, mainly gruffs and chuffs.

"What does she want to play with?" I asked, glancing between them.

"You understood that?" Gene answered.

I shrugged, my throat tightening with worry. "I don't know. It seemed like she said she wanted to play."

Gene nodded. "She asked Zara to play. Being around Zara soothes them."

I turned to my mate when Arielle dropped to all fours again, both of the young wolves continued to weave around our legs. "Go ahead, baby. If you want to."

"For a minute," said Zara. The wolves leapt happily then trotted over to the blankets, leading Zara a few paces away.

Gene ushered me to sit with the two other children who played with blocks together. All of the kids appeared unaware of whatever danger going on. Anadaya and Adia sat together at the kitchen table, neither of them saying much.

I drew my gaze away as Gene settled with her skirt tucked under her legs. "Is that one yours, too? I've never seen her before." I gestured to the kitchen.

"Adia?" Gene shook her head. "She looks young, but she's about thirty."

"Jeez. I thought she was a kid."

"That's part of her abilities. Shaman like her don't age much. She'll be a very old wolf one day, and look better than we do now."

"She called me a weaver. What's that mean?" I kept my eyes on Zara who, despite her terrible nerves, engaged with the young wolves. She crouched down with them, her body freezing for a moment. I watched as the change came over her, rolling up her body and coating it with fur. She seemed unfazed by it, and yet some relief filled our mate bond as well. I blinked a few times to clear the haze from my eyes as I watched her shift. It seemed painful, though she never exhibited any signs of such. Her fur, an even honey color, sprouted all over her body, and I stared at the thick tail that appeared at her back. In less than a few seconds, she was a full-grown wolf. A beautiful, elegant creature that warmed my heart and brought mist to my eyes. Had I never seen her change into her wolf form before? The sentiment overwhelmed me. "Wow."

"She's breathtaking, yes," commented Gene. "You've never seen her shift?"

"Not to wolf form, no. Only beast."

"Much different. Zara is a very special wolf." Gene

smiled gently as she watched Zara roughhouse with the two young ones. Paws and bones thumped on the floor as they wrestled about.

"She's a special everything..." I stared at Zara then turned back to Gene after. "I love her so much."

"We know." She patted her chest. "A weaver is a Breeder who can deeply sense the Sept and pack bonds. Weavers can trace connections, family lines, and map out the inner workings of order. They can tell weak bonds, and point out taint, or descent."

"I don't think I can do any of that..."

"Give it time." Gene smiled and I sat on the floor beside her kids. The older boy, Cote, turned to me right away.

"Mack, you wanna build a castle wif us?" He wiggled his fingers at me. At this point, he was probably about four or five. I couldn't remember.

"Okay, sure." I scooted a bit closer and listened to his instructions on how to build the castle. While we did so, little Isabelle worked diligently to knock some things down.

"There. Put the cannon." Cote pointed to the pointy roof.

"If you say so." I clicked the round, gray block into place. Imogene chuckled while she looked on.

Occasionally, I looked over to find Zara continuing to romp about with the two cubs. In time, they settled. Zara lay between them, while the young ones batted at each other.

"Have you considered having kids?" Imogene asked, drawing my attention.

"Um...not really. I mean, I would if Zara wanted to. She seems good with them." Nervousness tightened my stomach. Zara and I hadn't talked about wanting children, or not wanting them. What else hadn't we considered?

"Mom!" Cote dropped himself back on the floor and threw some blocks back into the rubble. "She keeps knockin' it!"

Imogene picked up Isabelle and plopped her in my lap. "Here. Start with this one. Cote, come with me and get a snack."

"Fine." He huffed, taking her hand when they stood together and headed to the kitchen.

I propped Isabelle to stand on my knees. The one-year-old made all sorts of funny noises when we were face to face. "You're gonna be a troublemaker. I can tell."

"Gah!" she exclaimed, grabbing fistfuls of my hair. She giggled after, letting the strands move through her fingers.

"Yep." I grunted when she gave a great yank. "Trouble." I turned her around in my lap, perching her in the center of my crossed legs, then handed her two blocks. She banged them together while sputtering and humming something. I smiled while I stroked her ear-length hair, nearly as black as her brother's.

You're good with her, Zara's voice entered my mind a moment before a warm, furry muzzle met my neck. I shuddered hard as her breath puffed against my skin.

You're equally good with those cubs. I nodded toward the now human tweens sitting at the table with Adia and Ana while Imogene fixed snacks. They chatted amongst themselves about comic books.

They're easy to manage. Not all are. They only like me because I make them feel calm.

They like you because you're you. I reached up and ran my fingers through her fur. *Your wolf is beautiful.*

Zara leaned down and nuzzled Isabelle. The baby buried her face in Zara's fur, returning her affection. It brought me great joy to see Zara relaxed with the children, and in an environment that previously made her quite nervous.

Babe, do you want kids? I blurted out.

I'm not sure. I never really gave it any real thought considering...

Would you not want kids?

No. I would if you wanted to.

If I didn't? I ran the tips of her ears between my fingers. Nothing in the world felt as soft as that portion of her body.

Then I wouldn't either. She met my gaze, her green eyes now more yellowish.

If I did? My bottom lip found its way between my teeth.

Then I would, too. It's us together, no matter what. She pressed her wet nose against mine and it made me chuckle. Below her, Isabelle squealed in delight and hugged Zara around the neck. Zara used her front paw to hold the kid to her.

You're very relaxed here today.

I can deal with this. We'll be leaving before the others return.

You'll be able to feel it when they get close.

So will you.

Oh. Right. I smiled at the way she hugged Isabelle who continued to nuzzle her. The little girl gripped fistfuls of Zara's fur and climbed onto her back. I gasped at the swift movement, rolling to my knees just in case.

She's okay, affirmed Zara. *She does this for a living.*

I watched as Zara walked Isabelle in laps around the carpet. The little girl giggled, lying on her stomach flat against Zara. *How come you don't give me horsey rides?*

Because I like looking at you and can't see you if you're on my back.

Clever save.

I laughed aloud which drew Imogene's attention. She smiled at the three of us, then called out, "Would either of you care for some beef patties?"

"I'm good. Thank you though," I answered.

"*Be!*" Isabelle rolled off Zara, catching herself in a wobbly stand before toddling off toward the kitchen. Zara chuffed at her, then returned to my side.

She sat on her haunches, pressing her nose to my cheek before the warmth of her radiated and arms slid around my middle. I leaned into her, watching as her clothes melted over her body at the same time that her fur faded. This close, I heard her bones snapping and popping, similarly to when I crack my knuckles.

"You're amazing," I whispered against her cheek.

"Like you." Zara hugged me from behind, but in a flash, her hug turned to a hold. At the same time that our bond lurched, the Sept bonds inside me began a furious dance. Anger teetering on rage shot through me and I drew in a deep breath.

"I feel them."

"Let's go." Zara lifted me to stand with her. Anadaya rose with us, offering a solemn gaze. She nodded at the same moment Zara stepped with me toward the front door. "Close your eyes. Don't look."

"Okay." I buried my face against her chest. "Okay." And our feet left the ground, followed by a swirling sensation.

Wind lashed around us until we dropped on the thunking wood of our own cabin. Zara stroked my back when the familiar fragrance of lavender returned to my nose. The bonds inside me still thrashed about in a ruckus, but with distance, it wasn't as obvious.

"How come you tell me to close my eyes when we bend?" I asked, stroking her cheeks.

"It's safer. The inbetween is literally *in between* dimensions, and spirits can attach to you. The more you look, the more at risk you are. Mainly for Breeders. You don't want them attaching to you," she explained, her hands on my hips.

"What happened back there?"

"The fight didn't go as intended. No one's hurt." Zara's fingers pressed my sweater upward, urging it off. I let her, ducking out of it when she pulled it off my head. Her eyes lingered on my breasts, bare because of my rush getting dressed. Our mate bond swelled between us along with Zara's need.

"I'll be naked for you if you tell me why you need me to be," I said, letting her unbutton my jeans.

"Stressful." Her single word told me as much as she

could in the moment. She glanced to the front door to our left, and double checked the deadbolt. We both knew it wouldn't stop any of the Changers from barging in, but for Zara, it served its purpose in soothing her anxiety.

"It was, babe." I cupped her face in my hands. "And you can feel their chaos."

She nodded, kissing my thumb when I brushed it over her lips. "Yes. It's better now."

"Good." I wiggled out of my pants, my panties going with them, and ditched them along with my shoes. "And now?"

"You." She pulled me into a kiss, lifting me from the floor and urging my legs around her waist. It surprised me still, her strength and passion. I'd never been with a man, and any woman I was ever with couldn't lift me like Zara. Her fingers squeezed my rear, then brushed against my pussy. I ended the kiss when I sucked in my breath, quaking as her touch dampened my core.

"Zar."

"You get wet so easily." A soft growl left her, deepening her words. "I love it."

"It's your fault." I gasped when she continued to stroke me, her fingers teasing my clit while she walked with me toward the hearth. "Zar, I'm going to come in eight seconds if you keep that up."

"Who said that wasn't my plan?" She smiled as she lowered us to the carpet, keeping my legs around her. Her arousal pulsated through our bond, thumping all the way through me and ending like a luscious vibration against my clit.

"My God." I grabbed her face, kissing her deeply and at the same time, she slipped two fingers inside me. My cries ended our connection as I tossed my head back, my nails digging into her shoulders. Her clothes had disappeared at some point during, and my thighs fell around her bare middle.

You're so tight, her voice burst into my thoughts. *Is it okay?*

Yes. I'd tell you. I dropped my head against hers as I rocked my hips, urging her to continue. *Don't stop.*

Zara's mouth claimed mine and her reserve faded, she slid her fingers in and out of me while I rolled myself against her hand. Her free hand held tightly to my ass and I grabbed both of her breasts, pinching her nipples as I neared losing myself.

It took barely a few seconds before the deep, even thrusts brought me to a delicious, rolling orgasm. Zara nipped my lip, growling as my body tightened around her. I moaned against her mouth, bucking right through my explosion.

Fuck, Zar. I gasped, dropping against her as I slid down the curve of pleasure. She didn't allow me a moment to breath before she moved me backward, dropping me on to the carpet. Rumbling continued as she lowered me down, shoving my knees apart when she crawled over me.

Taste you, she threatened, in the most amazing way.

Yes. Please.

She slid down my body, grabbed my hips, and dropped down between my thighs so quickly that I squeaked, expecting a bite. Her mouth met my pussy, lifting my hips from the floor as her tongue lashed at me. No one in my life took me like Zara, so completely and so easily. She knew everything I wanted, everything I needed and she didn't hesitate a beat to bring me there.

Every stroke, every lash, every lick taunted me, lifting me toward the thralls of pleasure so deep, and so complete that I lost myself over and over under her tantalizing tongue. Sweat beaded my brow, casting a humid air between us as heat fueled our passion. My body writhed, thrashed, and contorted under her beautiful assault until I collapsed under her, panting like I'd completed a marathon. Zara kissed my clit, then each nipple before moving over me again. I grabbed her breasts, thumbing her nipples.

Sit on me, I told her. She listened and straddled my stomach. Her hot, saturated pussy nearly burned a hole in my abdomen.

I could taste you all day, she said, her voice husky even in my mind.

How do you think I feel? Come here. I gripped her hips, urging her forward as I slid under her. She tensed a little, but I didn't let her get away with any worry. Before she had a chance to think too much, I wrapped my arms around her thighs and took her.

Kay! She gasped, her hand falling to my hair as I assaulted her folds with my tongue. I moaned into her sweet, luscious core, holding on to her so tight that she couldn't squirm away out of shyness. My magic worked and before long, all tension washed away and she dropped her head back, her hips moving against my face.

Zara's mouth fell open slightly, her eyes closed as she finally allowed herself to let go. Her body moved fluidly with each revolution I made around her clit. Soft moans left her lips, and she closed her eyes, surrendering to the pleasure that she craved from our connections. In this position, a mix of vulnerable and controlled, she allowed me to take all of her.

When I thrust my tongue inside, deep vocalizations left her, only growing as I used my fingers to toy with her clit. I swirled my tongue inside her, flicking and curling against each erogenous spot. Her bucking grew, and her fingers gripped my hair. Her back arched and a strangled cry left her as she came, a sound more human and freer than she'd ever made before. She soaked my lips as I lapped at her.

Her body fell forward, and she caught herself on the floor, propping herself up. I took the opportunity to hold her against me and continue to devour her. Zara cried, writhed, and rocked against my face with a new fury. Her nails tore at the carpet, and out of sheer exhilaration, I slapped her ass, grabbing thick handfuls as I took her clit in my mouth and shook my head.

"Kay!" She screamed, and this time when she came, she lost all of herself. Mind, body, and bond. Our connection widened and her pleasure forced itself on me. I cried out against her as I came against the air, my hips thrusting against nothing as ecstasy swallowed us whole.

Zara's orgasm lasted seconds, towering toward a minute and so did mine. It was almost as if she fucked me at the same time that I had her. My heels dug in the floor, lifting myself toward nothing while she moved against my mouth.

Zara collapsed, her elbows hitting the floor as she heaved for breath. Only then did my pleasure quell, and she rolled off me, dropping beside me as we both panted. I reached between my legs, touching my pussy as if searching for her until I turned to hug her beside me. We moved to meet each other with a kiss. Zara's hand cupped my pussy at the same time that I moved to do the same to her.

In that moment, we melted together. From lust and passion, to lovemaking. Our bodies and minds connected, and our matebond thrummed with happiness. Equal sounds, equal movements, as if we were built as synchronous as the gears of a fated clock. Moving and loving in unison.

Zara told me, forever ago it seemed, that Gaia's greatest gift was the matebond between a Changer and their chosen mate. I believed her then, because I trusted her. Now, I believed her because I knew the truth. Zara was Gaia's greatest gift to me, and our love a complex extension of that. I never thought I could want and love so deeply until the full capacity of it slammed down on me, erasing any doubts or thoughts I had about never finding true love.

Zara was my true love. She was my soul mate. That concept, lost in ways to the pain and doubt of humanity, solidified itself the moment we chose to unite our bodies, minds, and souls. The same moment that I chose her as my forever. Because she was mine.

CHAPTER FOURTEEN

"Parker!" The chief tossed last week's paper down on my desk. "Your stories are boring. What happened to your irksome tenacity for bothering the cops?"

"I've been busy." I grumbled. Ian shot me a glance and snickered. "What?"

"Nothing," he said, still grinning.

"Parker, focus. What've you got on your plate?" My attention returned to the chief.

"I'm interviewing the doctor who was recovered after the hospital *terrorist* attack," I told him. "An exclusive."

"Good. Then you're back on book reviews until you find some sparkle in this dreary town," he said, walking off to yell at Heather about something.

Ian rolled his chair closer. "You're not bothering the cops anymore because you're too busy being buried between her thighs."

"Shut up, douchebag." I kicked his chair and it rolled him a few feet away. He laughed at me then paddled his way back.

"How are things going with Zara?"

"Really good." I smiled at the thought of her as I clicked through my emails for the books to review. "She's amazing."

"You're in love. I see that love sparkle in those shimmery hazel eyes." He wiggled his fingers in front of his face. "So...does she have a guy for me? I could really use a guy…"

"Nope." I smacked his hands away. "You're the only gay guy in this entire town, doomed to live a celibate life."

"Jerk." He sighed dramatically. "I was thinking about trying out that new club downtown—"

"No." I spun around to face him. "Don't go there."

"Why not?" His bushy brow furrowed. "What's wrong with it?"

I glanced around us, then lowered my voice as I devised a cover story. "It's a huge drug den. The cops are all over it. You've got to stay away. Don't get yourself in a position to be questioned."

"Jeez… Then come with me to the gay bar in Salt Lake this weekend?"

"I'll see if Zara wants to…"

"Aw, come on. Even if she doesn't want to, come with me." He bat his lashes as he tilted his head. "Please?"

"I'll let you know." I closed my laptop and glanced to the clock. "I'm heading to my apartment to finish packing while Zara's still on shift. Want to help?"

"You mean move thirty-thousand books into boxes? Sure." He smirked, rolling back to his seat. "Let's order food while we do it."

"Okay," I agreed.

Ian and I bustled through the snowy, Christmas-laden streets toward my apartment. Carolers sang *Silent Night* around the base of the pretty Christmas tree in the town square. We stopped briefly to listen and take in the sights before continuing on to my apartment.

Once inside, he glanced around at the nearly empty unit with a few boxes packed by the front door. "Just books left. I knew it." He pointed to the three shelves lined along one entire wall.

"Very funny. Get to work. What do you want to eat?"
"Chinese."
"Mmmkay." I picked up my phone to text Zara a warning about Ian being over and ask if she wanted dinner.

An hour later, Ian and I had nearly everything packed, and Zara arrived five minutes after the Chinese delivery. While the three of us sat on the floor, surrounded by boxes while eating, I took a moment to gaze around the little loft. It served me well over the years, and I would remember it fondly.

Zara gave my knee a squeeze and I turned my attention to her. She smiled softly, as if she could feel every sentiment I shared with the little place.

"Commuting to work will be the most annoying thing," offered Ian. "Luckily your law enforcement girl doesn't need to worry about speed limits."

I laughed, and so did Zara.

"It's my main reason for loving her; speed racing." I grinned and gave Zara's cheek a light pinch. "Right, babe?"

"Only reason." She nipped my finger.

"You two are adorable." Ian snapped a picture of us on his phone. After the first shutter sound, I promptly flipped him off before the second. "Classy."

"Always." I tossed my empty plate in the trash bag near us. "It's getting late. I need to give Imogene the keys before she closes up."

"What time are the movers coming?" asked Ian. Zara and I shared a glance while I fought the smirk that tugged the corner of my mouth.

"About an hour," I said. "We're heading out from there."

"Well, ladies. It looks like quality gay time is coming to a close." Ian tossed out his trash before he stood. "When you're settled, we'll have a gay house warming."

"That sounds like a lot of gay," said Zara as she stood with him. "I'll walk you home."

"Erm. I live down the street, Officer." Ian thumbed over her shoulder, his brow cocked. "Like, literally."

"She's chivalrous." I packed up the rest of the trash then picked up the bag. "Meet you downstairs?"

Zara nodded and turned to Ian, resting her hands on her gear belt. In that moment, she appeared stocky and brooding.

"Jeez!" Ian hugged the wall in a theatrical display as he made for the door. "I'm going!"

Zara and I laughed at him, and I blew her a kiss when she glanced at me over her shoulder. They headed off and I busied myself tying off the trash bags and bringing them down to the dumpsters. Afterward, I found Imogene in her shop, closing up the register for the day.

"Hi, Gene."

"Hello, sweetie." She offered me her usual kind smile. "All packed up?"

"Yup." I hopped up to sit on the stool beside the display counter near her. "Brought you the keys. I really liked that little place."

"Well, we really liked having you in it." She gave my forearm a pat after I handed her the key ring.

"Did you know I was a Breeder when you rented to me?"

"I did not." She chuckled suddenly. "However, there might've been a motive."

I perked at her exposition. "Oh yeah? What?"

"Well, Steve figured having the town's most nosey reporter living in our territory and right above us would help us keep an eye on your snooping. There are dangerous things out there and you, Mack, have a knack for stepping in it." Gene's hands fell to her waist and she grinned.

I cracked up, nearly tumbling from the stool. "Imogene! That's so sneaky."

"Oh, indeed. And it was also my idea." She nudged my chin with her knuckle. "One of my finer ones, I must say."

"Me too." I smiled at her affection, and returned the squeeze she offered my hand after. "You've taken good care of me. Like the mom I never had in my later years."

"I know, love." She then gave both my hands a firm tug. "She doesn't know what she's missed, but I am grateful to be a part of who you've become. Thank you for letting me."

"Thank you for bringing me Zara. Even if not directly." I sniffled at the sudden emotions that overwhelmed me.

The shop door chimed when Zara entered, her footfalls tentative on the wooden floor as she approached us. "What's wrong?" She stroked my cheek and glanced to Imogene.

"We're being sentimental fools," she said. "I'm going to miss having her upstairs."

"I'll literally be on your territory now," I told her, leaning back against Zara when she hugged me from behind. "You get to keep me around forever."

"I reckon Zara had most to do with that." Gene grinned at Zara, and gave her shoulder a squeeze on her way to the safe. "We are happy to have both of you."

Zara tensed out of nowhere, her grip on me tightening in a scary way. She glanced to the front door a few yards away, then the door to the back room which was even further. I held on to her arms as she urged me from the stool.

"What is it?"

"We have to g—"

A step away from the safe where Gene locked up the day's earnings, Hank appeared just in front of the doorway to the storage room. Beside him, another Native man, clad in a casual T-shirt and jeans, appeared. The second man towered at least two inches over Hank, and shared the girth of a Redwood tree at least.

"Genie, baby, Caden here's got a— Oh boy." Hank's wide eyes fell on me and Zara.

Imogene scurried across the floor, coming to stand

beside us. She placed her hand on Zara's shoulder again, but my mate remained frozen behind me. Her arm squeezed my middle so hard that my ribs threatened a crack. Zara's panic flooded our connection, screaming and thrashing through the center of our bond. *No escape*, it shouted.

"You're Caden?" I asked, patting Zara's hand as I attempted to intervene before we lost her completely.

"I am. You must be Mack." He smiled, a kind, copper-lipped smile that sent warmth through the bonds inside me that belonged to him and his pack. He felt like them; like Xany most, and Mal second, followed by Shawnee. Like they all shared the same pulse-beat of a drum.

"That's me. You know my mate, Zara." Again, I patted her hand. She stood stock still, though her fingers trembled against my stomach.

"I do. Hi, Zara." Caden kept his eyes lowered, and took a step backward as if giving her more space. She didn't answer him, and a quiet stalemate fell around us. Caden's nostrils flared for a moment and I watched as his lips curved into a smile. "Your mate is a Breeder."

"I have a glyph," I told him, still stroking Zara's bare wrist. "I'm glad you confirmed it though."

"Me too. I'll go wait in the back room, Hank." Caden clapped Hank on the shoulder before taking his leave. "Good to meet you, Mack. Welcome to the Sept."

"A'right." Hank nodded, but like Caden, he remained very still. We watched as Caden disappeared behind the door of the store room. A second later, squeals of delight rang out as Gene's children greeted him.

"Caden! I gots a crossbow, look at it!" Cote squealed just before the door shut.

"We should get going," I said, sliding from the stool, though remaining firm against Zara. "We have boxes to move."

"A'right, young ones. Best be takin' care of ya business." Hank tipped his head forward as if he wore a cowboy hat. "G'night."

"Night." I pulled Zara away from Imogene toward the front door. Her feet moved with mine and as soon as we neared the entryway, the yanking jerk of bending pulled me from around the middle.

We landed in the living room of the cabin, and right away I turned in Zara's arms. She remained frozen, her lips pursed and eyes raging red.

"Baby..." I placed my hands on the center of her chest. Beneath my fingertips, the rumbling of growling emanated even though I couldn't hear much of it. Our bond rattled, slamming inside of us and striking a chord of fear. "Zara." I grabbed her face, forcing her to look at me.

Fur bristled along her forearms. Her panic turned to rage, and fear tumbled to uncontrolled levels. I'd never felt our bond so out of whack, so angry and afraid. Zara's upper lip curled back and she snarled, grabbing my wrists in her clawed hands. She grew inches taller, slowly as war raged inside both of us. Images burst into my mind. I saw myself crying, being forced into a dark cement basement, a heavy metal door slamming on top. I saw myself thrown into the arms of a brawny man, who ran his fingers through my hair. His lips moved, and I read the phrase, "meant to be" from them.

I cried out when Zara's tightening grip lifted me from the floor. I managed to wiggle away, landing on my feet. "Zara! You...you need to run!" Anadaya's warning struck a chord in my memory. "You have to run."

Zara's gaze snapped in my direction, as if the word *run* unlocked her from whatever torture that captured her. I shifted away from her and opened the front door in a swift movement.

"Listen to me, Zara. Run. You have to run right now." I pointed outside, my brows narrowed as I forced my will on her the way Ana told me to. Zara's work gear disappeared, save for her gear belt which thudded to the floor. Again, I pointed outside. "Go. *Run!*"

A growl rumbled up her torso, leaving her mouth at the same time her lips and nose turned to a muzzle. In a blurry rush, she leapt for the door, landing in a crouch on the front porch. I hurried after her as she glanced over her shoulder at me. Saliva dripped from her huge fangs, and her eyes glowed an eerie red. Her muscles bulged under the full coat of fur belonging to her beast.

"I stay here, you run." Again, I pointed toward the woods. "Run. Now."

A roar erupted from her, rattling the window panes and my soul. I shuddered as my heart pounded in my chest. Zara took off, bolting from the house at the speed of a runaway train.

I stood on the porch for minutes, in the darkness, waiting for any sign of her return. Our matebond told me she was okay, and rushed me with sensations of flight. It reminded me of the moment a speeding plane lifted from the tarmac, taking my breath away and squeezing my stomach in knots.

Snow fell heavier and heavier as time passed, and I shivered with the door open. I bit my bottom lip, and retreated into the cabin.

Why did I make her do that? With all the leeches out there, how could I know she'd be safe? Why did Anadaya have to tell me to make her run?

I looked around the place for my phone as tears prickled my eyes. There was no phone, not mine or Zara's. Then I remembered that my purse remained at the old apartment. Zara didn't have a house phone, and so I sat there, worried and afraid, in the dark.

Silence never sounded so silent to me before. The snow muffled the sounds of nature that usually happened around the cabin, even at night. Gusty wind replaced the silence after a few minutes. I sat down on the sofa after turning on the lights, and stared at the hearth in contempt. Did I even know how to start a fire? With my luck, the whole placed would go up in flames.

I took a deep breath, focusing on keeping my anxiety lower and not reactive to the matebond that continued to flounder inside me. I closed my eyes, and concentrated on the Sept bonds, and was struck by the memory of calling Mal to me a few weeks ago.

It took a moment to direct my focus to the silvery tendrils that wiggled from me to Hank, to Caden, from Caden to Mal. I concentrated on his connection, thinking his name over and over in my head. The threads belonging to him became clearer, and I could've sworn I heard him call my name.

I opened my eyes, expecting him to appear in front of me, but he didn't. What was I supposed to do now? Wait? Sit here and wait while Zara's beast took her over? I thumped my hand on the arm of the sofa.

"Well, don't blame the couch," Mal's voice rang out at the same time that he opened the front door. He had Shawnee with him, both of them clad in sweats like I'd interrupted an early night movie binge.

I jumped to my feet and choked on the sob that rose in my throat. "Zara, she—"

"Frenzied, we know. Caden told us she might." Mal gave my shoulder a squeeze as he guided me back to the sofa. "Don't pass out."

"Slow breaths, Mack." Shawnee grabbed my elbows, pulling me with her as she sat down with me. I held on to her arms while I attempted to get a hold of myself. "Easy."

"Will she be okay?" I asked, sniffling and accepting the tissue that Shawnee offered me.

"She will." She nodded, cupping my hand between hers. "Running soothes her beast. It soothes all beasts and wolves."

"She was so afraid." I sniffled, leaning back into the pillows with my knees tucked against me. "I think she sent me pictures. Of bad stuff happening to me."

"She's a telepath like Mal. It can happen," Shawnee explained while Mal got a fire going in the hearth. "What did you see?"

"Me being locked in a bomb shelter or something. Then getting manhandled by a dude who was saying it was meant to be. I think she's experienced that and is afraid of it happening to me," I confessed, sighing after. "I met Caden today. I can tell he doesn't have any ill will. How come she can't?"

"Fear distorts things, Mack. It takes time to heal from that." Shawnee's cool, calm demeanor soothed me some. For awhile, I thought I knew everything I needed to know about the preternatural world I'd stumbled into. I thought I learned what I needed to know about my mate. Turns out, I knew only the bare minimum.

"Anadaya told me to make Zara run when she freaked out. She listened to that."

"It's good advice for anyone newly mated to werecreatures. Especially wolves. Running reminds us of our power, and calms down the rage. It usually involves hunting and eating until we're full as well." Mal joined us, taking a seat on the coffee table.

I nodded, closing my eyes for a moment as I took in everything they said. My matebond felt calmer now, more like Zara's less rage self. I listened to the crackling fire, and the soft breathing of the people beside me. When I peeked my eyes open, Mal and Shawnee shared glances and I could tell that they were mind talking. Shawnee glanced at me, offering me a soft smile before standing and heading to the kitchen. I watched her for a moment while she fixed a cup of tea.

"She'll be back soon, Mack. This is normal for werewolves," Mal assured, though his words did little to soothe me.

"How come I couldn't make her feel better? Normally, if she's upset being close together makes her feel better. Especially when we're both naked or if I'm touching her skin."

"Skin to skin contact is everything for Changers; you're

right on that." He nodded, gesturing toward me. "You figured that out. Sometimes though, the rage of the beast takes over and only our deepest instincts—to run and hunt—can help. When Zara gets back, she'll need your closeness even more so than usual."

"I wasn't afraid of her or her beast. I'm still not," I confessed, sniffling a little.

"There's no need to be. Her beast recognizes you as she does. Mates are special in that manner, and she'll listen to you."

"She did." I looked up to Shawnee when she returned with a hot mug of tea and handed it to me. "Thanks."

"We'll have to go before she returns," said Shawnee as she sat beside me. "She won't be happy to see us."

"I'll feel her getting closer and tell you," I told her, then sipped my tea. The warmth of it soothed my throat and warmed me up a little. "Thanks for coming to see me and explaining things."

"It's what family does," said Shawnee, her expression as kind as always. "Sept is family."

We waited for nearly an hour before I had even the tiniest inkling that Zara would return. In that time, Mal had made two quick trips back and forth to my apartment for all the boxes. Shawnee and I unloaded most of my clothes together, leaving only books and a box of random house stuff.

My matebond gave a great tug and I turned to them. "She's coming back."

"Okay." Mal stood with Shawnee. "If you need anything, you know how to reach out."

"Thanks, both of you." I watched as they stepped toward the front door and faded from view.

Zara was still a bit away, but I could tell she was getting closer. Our connection widened and her fuzzy emotions returned to funneling through me. Sadness and fear tangled together, weighing heavily on my heart. In effort to keep things as normal as possible, I continued unpacking.

Under each window along the far wall behind the sofa, I made short, neat stacks of books so that the boxes weren't in the way. Zara and I would figure out what to do with them later.

The front door opened, creaking a little in the quiet cabin. Zara stepped in, soundlessly, and right away the sight of her brought me pause. Naked and covered with dirt and blood. Her hair, damp and soiled, hung heavily down to her waist. She kept her eyes to the floor as she closed the door, but I rushed her without giving her much of a chance.

"I'm sorry," she said, sobbing immediately as I touched her face. "I left you, I'm sorry."

"You didn't, Zar. You brought me home safely then did what you needed to do." I brushed the matted hair from her face, and kissed her forehead. "I love you, baby. I'm so sorry that you're hurting."

Zara lifted me into a hug and I wrapped my legs around her waist. She smelled of woodlands, and metallic from the blood. "Let's have a shower, then snuggle by the fire, okay?"

"I love you," was her only reply.

~~~

As expected, Zara slept in the next morning. Unlike last time though, she actually slept. All night, her body burned with fever, or at least it felt like it to me. And when we made love in the darkness, the heat of her overwhelmed me. She slept after, only when she was assured that I was okay and so was she.

While she rested, I unpacked the last box and found a few Christmas decorations. I stared at the bundle of twinkle lights, the tiny tree, and the pink star. I glanced around the room for my phone then checked the date.

"Christmas Eve? Shit."

My thoughts spiraled. Did Zara celebrate Christmas? I hadn't thought about gifts for anyone other than Ian for years, and even that was minimal. In a rush, I unpacked the little tree and set it up on the corner table adjacent from the fireplace.

Half a dozen ornaments, mainly ones gifted to me from work people over the years, a string of lights, the small skirt, and the star later, and we had a tiny Christmas nook in the cabin. I used the rest of the lights to string along the mantle, then lit the two candles that Zara had on either side. For once, I was grateful for Zara sleeping the day away so that I could set up the little surprise.

When the sun began to set, I made for the kitchen to fix a meal for the two of us. A rib roast, mashed potatoes, and vegetables would do. Zara would like something extra meaty, as she always did. While the roast cooked, I stole a quick shower before shuffling through my clothes to find a red skirt, white blouse, and green sweater. The combo suited my Christmassy desires and, even if Zara didn't celebrate, I hoped she would appreciate sharing the time together. I pulled on a pair of fluffy Christmas socks, and scurried back to the kitchen where the scents of the seasoned roast began to rise.

"That'll wake her up, just watch," I muttered to no one in particular.

In effort to appear casual about the whole deal, I sat down at the kitchen table, pulling a book into my lap while I waited.

I hardly made it through one chapter before the bedroom door opened. Zara emerged, clad in floppy linen pants and a loose tank top. The muscles in her arms remained as defined as ever in the dim light. She paused, glancing around the living room with her jaw slightly slack. I rested my book on my crossed legs and watched as the surprise rolled over her.

"What... Did you... I mean, you did all this?" She stared at the little tree before reaching out to touch the star, a smile tugging the corner of her mouth.

"It's our first Christmas together," I said. A languid warmth flooded inside me like a vat of comforting hot tea poured into a mug as Zara's emotions emanated through our matebond. It stole my breath for a moment with the sentiment attached. Appreciation, affection, and a tangle of joy.

"I love it," she said, drawing her gaze from the decorations to me. Her eyes widened when I stood to join her, and her focus flickered over me from head to toe. "You sexy little Christmas elf."

I laughed and bound over to her, sliding into her arms when she caught me. "Hi."

"Hi." She grinned, her arms around my waist as she leaned in to kiss me. I nibbled her bottom lip before we parted.

"I'm glad you like it. I didn't know if you would or if you celebrated." I stroked the space between her breasts, placing my hands where I could feel her heart beating.

"I don't usually, but this"—He gestured around us—"with you is perfect." Zara's eyes twinkled as much as the lights around us, and her smile brought great happiness to my soul. Her genuine response to my efforts made all the difference in the world.

"I made dinner," I told her, lacing my fingers behind her neck. "Because I knew it would wake you."

Zara's hands wandered down my sides, over my hips, then back down again. "You know how to entice me, don't you?"

"I do." I nipped her chin. "And how to make you feel better when you've had a rough day."

"I appreciate that, Kay. I appreciate everything you do." She pulled me into a firm hug, kissing my neck and shoulder.

"I know you do. And I do it because I love you and want to share things with you."

"Sometimes I think I need to cook more for you—" Zara's hand tensed against my thigh. "Are you pantyless under that skirt?"

I burst out laughing at the wide-eyed expression on her

face. "Yes. Thought you might like that." I grinned, giving her chin a tweak. "Hey, girl…"

"Hey." She smiled, swaying with me as if there was music playing somewhere. "Is that my gift? Do I get to unwrap you?"

"Actually…" I dragged my nail down the side of her neck. "I was hoping you would disappear beneath my skirt."

"Were you now?" Her smile morphed into a grin and her hand snaked around my hip to fall between my thighs. She snuck the hem of my skirt up so that she could reach under it.

"Yes." I shuddered the moment her fingers grazed my clit. "I mean…only if you want to."

"Do you know me at all?" She caught me in a rough kiss, claiming my mouth and my pussy at the same time.

Zara's desire and happiness thrust through our connection, flooding me with delight at the same time that it brought a wave of dampness to my core. Her fingers toyed with me as I groped her breasts through her shirt while she nibbled my neck.

"Zar, I'm—" I almost lost myself against her hand, but the sound of the oven timer blared behind us. It drew our attention to the kitchen for a moment, while I panted heavily against her shoulder. She made to retreat from me, and I grabbed her wrist, holding her in place. "It can wait five minutes."

Zara's hot breath puffed against my neck when she laughed. "Hmm. Your libido is delicious."

"It's your fault," I squeaked, then succumb to the moaning a moment after.

CHAPTER FIFTEEN

Zara and I sat together on the sofa, our feet tangled as we sat on opposite ends, each of us scraping ice cream out of pints. "Chocolate is better," I said, after tugging the spoon from my lips.

"Nope. Vanilla with gummy bears." She grinned around her mouthful. "Speaking of, we're out."

"You gobbled up all the bears, did ya?" I laughed and poked her hip with my toes. "On the shopping list they go."

"What if I globbed some of this ice cream and candy on your belly and licked it off?" She wagged her brows at me. Our laughter and frivolity had carried on for hours at that point, through sex and dinner, then sex again and dessert. Zara's continuous glee made me equally happy. Despite her hardship after seeing Hank and Caden, she appeared to recover better than she had in the past when faced with things that upset her.

"Depends. What part of me are we talking about here?" I motioned down my body, then back up again.

"I said *belly*, girl." She cracked up, swatting my foot. "Your dirty mind must've filtered that."

"Zara!" My face exploded with heat and I laughed so

hard I could barely breathe. She grabbed my ankle, and tugged me toward her. I slid down the sofa and, of course, it made my skirt bunch around my middle.

"Did I tell you how much I love you pantyless under that skirt?" She eyed my girly bits while taking another bite of ice cream. "Damn, Kay."

"Hey!" I laughed, pushing my skirt between my thighs. "And you said *my* mind was dirty."

"Oh it is. Mine is just as bad. Wolves think about food and sex a lot." She caressed my inner thigh then rested her chin on my knee. "I think about *you* all the time."

"I think about you all the time, too, baby. And about having sex with you and sharing meals with you." I laughed at the confession. "If that's any consolation."

"It is." She smiled, reaching up and patting my stomach. "Always."

I winced when her knuckles brushed my ribs, but ignored it for the most part. "You make my libido ragey. I really like it."

"My ragey libido likes that you like it," she said, rubbing the spot where her knuckle connected with my rib. "Was I too rough?"

"What?" I glanced down at her hand. "No, why?"

"You made a pain face."

"I'm not in pain." I placed my hand on top of hers. "I just felt a pinch. Maybe my sweater."

"On your ribs?" Her brow furrowed now and a twinge of nervousness poked into me through our bond. Her worry made me worry.

"A little, yeah. I'm okay, babe."

"Let me have a look." Zara didn't wait for permission before she pushed up my sweater. Along my middle, a band of deep purple bruising appeared at the bottom of my rib cage and wrapped toward my back. My eyes widened and I leaned up on my elbows.

"I don't know how that happened," I said, letting her lift my shirt off.

"Did you fall?" Zara guided me into her lap. I straddled her thighs as she examined me, her pursed lips curved into a frown.

"Um...maybe. I can't remember. Hey!" I jumped when she poked it. "Ouch."

"This looks kind of bad, Kay. Breeders get delayed injuries and if we let this go, you might be really hurt or really in pain later on." She poked around with as much care as she could. "I think you have a broken rib."

"How can you tell?" I grunted when she pushed on a particularly squishy part. "That hurt."

"I'm going to call Shawnee. I want her to look at that." Zara placed her hand protectively on my side and I watched as her expression hardened as she summoned Shawnee or Mal.

"Babe, my shirt." I searched the blankets on the sofa until I found it. "They don't need to see my tits."

"Yes we do," said an alluring sing-song voice by the fireplace. I glanced over my shoulder to see Shawnee and Vanessa standing there, the latter holding tight to the former. I covered my front with my shirt and squeaked.

"Nosey cat," I muttered.

"You have perky little nipples." Vanessa sat down beside us on the sofa, a mischievous smile plastered on her face. Zara shot her a warning glare, but Vanessa kept it up.

"Mal was in the shower," said Shawnee, and nudged Vanessa's forehead when she approached. "Quit staring at another woman's breasts, Ness."

"It annoys her." The cat purred heavily while Shawnee nudged her out of the way.

"Ignore her completely. She gets a rise out of your reactions," Shawnee warned. "What's going on?"

"Makayla's hurt," Zara jumped right to it. "I think her rib is broken, but we don't know how or why."

"Let's have a look." Shawnee looked to me, scooting closer to us. Zara tensed under me, though not as much as usual. Shawnee turned to Zara as if she felt her recoil.

"Permission to examine your mate?"

"Yes," said Zara, tersely.

"I'll have to touch her, okay?" Shawnee's continued questioning made me wonder what kind of energy Zara gave off to other people.

"I know." With that, Zara calmed some.

I turned in her lap so that my knees faced Shawnee. She took hold of the sweater and gently pulled it aside. I let her do what she needed to. Her expression smoothed to a gentle stillness while she looked over my bruises. Her warm, firm fingers skittered over my flesh in a practiced fashion.

"Rib is definitely broken," she said, glancing between me and Zara. "I'm going to heal you. You'll feel some warmth, and a quick strike of discomfort. It won't last, but it might be surprising, depending."

"Okay." I held my breath as my heart pounded in my chest. No one had ever healed me before with anything more than some antibiotics or a bandage. Magical healing was a whole new ballgame.

Shawnee placed one hand over my ribs, and the other near my navel. Her hand warmed up super fast, and a purplish glow surrounded her fingers. Shivers ran up my spine and goose bumps formed over my flesh as a feathery tickling sensation slithered around my midsection. I felt my muscles contract, followed by a faint pop somewhere inside. A strange squeezing sensation scared me for a quick moment before that, too, faded away. On my flesh, I watched as the bruises faded, shrinking away to nothing.

I let out a deep breath when Shawnee removed her hand. "Whoa."

"All done," she said, leaning back to survey me. Her eyes continued to wander over me along with her left hand as if she scanned me for some sort of energy disturbance. "No other injuries."

"Maybe I did it while moving books the other day." I slipped my sweater back over my head and tugged it down over my hips. "Thank you, Shawnee."

"You're welcome." She smiled and gave my hand a squeeze before leaning back against Vanessa when she hugged her. "Breeder injuries are tricky. When you were little, did you have incidences where you had unknown or delayed injuries?"

"Only a few times with random bruises. Once though, when I was in one of the conversion camps my parents sent me to, they tied my wrists to a chair. I was fine while sitting there, but a few days later I remember waking up in pain with bruises and cuts on my wrists," I told her, looking down at my arms. "It went away pretty quick though." Zara ran her fingers through my hair as a sad expression replaced the formerly worried formerly jovial one.

"They did that to you?" asked Vanessa, her brow narrowing.

"Yeah...I don't talk to my parents anymore," I told her, lacing my fingers with Zara's.

"Where are they?" Vanessa's hands balled to fists in Shawnee's lap.

"Baby, we're not going to kill Mack's parents." Shawnee brought Vanessa's hand to her lips and kissed her knuckles. "Though I'm sure she appreciates your convictions."

"I do, Vanessa." I laughed a little. "Thank you."

"If they come near you, I'll kill them." She nodded her affirmation and it made Zara chuckle.

"Me first," she said.

"Together." Vanessa perked up at that and lifted her hand to Zara.

"Deal." They high-fived, leaving me and Shawnee laughing.

"First, you'll need my permission, yes?" Shawnee cocked a brow at Vanessa, then cupped her hands over her cheeks. Vanessa returned the gesture, lifting both of her arms and grabbing handfuls of Shawnee's hair.

"Yes, baby."

"Whoa." I pointed at Vanessa. "Are you pregnant?" Her round belly became visible only when she lifted her arms enough to force her sweatshirt to rise up with them.

"A little," she said, dropping her arms into her lap.

"How can you be a little pregnant?" I chuckled when Shawnee tried to hide her grin. Zara rested her chin beside me, a light smile on her lips. I glanced at her. "You knew?"

"I did." She nodded, nuzzling my cheek with her nose.

"How come I didn't know?"

"Cats are very secretive." Zara glanced to Vanessa.

"Did you tell Zara?" I asked Vanessa who shook her head. Shawnee ran her fingers through Vanessa's hair, her smile continuous.

"I can hear it," Zara told me. "The baby's heartbeat."

"Well, why aren't we having a baby shower already?" I tossed my hands in the air. "Come on, you mean to tell me Mal's sister isn't throwing a huge giant shindig? She seems like the party type. Oh wait. Was I not invited?"

Shawnee burst out laughing at the same time that Vanessa snickered. "Mack, you and Xany might make good friends one day," said Shawnee.

"No party." Vanessa shook her head. "But monkeys aren't invited."

"Hey, I'm not a monkey. I'm a *Breeder*." I huffed at Vanessa and it only made her laugh more. "Confirmed now, thank you."

"You're less fun now that you're not a monkey." Vanessa grinned, pulling Shawnee to her in a tender hug. Her mate melted into her, nuzzling her cheek. "Take your shirt off again."

Zara's quiet laughter bounced me a little in her lap. She got a kick out of Vanessa teasing me and it showed.

"No way. I know your games now, cat. I'll be the least fun target you have." I folded my arms over my chest.

Vanessa looked to Shawnee now, nearly pouting. "She's like Xany."

"Glad you caught up with what I insinuated before." Shawnee leaned in and pecked her on the lips. "Behave."

"Let's go home so I can make you take off your shirt." Vanessa's purrs filled the space between the four of us. "And panties."

"That's our cue, before things get way too interesting around here." Shawnee gripped tightly to Vanessa's arms when she wrapped them around her. "Mack, if you feel unwell or have any more bruises, call me."

"We will," answered Zara, her arms falling around me like Vanessa's on her mate. "Thanks for coming here so fast."

"Of course." Shawnee nodded, then patted Vanessa's arms. "Say bye."

"Bye." Vanessa bit down on Shawnee's shoulder, though her gaze flickered to the front door. In an instant, they disappeared.

"I'll never get used to that vanishing people thing." I turned in Zara's lap to face her.

"It takes a while," she said, rubbing my sides affectionately. "Do you like hanging out with them?"

"I do, yeah." I rested my arms on her shoulder and toyed with her hair. "Do you?"

"Starting to. I don't know any other lesbians or gay people anymore. It's...I dunno." She searched for the word, glancing around us while she thought about it.

"Comfortable," I suggested. She nodded, meeting my gaze again.

"Yeah. Even though Vanessa is provocative."

"It's kind of funny. Ian's gay, you know. He wants to go to that gay bar in Salt Lake City. Would you go?"

"I'm not sure...maybe?" She bit her bottom lip as nervousness tightened her muscles. "Maybe after we deal with the leech situation around here."

"Oh. Yeah. After that for sure. But if it was safe, would you consider going?"

"I've never been to one..."

I chuckled as I tucked her hair behind her ears. "Me either."

Right away, her tension relaxed. "You haven't?"

"Nope. I met all my women at conversion camps and crime scenes." I grinned and it made her laugh. "How about you?"

"High School, in the old pack, then at the police academy. None since then, though."

"Well, I'm glad I could be the one to break you out of your stasis. And be your mate." I kissed her before she could respond.

"Me too," she said after we parted. "I'm sorry you had bruises, baby...I'm worried that I hurt you by accident."

"Like you said before, you won't hurt me seriously no matter what. All of your forms will know me. Small injuries are part of the relationship with a Changer, right?" I stroked her cheeks.

"Yes," she said, turning her face to kiss my hand. "I did say that."

"You did. So worries go out the window. I'm fine and so are you." I smiled and her return was equally warm. "Now, we need to figure out what to buy Vanessa for her baby. When is she due?"

"Not long. A few weeks. Weretigers have a much shorter gestation than other Changers." Zara seemed to relax into the conversation.

"What's it for werewolves?"

"Same as humans, nine months. All Breeders are the same. It's the different species that vary. Wolves are closest to their human parts so the pregnancy period is the same." Zara shifted me around so that we could lie on the sofa together. I rested my head on her shoulder and she pulled the blanket over us. "Thank you for everything you did for Christmas. It means a lot."

"I'd do anything for you." I tapped my finger on her chin. "How about for Christmas dinner we go to the fancy Chinese place outside of town?"

"I got a better idea." A broad grin stretched across her lips and her eyes twinkled with mischief. "How about we go for a fancy Chinese dinner in China?"

"What?" I nearly gasped. "You can bend to China?"

"Oh yeah. What do you say?"

"Yes!" I squealed with delight. "Oh my God. What will I wear?"

Zara cracked up, grabbing the pillow and nearly smothering me with it. "Oh my Gaia. I can't. 'What will I wear?' she says."

Giggle fits followed our excited planning. Zara made every moment an adventure, and the best part about it was that she didn't even realize it.

～～

"She took you where?" Ian's mouth hung open as he stared at me from over his laptop.

"China. It was incredible. A surprise trip for Christmas." I couldn't stop grinning as I boasted about Zara's amazingness. I wasn't someone who bragged as a general rule, but with a partner like Zara, how could I not share my happiness?

"What was it like? It must've been a whirlwind to be there for only a week."

"Oh yeah. The flights were wicked so close together." I laughed at my own secret. "We spent most of the time in Hong Kong, eating and shopping."

"It sounds great." Ian leaned back in his chair. "You're so in love. It's great."

"Yeah." My smile must've been a beaming one. "I am."

Ian and I spent our lunch hour chatting about the China trip, then focused on planning an adventure to Salt Lake to one of the gay bars. He seemed excited to spend a night getting to know Zara.

For the remainder of the day, I worked on my article with the exclusive interview provided by Shawnee. She really helped me put a great spin on it, and yet stuck to the facts as much as possible. We used the domestic terrorism angle, but encapsulated it in the process of healing from difficult experiences and finding community. It spoke for both of us, and hopefully for Zara too some day.

As day rolled to a close, casting longer shadows in the office the way it usually did in the winter, a sharpness struck my chest. A pang of anxiety followed and I gripped my shirt. Every day, my matebond with Zara thrummed contentedly, reminding me that she was there and that we could feel each other. Never before had it jolted me so while I was at work. I focused inward, our indigo connection bouncing faster than I expected. It reminded me of the day Zara's beast went into frenzy and she had to run. However, this time I could tell she was present and in charge, not her beast. I wasn't sure how I could tell that though. Again, our bond seized and I let out a small gasp.

Ian looked up from his computer. "You okay?"

"Yeah. I just need some air I think." I snatched my phone from the desk and headed outside. I poked Zara's number into my phone and listened while it rang. With each ring, my heart pounded faster in my chest and our bond tensed in dramatic fashion. My call went to voicemail and panic nearly swallowed me.

My boots thudded on the snowy pavement as I hurried down the street. I had no sense of direction, I just ran, my phone clutched in my palm. All I could think about was Zara, and my fear for her rose.

Sirens wailed in the distance, echoing under the thick clouds and falling snow. I bolted toward them, just in time to see a police car skid to a stop beside the big branch bank on the edge of the town just off the highway. Four cruisers, two from our local department and two from the state police, surrounded the front of the bank. Half a dozen cops stood, guns drawn and shouting at a group of masked people exiting the bank.

I saw Zara, the first and closest to the bank, her weapon held in front of her as she shouted, "Drop your weapon!"

Laughter rang out, someone screamed, and a gunshot exploded from somewhere.

"Zara!" I cried out as our bond thrashed inside us, my panic mixing with hers.

Rapid blasts ricocheted through the streets, the people in masks exchanging fire with the police. I covered my ears, and huddled against the brick building as I watched. Tears poured down my face as I trembled, fearing for Zara.

Bullets slammed into the torsos of the masked people, blood splattering on the walls behind them. None of them fell, however. They continued shooting and laughing. One of the police officers hit the ground, and someone yelled, "Officer down!"

My eyes searched the scene for Zara, but I couldn't find her anywhere. Inside me, all the connections screamed and thrashed. My bond with Zara tightened, the Sept bonds raged, and I couldn't do anything except remain frozen in a crouch beside the cold bricks.

Pops continued to sound, and I kept my hands on my ears. A searing pain stabbed me in the chest, radiating through my back. I cried as I held my side, gasping as it stole my breath. Footsteps stomped nearby. Before I could look up, someone slammed into me, grabbing me and holding me against the bricks.

"Don't move, stay down." Zara's husky voice demanded against my ear. I cried as I held on to her, every bit of me shaking. When the gunfire slowed, I leaned back to see blood smeared all over my front.

"*Zara!*"

"We're okay. Stay down." She held my head to her chest, my entire body clutched against hers. Despite being in her work uniform, she felt larger to me. The sounds of her breathing heavily drew my attention upward. She held me with one arm, the other gripping her gun as she scanned the area around us.

When everything quieted, Zara rubbed my back. In the

snow at our feet, drops of blood made a small pool, spreading from deep crimson to pinkish. I sobbed as I held on to her, her lips pressed against my forehead.

"Easy, baby," she said, her voice soft.

"Fucking vampires with guns. Are you kidding me?" Lightfoot stormed down the street, stopping beside us. "You good, Weston?"

"We're okay." Zara stood slowly, pulling me up with her. "Where's Steve?"

"He went with Caden to chase down the last one." Lightfoot holstered his gun. "Wood-infused bullets were a smart idea. Glad they listened to you."

"You're bleeding." I sobbed, touching Zara all over. "Am I bleeding?"

"We're okay," Zara continued her mantra. "I need to get her out of here."

"I got this. Hank's here. You go." Lightfoot glanced around us. "Use the alley."

"Come on." Zara lifted me, my arms around her neck. "I'm sorry, Kay. I should've warned you."

I could hardly get a hold of myself while Zara bended us somewhere, the swishing swirl of the inbetween detectable only in the pause in sound. When I opened my eyes, we were in the back room of the police station. A makeshift locker room, first-aid area all rolled in one. Zara set me down on the bench where I continued to sob and tremble. Fear continued to bounce around inside me, mixing with the anger the Sept felt over the assault.

Zara sat down, straddling the bench in front of me, her hands cupping my face. "*Calm*," she said, and a slithering sense of comfort poured over my shoulders. I sniffled, meeting her gaze and nodding when my breathing slowed. "We're okay."

"Blood."

"It's mine. I'm fine." She stroked my face, cooing to me until I was able to move on my own again. I nodded, rubbing her arms as I gulped down the remaining sobs. I looked down at her shirt and saw the multiple bullet holes in the front. It only made me cry more as I touched her.

"You got shot."

"I always get shot. Easy." She placed my hands on her face. "I'm fine, baby."

"You're bleeding." I sobbed, caressing her face as the reality of her words struck me, sobering me in an instant. "What do you mean you always get shot?"

"Regular bullets don't do much damage to wolves. I need to remove them though." She released me to unbutton her shirt. "How did you get by the bank?"

"I don't know." I sniffled as I watched her, using my sleeves to clean up my tears. "I felt something. Our bond going crazy, and your emotions. Then I just ran and ended up running right to you. I couldn't help it."

"I know. I understand. I should've warned you about that." In her white tank top, the bloody holes became alarmingly apparent. She pulled it over her head, leaving her in just a sports bra. Two wounds oozed blood down her stomach and one in her chest that scared me because of its position over her heart.

"Oh my God." I sniffled as I placed my hand on her shoulder. "Zara."

"I'm okay. Watch." She reached for the first aid kit on the shelf and removed a pair of long, thick tweezers. Without an ounce of hesitation, she jabbed the ends into the spot on her chest then twisted. A moment later, she extracted a nearly flattened bullet. Her skin melded back together a second after, leaving her flawless as if nothing happened, save for remnants of blood.

"Shit." Immediately, my insides calmed and I touched the space where the bullet was. "How?"

"Werewolves are very dense. Only silver really hurts us. That part of the stories is true."

"What if those bullets were silver?"

"We'd be in trouble."

I watched as she removed the last two, then stared in

awe as her skin melded together, like a melting weave of flesh and tissue.

"See?"

I let out a shaky breath. "Scared me."

"I know. I'm sorry." She used a nearby towel to wipe some of the blood off her torso.

"What if you get shot in the head?"

"Same thing with regular bullets. It won't penetrate the skull."

"Silver?"

"Bad. But silver is a soft metal. It's more the poisoning factor that damages if the bullet isn't removed right away." She tossed the materials in a nearby biohazard bin and then returned to stroking my face. "Are you okay?"

"I'm still scared." I scooted closer and pulled her into a hug. She rubbed my back, nuzzling her nose against my neck.

"I'm sorry you got drawn to me like that. I should've tightened down our bond while I'm working. But I like feeling you…"

"I do, too." I settled against her, her body burning around mine as usual. It soothed me, comforting me in the fact that she was safe. "I bolted from work."

"We need to get you back."

"I'm all bloody."

"I'll go pick up your stuff and tell them you got sick or something," she said, leaning back to look at me.

I nodded my agreement. "Vampires again?"

"It's been going on for weeks. Random attacks mirroring human crimes. Bank robbery this time. When I first met you, it was kidnappings and sexual assaults," she divulged.

"How do you guys keep it out of the news?"

"The Sept is good at clean up."

I sighed, leaning into her embrace. "This was scary."

"I know, baby. And I'm so sorry for all of this." She rubbed my back while I held on to her.

"You don't have to apologize, Zar. It's not anything that happened on purpose." I kissed her cheek and let out a deep breath as I truly began to calm. "So you've kind of been forced around Caden and Hank more lately, yeah?"

She nodded, her lips against my cheek. "Yeah."

"We'll talk more about that later. You have to go back, right?"

"I do. First, let me take you home. Or to Mal's. Your choice."

"Um...home. I need to change."

"Okay, but you can't leave unless we come and get you," she said, standing with me after she grabbed a clean shirt from her locker.

"I understand."

Zara brought me home and, after a painful, "See you later," I forced myself into the shower. Even though brief, today was one of the hardest days of my adult life. I hadn't been scared like that ever before, it seemed. The warmth of the shower soothed some of my leftover anxiety.

As I pulled on a pair of sweats afterward, the chattering of muffled voices in the living room reignited it. I emerged from the bedroom to see Shawnee and Vanessa in the house.

"What's going on?" I asked as I hurried to pull on a pair of socks.

"Mal sent us to get you. Zara's going to be longer than expected," answered Shawnee. "No one should be alone when patrols are active."

"Is everyone okay?" Worry pooled in my gut again as I thought of Zara with bullet wounds in her torso.

"Yes. They haven't tracked down the last leech yet. C'mon." Shawnee waved me over. Vanessa held out her arm and, with caution, I stepped closer to them.

"Close your eyes," Vanessa muttered as her arm encircled my waist.

"I know." I squeezed my eyes tight and hugged on to her arm.

A moment later, my socked feet hit the floor of their cabin. The kitchen smelled of freshly baked something, and pizzas lined the kitchen table. Xany iced a cake, perking up and waving to me when I arrived. A blonde man sat with her, devouring a pepperoni slice.

"Who's that?" I asked, letting go of Vanessa.

"Vanessa's brother, Gavin. Gavin, this is Mack." Shawnee gestured between us. "Mack, Gavin."

"Hey, lass." His Irish accent threaded heavily through the greeting. "We've got plenty. Grab a squat."

"Okay." I laughed a little.

Shawnee gave my shoulder a squeeze, drawing my attention to her for a moment. "I'm not hurt," I assured her when I felt her hand grow hot against my shoulder.

"Good," she said. Emotions tangled in my throat the moment my gaze met hers. She offered me a soft smile then rubbed my back. "Come have a seat with us."

"Thanks." I tried to swallow the lump in my throat, and blink away the tears that threatened to fall. Everything seemed so overwhelming all of a sudden and I didn't have time to process any of it. Shawnee urged me into a seat between her and Xany.

"We know you've had a hard day, Mack," said Shawnee, her hand still on my back in an almost maternal manner. "And you're worried for Zara."

"Who's the empath here, me or you?" Xany huffed at Shawnee. It made me smirk as I swiped at the fat tears that tumbled down my cheeks. I hated crying, mainly because it made me look like a pathetic Precious Moments doll with giant tears. Over the years, I learned how to cry silently, however.

Vanessa's heavy purrs filled the kitchen, and the sound of it relaxed me some.

"Have at it, Xee." Shawnee scowled, but it was easy to tell that it was playful.

Before Xany could speak, I burst forth, "Is this what we're supposed to do?" I glanced between everyone. "Sit here and wait for them to come back? I saw Zara get *shot*. Is this what's supposed to happen? The Changers go out and purge the scourge of vampires threatening to kill us and Breeders bake cakes and eat pizza?" Frustration bound my insides, tangling with the fear I already carried. "It doesn't seem fair that Zara is out there fighting and hunting while I sit here and do nothing."

"You aren't doing nothing, Mack," Xany began, but I cut her off.

"I'm literally doing nothing." I gestured around us. "I want this to be over so we can go back to our normal lives."

"Not finished yet here. This *is* our normal lives. What we are doing is supporting our mates by holding things together and making sure that none of their wolfy parts start sprouting up out of control." Xany turned to face me, her eyes bright as if she just declared today a holiday.

"But you people have gifts. Shawnee can heal bodies, and you can heal minds. What good am I?" Heaviness fell around me as I slouched in the chair. "What good am I to Zara when she's hurting?"

"Who's to say that you don't have any gifts? Maybe they just haven't been needed yet. That's all." Xany shrugged, though her gaze softened. "Took me forever to figure out mine."

"Ana called me a weaver. What's that even mean?"

"It means your ability to connect with your pack and Sept is strong. Did you ever see Harry Potter?" Shawnee asked, drawing my attention to her.

"Yeah." I blinked away the remaining tears.

"Do you remember Mrs. Weasley's clock? She had her family on all the hands, and it told her where everyone was and if they were safe."

"Yeah. I remember that. She was always worried for everyone."

"Right. A weaver is like that. You can weave the bonds. Whether that means navigating them, checking on people, locating them, helping fix rifts, or call on people. It can become really strong over time. It's an important gift."

"Like a walking, talking *Tom-Tom*." Xany snickered, giving my shoulder a nudge.

"What's a Tom-Tom?" I asked, huffing at her for laughing at me.

"Geesh. I'm not that damn old." She mimicked my huff, and crossed her arms over her voluptuous chest.

I laughed at her, glancing between all of them. "I still don't know what it is."

"Oh, Great Gaia. Like a freakin' GPS. You can locate any of the pack or Sept." Xany grumbled at me, her scowl pretty dramatic. Vanessa and Gavin both sniggered at her, and Shawnee's smirk made me wonder how much of her true emotions she held on to.

"Oh. Like a supernatural *Google Maps*. Got it." I sighed, slouching in my chair. "I don't feel useful or helpful in any way."

"Eat some pizza, lass." Gavin shoved a pie down to our side of the table. "That'll be helpful."

"He thinks he's funny that one." I jabbed my thumb in his direction, but didn't refuse the offering.

"He's very handy to have around. You'll see." Xany perked up again, a minor giggle returning to her.

"I'm handy *and* funny." Gavin grinned as he crunched on pizza crust.

"Are you a cat?" I asked him, noting that he moved similar to how Vanessa did; fluidly and with grace.

"She pegged you." Xany flicked Gavin's ear.

"I'm easy." He shrugged, grinning at Xany and wiggling his fingers. "Is the cake ready? Can I eat it?"

"Only if you share. I have to get the meat ready for when the wolf folk make it back." Xany stood from her seat and began fussing over something by the oven.

"You're nothing like Vanessa." I glanced at Vanessa. "She always looks at me like she's thinking about how easy I would be to swallow."

Vanessa grinned and Shawnee laughed for once. "Good observation."

"So why do Breeders and cats hang back?" I asked, turning my attention back to Shawnee. Even though Xany was meant to heal emotions, she did little to make me feel better. Her energy bounced all over the place, and made me nervous. I preferred Shawnee's steady quality and her frankness.

"I prefer the sidelines, lass," answered Gavin. "There's more cake." He grinned up at Xany when she handed him a cake knife.

"There's no rule about that with our Sept. Though with general matters, they handle it. Vanessa and Gavin are our allies," explained Shawnee. "With Vanessa being pregnant, staying out of unnecessary fights is best. And Gavin is comfortable letting the others handle it."

"Like Zara, mostly," I said, nodding to him. "Are you submissive?"

"I am, lass. Can ya tell?" He wagged his brows at me from under the fringes of his frosty blond hair.

"A little." I turned my attention to Vanessa. "His accent is stronger than yours."

"Yes," she said, purring heavily as she leaned her chin on Shawnee's shoulder.

"It's also probably because you hardly say anything that isn't obnoxiously provocative," I told her, flat out.

"Does it bother you?" She smiled, her pretty face lifting with it.

"Don't answer her," Shawnee warned, holding up her hand. "Don't pick on her, Ness."

"But I like to." Vanessa pouted at her mate which made her chuckle.

"Tough shit." Shawnee grinned and smooched her cheek. "Behave yourself."

"How come I can see Vanessa's bond to Shawnee, but not yours, Gavin?" I met his gaze, as he was the most comfortable person in the room to talk to for me. Xany set a glass of iced tea down on the table beside me, then she patted my shoulder a few times. The gesture soothed me as if I took a swig of the tea on a hot summer day.

"I'm not part of your Pride—no, Sept," he said, gesturing to Vanessa. "Vinny is."

"Vinny." I perked at the nickname, grinning at Vanessa. "That's cute."

"Don't call me that." She hissed at me and I laughed right in her face.

"I won't if you stop picking on me. If you pick on me, I'll call you Vinny."

Gavin burst out laughing and clapped a few times. "Ah, lass, you win." He patted Vanessa on the back and she sent a hiss in his direction as well.

"Clever," said Shawnee, chuckling at the exchange. "You've figured out cats pretty fast."

"Well, it's survival in this sense," I confessed.

"It is."

"So, deal, Vanessa?" I lifted a brow at her. She twitched her nose, blinked, and lifted the corner of her lip in response. "Well, I'll take that as a yes."

After some time, Gavin convinced me to eat a slice of pizza while our conversation continued. All the while, I paid attention to my mate bond that thrummed in the center of my chest. Unlike before, it wasn't as wide opened where I could feel Zara so closely. Now, it was tighter, and I could tell she was highly focused and busy.

As the night wore on, we moved to the living room area where I perched myself on the sofa, tucked closely against the arm of it. Xany curled up in the giant armchair, while Gavin sprawled on the fluffy carpet. Shawnee lit a fire in the vast hearth while Vanessa picked a movie to watch. In a moment like that one, we all seemed like normal people on a normal night. Just a bunch of friends hanging out. The world would never expect that all of us waited for our supernatural mates to return after a night spent chasing vampires. With the lights dim, and everyone settled, I pulled my knees to my chest and rested my head on them while we watched the show, my worry for Zara never fading.

I must've dozed off because I opened my eyes when I felt someone draping a blanket over my shoulders. I looked up to see Shawnee's caretaking continuing. I allowed her to, and pulled the blanket tighter. "Thanks," I whispered. Everyone except her seemed to have fallen asleep as well. Soft purrs emanated from both Vanessa and Gavin, creating a calming lullaby for the room. Shawnee sat beside me, in between me and Vanessa who slept curled up at the other end of the sofa.

"They'll be back soon. They found the leech," she said, her voice quiet.

"How'd you know?"

She placed her hand on the center of her chest. "Mal."

"Right." I ran my fingers through my hair. "You're exceptionally nice to me."

"You're someone who needs exceptional niceness," she said, tugging a blanket around her own shoulders.

"So do you."

"Mutual agreement then."

"How long have you lived here?" I asked, sniffling a little when emotions surged again. I couldn't get the images of the bullet holes in my mate out of my mind.

"A little over a year." Her response surprised me.

"Oh. It seems like longer."

"To me as well."

"I feel like I've been here longer than a few months, too."

"Do you have family, Mack? Other than Zara."

"None that want me around," I told her. "Left them when I was eighteen. Never talked to them again."

"How long ago was that?"

"About ten years."

"Because they didn't accept you." The way she said it wasn't a question at all. I nodded, affirming her statement.

"I've been alone since then. Except for my friend Ian."

"You're not alone now. With Zara and the Sept. We're here." As before, she reached to give my forearm a squeeze.

"It's hard to accept that sometimes. Zara I know, I feel her and we have each other. Knowing that so many people welcome us is very strange. I feel bad for Ian though. What do I do about him? He's a human. He can't know..."

"It is hard keeping our human connections. But not impossible."

"I feel like I've kept away from him more often lately because of it," I said.

"You'll find a way to balance it. Trust him a little bit. Humans become delirious if they see a Changer shift, but what keeps them safe from finding out is their uncanny system of denial. If they see anything, they pass it off as something else. Ghosts, vampires, magic." She shrugged. "It's Gaia's way of protecting them."

"I'll keep that in mind. Do you think anyone in my family was Changers or Breeders?"

"Someone somewhere must've been. Most likely an unknown Breeder."

I laughed at the notion of it. "Imagine my crazy parents actually being supernatural creatures? It'd serve them right to be something *different* than ordinary heterosexual Evangelical bigots."

"Even if they were, sounds like they'd never accept it." Shawnee sat up a little straighter. "I think they're heading back."

"Yeah, I felt that. I call it my proximity sensor." I patted the center of my chest. "Here."

She nodded, her hand brushing over the same spot on her own torso. "It is." Vanessa shifted beside her, turning so that her head fell in Shawnee's lap. Right away, Shawnee stroked her hair, running her fingers through it.

"When is the baby due?"

"Soon. Just a few weeks."

"Wow. Zara told me cats have babies faster than we would," I said.

"Yes. Cats in the wild don't fare well alone so being vulnerable with pregnancy isn't good. Evolution has a way of helping us, mostly."

"Seems to." I rested my head on my knees again as fatigue pressed on me. "Thanks for talking with me. You're becoming a fast friend."

"I don't have many, save for my pack."

"Me either."

"I read your article in the paper." Shawnee pointed toward the folded up newspaper on the coffee table. "You did a good job crafting it how we wanted."

"Thanks. It was easy with your interview pieces. Have you ever given an interview for the paper before?" I asked, yawning into my arm.

"Not like that, no. I've made comments on studies or medical reports in the past. Nothing unusual," she said, reaching over and grabbing a throw pillow. "Here." She tucked it beside me. "You look about ready to pass out."

"I wish Zara would come back already." I leaned against it and pulled the blanket tighter around my shoulders.

"She will. Rest for a bit. I'll be awake to wait for them."

"Do you ever sleep? You always seem to be up at night."

"I'm still used to night shifts." She chuckled, and returned to stroking Vanessa's hair while she purred.

"Makes sense."

Shawnee turned the television to an old sitcom, the volume soft due to all the sleeping people around us. We settled in to watch it, though my focus was split between it and paying attention to my matebond.

After one episode, I closed my eyes to rest them. The next thing I knew, something tickled my forehead. When I awoke, Zara crouched in front of me, a soft smile on her lips. Her hair hung to her hips and she wore her leather-on-leather outfit. My heart gave a great leap and she laughed softly as if she could see my excited rise.

"Hi, baby," she whispered.

"Hi." I pushed the blanket off of me and rolled forward to hug her. She slipped her arms under mine and lifted me clear of the sofa. I curled up against her as her arms encircled my waist. From over her shoulder, I saw Mal leaning over the back of the cushions, doting on Shawnee. They shared soft words, and gentle touches, but his fingers never left her hair.

To my surprise, Caden had woken up Xany, and she was perched in his lap. He held her hip in a possessive grasp, and they spoke animatedly about the events of the night. Caden's brown eyes twinkled when he looked at her, and Xany's hand pressed the center of his chest the same way mind did to Zara's. I looked back to my mate, both brows lifted.

"Caden's here," I whispered.

"You're more important," she told me, confidence laden in her tone.

In that moment, I knew what it meant to be a Breeder. The way I reunited with my mate mirrored the way the others had with theirs. For all three of us, nothing mattered more. No fear or worry, no obstacle or challenge could keep us apart and, most importantly, our Changers had someone to come home to. Someone who waited for them unconditionally, with open arms, and welcoming smiles. We were their foundations, the solid ground that they could rely on while they fought for our salvation, so to speak. Warriors, Anadaya told me. Werecreatures are warriors, and Breeders are solace; Gaia's greatest gift in that connection.

When I looked back to Zara, her smile continued despite the tendrils of anxiety that wiggled from her end of our mate bond. All on her own, she faced her fear of being in Caden's presence. Pride swelled in my heart as I stroked her cheeks, brushing my thumb over her bottom lip.

"Let's go home," I said, leaning in to nibble her bottom lip.

She nodded, pressing her lips to mine as her arms tightened around me. A quick step to the right and the wilds of the inbetween swirled around us, taking us to our favorite place to be together. Home.

CHAPTER SIXTEEN

"You're beautiful in the morning," I told Zara when she returned from a quick trip to the bathroom. She stood at the edge of the bed, naked and taut, as she ran her fingers through a tangle in her hair.

"Only in the morning?" she teased, chuckling with it. Once she worked the knot from her hair, she dropped down to sit on the bed, bouncing it a little.

"Only *always*." I reached for her, running my hand over her firm belly. "But especially in the morning." Her stomach quivered under my touch and it made me smile. "C'mere." I grabbed her hand and tugged her as I moved onto my back. She followed, rolling to her knees until I guided her to straddle my stomach. "Perfect."

"I like when you sit like this better," she said, holding my hands as she smiled down at me. The heat of her core against me brought the ache of desire back to my center.

"I know, because you're shyer." I kissed her knuckles, and her cheeks flushed with bashfulness. "You'll have to deal."

"For you, I will." She poked her toes into my hips.

"Like yesterday, with Caden. You surprised me."

"You're more important," she said, squeezing my

hands. "I can't be so afraid of him, or anyone, if I have to keep you safe." She fell from me, dropping down on the bed beside me with a firm bounce. I turned to face her, gathering her hands against my chest. I draped my leg over her hip and I felt her body shudder against mine.

"It was a big change from Imogene's shop to last night. I'm really proud of you," I confessed, releasing one of her hands to stroke her cheek.

"Thank you," she whispered, smiling softly. "I hurt you in Gene's shop." She glanced to my middle then back to me. "Your bruises and broken rib. I did that. I only remembered last night when I lifted you. My fear made me hold on to you so tight that I hurt you. That can't happen again."

"I don't...remember that happening, baby." Concern wrinkled my brow and I tucked her hair behind her ear. "I remember you squeezing me, but not *that* tightly."

"You're a Breeder. Injuries are delayed. It can't ever happen again, Kay. I have to be able to tolerate discomfort," she said, her tone firm.

"What else happened last night to make you feel confident enough to plunge in?"

She took a deep breath, her eyes darting back and forth between mine while she appeared to search for her words. "I caught the leech. Second one I've killed from that nest. No one else could catch it." She paused, brushing her lips over the back of my hand. "They were going to ask Vanessa to help, because she's the fastest of any of us. But Steve said to let me lead, because he knows I'm fast."

"And?"

"Caden said that he trusted me to lead, even when Hank was worried about it."

"Ah." My smile broadened at that. "And you didn't expect that, for him to stand up for you."

"No. His father would have never allowed a submissive to lead anything. His father would have never let me even out with them." She rubbed my arms as if she was soothing me, despite the fact that in that moment, neither of us needed soothing.

"And Hank agreed. I felt their..." She drifted off, again searching for the word. "I'm not sure. Something in the bonds. It was uplifting, like a sureness or a confidence from both of them. And instead of doubt, it was worry. They were both *worried* for me. Not hateful of me."

My eyes grew misty at her declaration, and I couldn't pull the smile off my face. "Of course they are, baby. Of course. We all care about you. We value you."

"Yeah." Her voice cracked and a thick tear trickled from the corner of her eye. "I felt that. It was very real."

"I'm so very happy for you, Zara. I'm happy you got to feel that." I pressed my lips to hers. "I'm glad you felt wanted and valued."

"Yeah." She sniffled, still smiling as she took a swipe at the stray tear. "I felt like that."

"Good. Now, you can add wanted and valued to loved. Which is all I have for you." I cupped her face and she nodded, brushing her lips over mine.

"I love you, too," she confessed, smiling through it as she rolled on top of me again. I squealed at the quick movement until she captured me in an impassioned kiss. My body melted under her as we tangled in each other again. Zara's hand slid down my stomach, then paused an inch above my pussy. She leaned back, her facial expression changing from smoothly sensual to concerned, tightening her forehead and mouth.

"What is it?" I placed my palm on the space between her breasts.

"Hank's calling a Clash, thirty minutes. Something must've happened." She slid from me, her body recoiling with her worry. "Can you feel it?"

"I don't know. What's a Clash?" I focused inside myself and the tangle of silvery threads pulsed around the large throbbing one in the center that belonged to Hank. "The bonds seem okay. Louder than usual. All alert."

"A Sept meeting. No one died. I would feel that," she said. "We better get ready."

I slid from the bed, rushing to join her. "Has this ever happened before?"

"Sept meetings?" She nodded. "But I'm usually exempt."

"And now?"

"Things have changed, it seems."

We grabbed towels, and rushed off to shower and dress. It took us all of fifteen minutes before we hurried off to Caden's house. Zara and I stood together at the front door. Her fingers balled to fists while we lingered on the top of the stoop. The group clamored from the other side of the door and Zara gulped, glancing at me to see if I'd notice.

"Are they both in there?" I asked. She nodded and her shoulders broadened a bit. "You can do this, baby." I held my hand to her. "We can do this."

She took it without hesitation, and I gave her a firm squeeze. "Okay," she said on a long exhale. "Okay."

I gripped the doorknob, and opened it without thinking. No one seemed surprised to see us when we entered. A dozen strangers talked animatedly, some in fervor, others calm. On the kitchen table, various weapons lay out in a spread. Crossbows, composite bows, arrows, guns, and wooden spears all made my insides clench. Zara seemed relaxed by the sight. Battle didn't scare her the way certain people did. Part of that worried me. Were people really more to fear than entry into a weapons-war?

Shawnee and Xany both greeted us, as the voices filled the room. I waved to them, then stood by Zara's side while she looked on. Mal met her gaze, and she nodded while he gestured to the spread on the table. Zara's eyes gleamed and Mal picked up one of the thick wooden spears, and threw it in her direction. I gasped, ducking to the side, but Zara snatched it out of the air without so much as a second thought.

"What's going on?" I asked, finally, to Zara, to *anyone*.

"We're going after the leech. The big one who has been causing all the chaos," she explained. I watched as Shawnee strapped herself in a shoulder harness, tucking a gun in the left holster and some weird round object that looked like a small canteen, in the right. Xany tossed a crossbow over one shoulder, and a quiver with arrows over the other.

"Is *everyone* going?" I squeezed Zara's hand.

"Not everyone. You can stay with Imogene and the cubs." Zara turned to me, her eyes flashing red on and off as she responded to the energy of the Sept. The bonds trembled with adrenaline, mixing with rage and excitement. It set my heart to pounding and all I could think about was Zara's last fight.

"No. I can't. I'm coming with you." I clenched her hand in a death grip. "Zar."

"Kay, you can't…"

"I'm not staying here without you." Panic tightened my throat, and Zara pressed her forehead against mine.

"Kay…"

"Hey," Xany called out. "What's goin' on?" She approached and we both looked at her. When she was up close, I noticed the outfit she wore, almost like a suit of armor, but close to her skin like some sort of space-age getup.

"I'm not staying here. You and Shawnee are going." I couldn't stop the trembling in my body at the fear of leaving Zara to fight a battle alone. She stroked my arm, holding on to my elbow in a protective gesture.

"Can you fight?" asked Xany, shrugging heavily. "Or shoot?"

"No…" I glanced from her to Zara then back again. "I'm a reporter. I *report* things. That didn't come with weapons training." Snark laced my tone, even though I didn't intend for it to.

"Bring a notebook and write stuff down." Xany

grinned, looking between the two of us. "The pencil is mightier, right?"

"Not exactly." I turned my attention back to Zara, our matebond seemingly quieter than usual despite our tense moment. "I don't want to stay here."

Our bond thrashed between us as an ache filtered through Zara's end. She cupped my face in her hand, and made to speak before a looming shadow approached us.

"What's going on here?" the booming voice of Caden asked.

Zara and I turned to face him. All I could do was stare at his hulking battle-ready bare chest as he towered over us. Zara's lips pressed tightly together, and her hand tumbled from my face to my arm.

"I...I want to come with everyone. Not stay here. I don't have cubs to look after. I want to be with my mate." The words burst from my mouth, sounding more confident than expected.

Caden met my gaze, and at first, the urge to flinch fell upon me. But the heaviness I expected never came. He looked from me to Zara.

"Zara, do you want her to join us?" he asked, his tone soft.

Zara hesitated, her palm growing clammy against my arm. She took a deep breath before saying, "I want her to be safe."

Caden nodded and turned his attention to Xany. "What are your thoughts, Xee?"

"S'gotta be up to them, TB," she chirped, her eyes twinkling when she looked up at him. "But ain't no one gonna tell me to stay behind. You know that."

Caden chuckled, his hand falling on the small of her back. "True." He kissed her forehead then met my gaze again. "Okay then. Come with me."

"Where?" With caution, I released Zara at the same time he relinquished his hold on Xany.

"I have an idea," he said, looking to Zara. "When we

return, you can both decide what to do. Okay?"

"Okay," I said, right away. We looked to Zara. Again, she hesitated and gulped. Her grip on my elbow slowly slid away. Her entire body tensed, but when I offered her an encouraging nod, she gave her blessing to Caden.

"Alright," she said, barely a whisper. "*Okay*."

I broke away from Zara, whose eyes widened as our distance increased. The last thing I heard was Xany saying, "It'll be cool. Just wait."

Caden led me down the hall toward the portion of their cabin where Shawnee's clinic attached. He paused just outside the clinic door, placed his hand on the wall, and a piece of the paneling slid away.

"Whoa. Future tech much?"

"Not really. It just slides back and forth." He laughed as he moved the rolling door back and forth a few times in dramatic fashion. "It blends well though."

"Yeah." I snickered as I watched him step inside the small closet and pull out what looked like a diving suit. "This is Xany's other suit."

"Is it special or something?"

"Bullet proof, difficult to tear, and most importantly, fang proof save for your exposed parts; face and hands," he explained. "Put this on in there and come back out." He nodded to the clinic.

"This is a little scary." I accepted the suit from him and headed into the clinic. It was heavier than I expected it to be and pulling it on over my clothes wouldn't do. I stripped down to my skivvies, wrestled myself into the getup, and zipped the front. My boots returned to my feet afterward. My heart continued to pound while I thought of the consequences to my decision to join Zara. If I stayed back, she would be out there, with the most dominant members of our Sept, and vulnerable to her fear. And her beast. If I stayed back, what if she got hurt again and I wasn't there? If I joined them, what if Zara got distracted by worrying about me? What if I got hurt? No matter what, the situation wasn't ideal.

I returned to Caden, holding out my arms. "Fits okay."

"Sure does. I know it's tight, but keep it zipped to your chin. It protects your neck from easy access," he said, despite the nerves thrashing around in the bonds, Caden remained a steady presence. "Now, hold out your arms."

I stuck my arms out in front of me, and Caden strapped something to them then tightened the bands. I bent my arms when he was done. "What is it?"

"Make a fist."

"What? Why?" I clenched my hands and started when light burst from my arms. "Shit."

"UV light. Relax your hands." He chuckled at my response. When my fists uncurled, the lights turned off. "They're activated by the muscles in your arms. Now, these are only repellent. Determined leeches can push through it if their blood frenzy is strong enough, but it will keep them back or deter them. Your job is to shine the light on any leech you see overpowering someone. If the person is on the ground with a leech on top, turn the lights on. Understood?"

"Yeah." I nodded, my chest broadening. "I can do that."

"But keep them off until that moment, or the leeches could get used to it," he said, his hand falling to my shoulder. "Good?"

"Yeah." I took a deep breath, broadening under his confidence. "I'm good."

"Good." He dropped his hand and nodded. A moment of silence passed between us before he said, "What you've given Zara is commendable."

"I didn't give her anything." My brow furrowed at the statement.

"You gave her love, Mack. Nothing less than that could've gotten her out of the cabin and out here with us. She's been locked away for years, only speaking to Mal by sheer requirement at times." Caden's features softened in that moment. "No wolf like her deserves to be a ronin."

"What's that?"

"A lone wolf without a pack. Wolves thrive in groups as social animals."

"It means a lot to hear you say that. I mean, not that I know you or anything." I smirked, shrugging away the discomfort. "She's more confident now."

"Very much so. And most importantly, she's grateful." He smiled, gesturing for me to head back to the main room of the cabin with him.

We returned to the group, and I felt like some sort of super human. Xany, Shawnee, Mal, and Zara all turned in our direction. Zara approached first, her footsteps tentative. I held my arms out to my sides, and spun in a circle.

"Hey, twins," called Mal as he pointed at Xany and I. He laughed as some of the others in the room snorted. "That's dangerous."

"What do you think?" I held up my arms to Zara and made fists to show her the UV lights. She flinched at first then smiled when she realized the nature of my outfit. I turned off the lights and moved into her arms.

"I think it suits you." She pressed her lips to my forehead.

"Is it enough to convince you to let me go with you?" I hugged her, carefully, while she touched me all over.

"It's enough." She leaned back, cupping my cheeks. "You'll stay close to me? And listen to what I say? If not me than..." She swallowed painfully. "Caden or Mal or Hank?"

"I'll listen." I took her hand when she offered it.

"Breeder power!" Xany shouted, giggling afterward. "Okay, people. Let's get a move on."

Everyone joined elbows, weapons held sharp against their bodies. I closed my eyes when Zara wrapped her arm around me, gripping the belt of my new outfit. Against her chest, I nestled into the familiar comfort of her leather bodice.

Our bodies swirled and the bonds inside me burst to life. I could see them, feel all of them, as if they beat next to my own heart. Tension gripped the Sept, worry tangled the bonds, for themselves and their families, but I knew they were all okay. Somehow, I just knew.

The minute our feet hit the ground, twigs and grass crunched under my boots, along with the bits of leftover snow. A huge, blazing bonfire burned in the center of all of us. It was still morning, so I knew we must've still been in preparation mode.

Hank turned to address the crowd, but commotion burst forth. From around Zara, I saw Shawnee go flying toward the tree line as if someone tossed her away from us. Pandemonium exploded inside and out. Mal grabbed for her as her body flailed out of control. He caught her wrist and the two of them soared across a stretch of land, then tumbled to the ground. Mal lifted Shawnee to her feet at the same time that he rolled to his. The Sept raced forward. Zara grabbed my arm, holding me in place. Roars mixed with gasps, until Anadaya shouted, "*Don't!*" Her arms held out in front of her, palms forward.

Everything and everyone stopped, freezing in place like a creepy game of statue, some of them in half-run poses. Others fell to their knees, and a younger wolf hit the ground on his rump. For the first time in my life, I found myself unable to move. Paralyzing pressure squeezed my muscles, and my will to move proved fruitless. Only Vanessa continued forward, breaking away from the group to rush toward Shawnee and Mal.

"Zara," I gasped, holding tightly to the arm she had on mine. She offered me a squeeze, her eyes soothing and calm despite her frozen posture.

"It's okay," she cooed.

"We're good," Mal called out, his arm around Shawnee's middle. "What the hell was that?"

Vanessa stood beside them, her yellowish eyes trained

on the area around us. Save for the caw of a crow and the crackle of the fire, everything seemed fine.

"None of you leave this spot," Anadaya demanded, pointing around us. She released her command and the Sept moved on their own accord again as she walked forward, her moccasin-covered feet paused about a meter in front of Shawnee and the others. "Step toward me together."

"What happened?" Shawnee asked as her mates guiding her forward. They crossed to where her mother stood, but when they tried to take her with them, her legs locked. She stumbled as Mal and Vanessa each had hold of one of her arms. "Stop, don't pull." She flinched, sucking in her breath.

"What's going on?" Caden came up behind Ana with Xany in tow.

"The protective barrier ends here." Anadaya tapped her foot on the ground. "She has been removed from it."

"Well, get her back in! Hurry up," Xany shrieked, grabbing Shawnee by the waist of her jeans.

Caden's worry made his bond inside me glow brighter as Hank moved toward them. Mal's panic wasn't any better, and Vanessa growled in a low rumble. She stepped outside the barrier to stand behind Shawnee, her back against her in a protective display.

"Give that to me, Shawnee. Right now." Caden reached his hand out, nodding toward the gun holster at her chest. "The heart."

"What? Oh." She removed the flask that I saw her hide in one of the holders and handed it to Caden. Mal yanked her inside the barrier so hard that her feet left the ground again. She held onto him as Caden's feet wobbled in place. As if someone grabbed him around the neck, his huge body soared away from us toward the trees. I gripped my shirt and Zara pulled me to her.

"Oh my God." My nails dug into her arms. "What's going on?"

"The protective barrier that Ana and Adia made. It's ejecting them for some reason," she explained, her arms around me tightened and I clung to her, fearing getting tossed out in the same manner.

Unlike Shawnee, Caden landed in a crouch while still holding on to the flask. Vanessa remained outside the barrier, instinctively snatching Caden by the shirt.

"It's the heart," Xany said. "It can't come inside."

"At least we know the enchantments work," Adia said as she approached. "Give it here."

"Good thing we showed up early. Last thing we needed was for Shawnee to get tossed right into Ileana's arms like a bouquet of wedding flowers." Xany huffed.

Caden handed Adia the flask as she stepped out beside him.

"Don't take it away. I want her to see it," Shawnee said, releasing Mal to stand beside them.

"Dia will remove the heart for safe keeping," she said, opening a leather pouch at her hip. Adia pulled out something red and white from it, then tipped the flask. She held the fabric at the mouth of the artifact.

The Changers around me cringed and I looked to Zara. "What is it?"

"Blood," she said, her body tensing around me. I didn't understand what was going on at all.

"What's going on?" Xany asked.

"Just watch," Adia said.

We continued to look on. After a few minutes, something slimy and black rose from the opening of the flask. It made a slight suctioning sound and inched like a pruney little slug. The shriveled thing made my skin crawl. The softest, grossest little slurping sound followed. Adia wrapped it up in something then tucked it away.

"That's human blood," said Shawnee, nodding at Adia.

"Yep. Leech heart can't resist it." Adia handed her the flask.

"That..." Xany gulped. "Was the most disgusting thing

I've ever seen."

"Where are you taking it?" Shawnee queried as everyone moved closer to the fire.

"Dia take it to the cabin and remain there with it. When you're ready, Anadaya will fetch me, okay? Okay," she said, answering herself.

"Don't go anywhere with it. It's... it's mine." Shawnee gripped the flask tightly in her fist.

"You can stake it when its time," Adia reassured her. After a glance to Anadaya, she was gone.

"Heart?" I looked to Zara as she urged me away from everyone. "What was that?"

"I'm not really sure," she admitted. A group of the Sept members gathered with us as Hank approached.

"I reckon I need to tell ya a few things as we enter this fight," he began, glancing over the group of us.

"Dad, that was gross." A younger man dusted off his jeans. "What the heck, man?"

Hank chuckled, clapping him on the shoulder. "Henry, I want you lookin' after this lot here." He nodded toward me and Zara. "An' don' go chasin' the others. You lot stay back here. Hold down the East side, ay?"

"Alright, Da. We will." Henry offered him a firm nod.

"And listen here." He glanced at him, his heavy dark eyes flickering in my direction. "None of you are to run after Shawnee, no matter what. Leave that to us. She and hers have a handle on this."

I glanced to Zara and she nodded, her fingers digging into my hip. With her urging, I nodded as well. The others offered the same affirmations, and Hank eventually joined Caden and the others again.

There must've been forty people gathered inside of the magical barrier. Zara pointed out the markers around the parameter that identified it; rock formations or vertical sticks. Some folks sharpened weapons, others sat on the ground eating sandwiches and drinks. I couldn't even fathom the idea of eating. Bile rose in my throat as I reconsidered my decision to join.

I sat down on a fallen log by the fire and allowed the warmth of it to sooth my cold hands. Zara joined me, kneeling in front of me with her hands on my legs. I met her gaze and she offered me a small smile.

"What else do I need to know?"

"Keep your eyes down. Don't make eye contact with the vampires. They can thrall you." She took my hands in hers. "Like hypnotize."

"Great. Just what I need." I started suddenly. "Do you think that other vampire did that to me? Am I dreaming all of this?"

"No, baby. Even if she did, the thrall ends when the vampire dies. All of this is real." She brought her hands to my lips and kissed my knuckles. "I'm real. And so are you."

"I had no idea what your life was like." I sniffled as fear and sadness overwhelmed me. "Fighting wars with vampires. Your friends at risk. People dying. A creepy little bloody thing crawling out of a jar."

"I'm sorry," she whispered, and I sensed the dropping sensation of her burden thrusting through our bond. "I'm sorry you're involved in this, Mack. I never meant to—"

"No, no. I've chosen this, Zara. As I've chosen you." I scooted closer so that I could kiss her forehead. "I just never realized the magnitude of existence. Of this world. How didn't I notice?"

"Sometimes not noticing is better," she said, reaching up to stroke my hair. "Are you ready to be a warrior of Gaia?"

"Like you?" I chuckled which made her smile.

"Yeah." She glanced around us. "Like all of us."

"Like every single one of you." I cupped Zara's face, kissing her softly before leaning back to gaze at our Sept.

Worried faces, tense shoulders, and fear-laden bonds mingled with smiles and friendship. All in one, these people belonged together, doted on each other, and found comfort in their connections. For the first time, it seemed like Zara belonged with them, and I belonged with her.

"Are you ready to fight vampires?" she asked, her lips curving into a wry smile.

I laughed, nodding my affirmation. "With you? I'd fight 'em every day."

"Well, not every day. When would we have time to sleep late and do other things?" Zara's smile, bright and wide, despite our dire circumstances, brought an epoch of relief to my insides. Our matebond, strong and fluid, coupled with the tendrils belonging to the Sept, shone in the darkness. Her strength, even while surrounded by the people who scared her the most, emanated from every pore of her being.

Zara never feared the monsters, the vampires, or the creatures of darkness. She feared connection and trusting that people would keep her will intact while preserving her best interest. One thing I didn't doubt was Zara's trust in me. While she crouched there amidst the bunker on the fringe of a war, we had faith in each other. With similar importance, we had faith in the people around us.

The day turned to evening under the guise of twilight. Surrounded by a bunch of werecreatures, the close proximity to each other seemed to build them up. Inside of myself, I sensed their connections tightening, and visualized the silvery strands moving closer together.

When the sky turned from cerulean to midnight, silence fell around us and a soft breeze wafted the flames of the bonfire to the east. The group quieted, as if a hush caught them all. Vanessa growled first, followed by several others. A shadow grew four times its size as a man shifted to beast form and Henry followed. The others caught on and they began to change as well. Some chose to remain in human form; Mal, Caden, Vanessa, and Ana among them.

A screech rang out from above, sending images of dying birds flashing across my mind. I envisioned the vampire from the street that perched itself on my window ledge, and later, the way it rose from the lake to attack us on our walk home. My eyes lifted to the sky, and Zara knew to look up as well.

Human-shaped bodies dropped from the heavens like fleshy bombs, flailing as they landed in the circle around us. They hissed and screamed as the protective barrier attacked them, burning their skin and dragging them toward the perimeter. Xany jumped out of the way and Anadaya grabbed her as one of the bodies hit the fire. It erupted in a flash as flames swallowed it, blackening its flesh as it screeched and whipped about. Reduced to ashes in seconds.

"Vampires, she's *throwing* vampires!" A woman with multicolored hair roared, bringing her hand down across the throat of a leech that tried to rise from the ground. I started when blood splashed to the snow at our feet. Zara's position beside me remained steady, her eyes trained upward. She jabbed her staff into the shadows and stabbed a vampire right through the torso. A wave of blood rained down on us and I shrieked, tightening my hands to fists. The UV lights turned on and the leech at the end of her staff squealed like a pig before it burst into flames. Without skipping a beat, Zara plucked it off the stick and tossed it in the fire where it continued to burn.

"They're jumping." Hank snatched a leech off Henry's back and tore it in two, its innards splashing on the snow at his feet.

"Holy fuck," I spat, relaxing my hands as I ducked when Zara swung around me.

"Eyes down," she instructed, her hand on my shoulder.

"Okay." I drew in a deep breath. My heart pounded, eyes widened, and never in my life had fear swallowed me so fully. The bonds inside me gathered together in a bright ball, tensing and flexing in unison as if choreographed to perfection. Their movements mirrored the fluidity of their real life counterparts.

Another vampire landed in the bonfire, though as his skin burned, it spit volcanic particles into the air. It landed on the arm of one of the men in the circle with us and caught his jacket on fire.

Chaos rained on us, drowning us in a sea of blood, fangs, and snarls. At the farthest part of the barrier, I caught a glimpse of Shawnee and her pack talking to a glowing-eyed leech in a white puffy jacket. I couldn't hear what they were saying, but no one looked happy as indicated by their angry faces, and sour scowls.

The attacked waged on, vampires arriving in droves. Some continued to jump down on us while a herd appeared to my left. Zara shoved me aside at the same moment that Hank and Caden swept in beside her, forcing me behind them. Hank pulled an arrow from the quiver on his back, loaded it in the composite bow, and fired at the same time that Caden began shooting two guns at once. Screams rang out when the bullets and arrows connected with torsos, only forcing the vampires forward. Zara tossed her spear like a javelin, spearing two in the chest at the same time as one rushed in front of the other. They fell to the ground, mouths held open as their skin blackened and peeled away until nothing remained save the brittle skeleton. Caden clapped Zara on the back before jerking his attention upward and firing in the sky.

Shouts rang out inside me, sounding an alarm in the form of a pulsating beacon. One of the bonds floundered and without much thought, I spun around, fingers twitching as I did so. In front of me, Henry, in human form, wrestled with two vampires that gnawed at his forearms.

"Hey!" I rushed them, forcing my hands to fists and blasting them with the lights. Both vampires freaked out, flailing and grabbing at their eyes. Henry got the advantage then, rolling up to his knees and punching them both in the chest. They flew out of the circle, landing in a heap a few yards away as they thrashed and clawed at their own faces. One of them stood up and bolted into the cover of the woods.

When I swung around to survey the Sept, every single one of them battled if not with weapons, in hand-to-hand combat. Blood and guts covered their bodies, fur, boots. The bonfire, laden with corpses and skeletons, burned higher and smellier than before.

As quickly as it started, everything came to a blazing halt. Caden's pack stared at Shawnee as she stood toe-to-toe with the small female leech dressed like a teenage ski bunny.

"A truce?" She hissed out the final word, her crimson eyes darting wildly over Shawnee as if sizing her up.

"A truce. You agree and we walk away. You don't agree, and I shove a tiny little stake into your slimy thousand-year-old heart like it was nothing more than an *hors d'oeuvre*," Shawnee said, holstering her gun and crossing her arms over her chest like she owned all of this. Her confidence, cocky and brave, had me standing up straighter in my boots. Zara's hand grasped my shoulder, her body burning beside me with radiant heat.

The vampires by the small leech's side protested, but she lifted her hand to silence them. Her eyes bore into Shawnee again, staring her down with little effect. The fight seemed to drain from the leech, her shoulders dropping from tension to ease. She gripped a flask in her hand, rubbing her thumb over the mouth of it in an affectionate caress.

"Truce," she said.

"Checkmate," Shawnee said, turning around to face the Sept.

The vampires retreated, melting away into the shadows as if they belonged to them. I glanced over the faces of the Sept, of Zara and Hank. For a fleeting moment, they all shared the same expression—wonderment and pride. In the battle, whatever war we fought, Zara stood among the other wolves, beside them and with them. She fought with the same bravery, the same skill and strength. Hank turned to her, their gazes meeting as if they shared a moment of understanding. His lips pursed, and he offered her the faintest nod. Zara's lip twitched as if she fought a smirk.

Despite her muted response, her inner world told a different story. Through the wide-open tunnel of our matebond, something else surged through it. Not the anxiety or worry that I was used to. Instead, confidence and connection reigned. Her shoulders broadened, and the silver tendril that connected her to the rest of the Sept thickened, drawing us both closer.

Something changed for her in that moment, though I couldn't tell exactly what it was. I knew it belonged to the type of magic that lifted you up, bringing you closer to people and the experiences of the world the way friendship would. Most importantly, it brought a fragment of trust. She no longer kept me glued behind her. For the first time since becoming her mate, she allowed me to stand beside her, rather than someone who needed constant protection. I stood beside her the same way she stood beside Hank; as an equal.

"It's your fault," I squeaked, then succumb to the moaning a moment after.

EPILOGUE

Zara's confidence passed well into the days that followed, and when we found ourselves in the same place that we started, curled up on her sofa with a snow storm raging outside, the laughter that left her brought nothing save for great joy to our connection.

"So wait. Let me get this straight." I held up my hands, gesturing dramatically as I postulated the tale of our lives. "Shawnee gave the kill order on a vampire that belonged to this Ileana character, who was some sort of ancient vampire that'd been walking around for thousands of years."

"Yep." Zara nodded, grinning around the spoon with a mouthful of ice cream on it.

"And she wanted revenge on Shawnee by making her name a human to replace her destroyed fledgling." I snatched the pint from her, and jabbed my own spoonful. "And Shawnee named *herself* because she knew she couldn't get thralled by Ileana. And we couldn't kill Ileana because of the *voodoo* magic she used to remove her own heart. So instead, we found her voodoo heart, and threatened to kill her by stabbing her disembodied heart, unless she backed off and stopped attacking us."

"That's about right." Zara laughed openly, dropping her head back on the cushions while she gazed at me.

"That is...the most ridiculous story ever. No wonder this whole world has been kept hidden from the humans. No one would believe it anyway!" I tossed my arms in the air then let them flop back down on the blanket in my lap, still holding on to the ice cream. "*Honestly*. Ridiculous."

"I never said any of this would make sense." Zara shrugged, the grin ever-present on her pretty mouth.

"You know what makes complete sense though?" I smiled after I set down the ice cream, then crawled toward her. Zara melted into the pillows, her gaze locked on mine though the smile never left her face.

"What?"

"You and me." I caught her in a kiss, both of us laughing through it. She ran her hands through my hair, grabbing it in playful fists.

"I agree," she said, leaning me back.

"I used to think I was dreaming. That all of this was unreal."

"It's real, baby." She leaned forward and kissed the end of my nose. "All of it."

"Yeah." I straddled her legs, bunching her hands against my chest. "I know."

"Hmm. Let's watch them." A gravelly voice drew our attention to the carpet by the front door. Vanessa appeared first, a wry grin curving her lips.

"Ness, don't tease them." Shawnee showed up a fraction later, swatting Vanessa. At almost the same time, Mal and Xany also turned up. Xany giggled right away as she bound over to us, releasing Vanessa's elbow.

"Hiya."

I rolled off Zara, both of us sitting up to greet them. "What if we were in the middle of sex or something?"

"Ness would be happy." Xany jabbed her thumb in Vanessa's direction. "We come with a proposal."

"Where's Caden?" asked Zara, her brow furrowed and

nostrils flared. The bonds inside me told me he was super close.

"Out here," a muffled voice said.

We all burst out laughing and Mal gripped the doorknob. "He begs entry, fair maidens."

"Yup. S'what I came here for. Am I allowed in, Zara?" Caden's husky voice, laden with laughter, had me grinning at the silliness of the situation.

"What do you say?" I lifted a brow at her.

Shawnee pulled Vanessa to sit in the chair by the fire, then helped herself to her lap. I recognized the gesture as her way of controlling the cat. Her round belly pressed against Shawnee's hip, now significantly larger than the night when we fought the vampires. Xany nearly bounced in place with excitement over something.

"Well, hurry up already!" She flailed, nearly squealing.

"Yes." Zara laughed, glancing between everyone. "He can come in." Despite her confident statement, Zara's arm slid around my middle in a mild, but protective, gesture.

Mal opened the door and let Caden in. He tipped an invisible hat to us before gliding in. In the quaint cabin, he appeared larger than life. Zara didn't shrink in his presence though, not this time.

"Okay, let's ask them!" Xany burst forth, bouncing over to Caden. "C'mon!"

"Ask us what?" I scanned the faces of our Sept mates. Each of them carried an air of lightness with them, which contrasted their previous conditions.

"Let's all have a seat," suggested Mal, gesturing around us. Caden perched himself on the edge of the coffee table, Xany beside him, with Mal taking a seat on the sofa beside Zara. I held her hand in my lap as nervous anticipation rumbled inside me. Zara and I belonged to the nervous part and everyone else carried the anticipation. Our silvery bounds wiggled along with it.

Caden glanced between us, his expression as soft as his brown eyes. "I know it's been a rough go, but we would—

"

"Will you join our pack or what?" Xany nearly erupted with the question, her bright eyes twinkling like a child.

"Wait, what? Join your pack?" I looked from Caden to Zara. "What's that mean?"

"We'd like you to be a part of our closer knit group. It's clear that you're both already bonded to us. Mal and Zara are buds, and Vanessa seems infatuated with you." Caden grinned at the latter, shooting Vanessa a glare.

"She just likes staring at other lesbians," I said, narrowing my eyes at Vanessa. She hissed, lifting her lip at me as everyone laughed.

"The rest of us are pretty fond of you as well," offered Shawnee. "Including my mother, who doesn't take well to strangers."

"She likes Zara…" I smiled at my mate, reaching up to stroke her cheek.

"She's a lone wolf, too." Zara leaned into my caress, her gaze on mine. "Guess I'm not so much anymore."

"Nope!" Xany grinned. "So you gonna accept our proposal?"

"How do we join a pack?" I asked, kissing Zara's hand before holding it again.

"All you do is agree, and the magics work themselves out." Mal clapped Zara on the shoulder and she looked at him. "No pressure. The offer is out there. We've found that a bunch of rogues and Lost Ones do better in groups."

"What do you think about that, Zara?" asked Caden, leaning his elbows on his knees.

"I think that'd make you my Alpha," she said, pulling me closer to her. "How about you guys join our pack instead?"

"Wait…" Xany perked up. "We can do that? Who'd be the Alpha?"

"Not me," said Zara, a smirk tugging the corner of her mouth as she looked at me.

"Who—what? Me?" I laughed as I shoved her shoulder. "Zara! I'm no Alpha."

"I am." Xany grinned at me, folding her arms over her chest. "What do you think, Mack? Wanna join?"

I took a moment to survey the people in the room. All of them had hopeful, light expressions as we considered them. Worry continued to tangle Zara's connection to me, at the idea of having someone in charge of us.

"I think," I began, giving Zara's hand a squeeze. "That we appreciate the offer and we'd like some time to think about it. Do you agree?" I asked my mate.

"Yes," she said straightaway, relief rolling over her. "I agree to that."

"I'll take it." Caden smiled, his cheeks lifting and brightening his face. "For now, how about close allies?"

"Deal." Zara nodded and when Caden stuck out his hand, she accepted it. Confidence sprung to life in her, broadening not only her shoulders, but her outlook as well. Gone were the moments where Zara faded away in the presence of a dominant wolf. It surprised me how little it took to transform her outlook and begin healing.

"I got an idea." Mal broke the quiet. "How about we get that Henry to deliver us buckets of wings and a few pizzas to celebrate our allyship?"

"I'm in." I hugged Zara around the neck when she released Caden's hand.

"Me too," said Zara, kissing my cheek. "Pepperoni and meatball."

"Sardine," Vanessa piped up from the peanut gallery.

"All the things!" Xany burst forth. "And mashed potatoes." She scowled at Shawnee who laughed, nodding her agreement.

"Sharing a meal is a good start. Do you agree?" Caden smiled at us as we all rose to head to the kitchen.

"Yeah." Zara hugged me from behind as Caden fell in step in front of us. "I'll agree to that.".

Titles by Max Ellendale

Four Point Trilogy
Four Point
Point Two
Mirror

Four Point Trilogy Tie-Ins
Anita

Lesbian Romance
(*in the same universe as the Four Point Trilogy*)
Wildrose
Rabbit
Anita
Mermaid

Lesbian Romance
Skyclad
Midsummer
Try Pink & Indigo

The Legacy Series
Glyph
Birthrite
Sacred
Bound
Marked

Paranormal Lesbian Romance
The Wolf's Consort

www.maxellendale.com

ABOUT THE AUTHOR

Max grew up just outside of New York City, spending most of her formative years outdoors creating wild ghost hunts with neighborhood kids, setting booby-traps to capture unwitting family members, and building clubhouses on top of ten-foot walls. Max wrote her first story at the age of twelve and titled it *Circles of Friendship*. Through the years, Max has written several short-stories and poems, all of which met the wrath of the "Not Good Enough" monster and ended in fiery demise.

Max regained her confidence when she began writing scholarly articles and research theses on her first trip through graduate school. It took several years for her to break the habit of the formal writing that marred her creativity. An additional Master of Fine Arts degree in Creative Writing was Max's biggest support in this. Max writes primarily sci-fi/fantasy, paranormal romance, and Young Adult stories.

Printed in Great Britain
by Amazon